Accidental Crimes

Accidental Crimes

JOHN HUTTON

THE BODLEY HEAD

LONDON SYDNEY

TORONTO

To my wife

British Library Cataloguing
in Publication Data
Hutton, John, b.1928
Accidental crimes.
I. Title
823'.914 F   PR6058.U859
ISBN 0-370-30498-5

© John Hutton 1983
Printed in Great Britain for
The Bodley Head Ltd
9 Bow Street, London WC2E 7AL
by Redwood Burn Ltd, Trowbridge
Set in Linotron Baskerville
by Rowland Phototypesetting Ltd
Bury St Edmunds, Suffolk
First published 1983
Reprinted 1984

1

The body was lying on its back. The sweater had been pulled up around the girl's neck and her left arm, awkwardly caught in its folds, was twisted at an ungainly angle. The skirt and brassière were missing, and her knickers had been pulled down her thighs. Detective Sergeant Rosen stood stolidly watching the neat, professional movements of the pathologist, and reflected that it was a piece of sheer luck that the girl had been found at all. Just over half a mile away was the road, with the cluster of police vehicles, the waiting ambulance, and the natty red sports car of the pathologist. Elsewhere the bleak Pennine landscape stretched in every direction, undulating, broken by shallow valleys, veined by small streams. The surface was a rough mixture of heathers, coarse grasses and reeds, broken by innumerable fissures showing the dark, peaty soil underneath.

It was in one of these fissures that the body had been placed. There appeared to have been an attempt to cover it with loose stones and tufts of grass, but either this had been half-hearted or small animals had removed them. In any case it had been unnecessary. You could only see the body by looking straight down at it. It could have lain there for months. Instead a party of schoolboys, in the charge of a master, had come that way, and two of them had been attracted by the activity of a pair of crows.

'Come back, you boys, leave it alone. It's probably a dead sheep or something. I'm not going to tell you again.'

But the boys had returned in a hurry, with white faces, wishing they had obeyed.

The master had behaved very well. 'Keep away from it.

I absolutely forbid any boy to go near. Nothing must be touched, the police will be looking out for footprints and things. No, Parsons, I do not intend to set a guard on it. We'll all stay together and we'll make for the road and get assistance.'

They had flagged a lorry and the driver had telephoned from the nearest kiosk.

The pathologist was intent on his work. He was good at it, proud of his skill, you could tell that, and pleased with the mental toughness that he showed. The constables standing near sometimes averted their faces, wrinkled their noses, turned away from the stench, but he held his face close to the disgusting mass and worked deftly, scooping and scraping, transferring deposits to carefully labelled envelopes, meticulously noting details. Sergeant Rosen allowed his gaze to wander. His subordinates, he knew, were watching, and he must seem as professionally unflinching as this medical man, so he shifted the distribution of his weight between his feet, swallowed the phlegm in his throat, and pressed his lips together against the noxious atmospheres.

'Dead ten to twelve days, I'd say,' the pathologist called over his shoulder. 'Difficult to be precise. Does that fit?'

It fitted very well, and this was a relief. The Sergeant had been afraid, from the state of the body, that it must have been there longer, in which case it could not be the girl they had been looking for. He asked the pathologist if he was certain.

'Decomposition is more rapid than most people think.' He paused in his work to demonstrate, as though the policemen had been a group of students. 'You see, in this case it is lying in a declivity facing somewhat south. Any heat from the sun will have been concentrated here and speeded the process up, and, of course, it is sheltered from cooling winds. The last few days have been quite fine.'

Quite fine, this was indisputable. The very last postcard the girl had sent to her mother had commented on the niceness of the weather. Ten to twelve days, it was perfect. The girl had last been seen in Abenbury, the nearest town, on Thursday, April the twenty-ninth, and it was now Tuesday, May the eleventh. It must be the girl. The details of the clothing tallied. In any case the identification would soon be beyond doubt. A message had gone out and her mother was coming over from Sheffield. There was a nice job for you. She was a widow, Mrs Watson. This was her only daughter, just eighteen, taking a holiday with a friend to celebrate completing her first year in a job. Sergeant Rosen was neither sentimental nor imaginative, but he was not unaware of the pathos of the situation. He had two daughters of his own, and he knew something of the problems of bringing young people up in the modern world.

'She promised faithfully that she and Denise would stay together,' the mother had said. 'Lucy was a good girl. She wouldn't have thought of going off by herself with a stranger.'

But Denise, now tearful and defensive, had met a boy in Abenbury, and Lucy, apparently, had done the unthinkable.

The Sergeant's daughters were good girls too. They were both married now, safely off his hands, no longer his responsibility. They had gone about quite a lot when they were young, hitch-hiking all over the place, pop festivals, demonstrations. 'Oh, Dad, don't worry. We can look after ourselves. We weren't born yesterday.' If you were a parent you had to take chances, and most young people came to no harm. He'd been lucky.

The pathologist was feeling delicately round the throat and neck of the dead girl, peering into the gaping mouth. The head lolled sideways. The eyes appeared to have been pecked out by birds. The Sergeant looked quickly away and caught a young constable eyeing him; he scowled back.

'Strangled,' said the pathologist, 'with what looks like her own tights. I'll leave the knot for you to look at yourself, see if it tells you anything. She must have been placed here pretty

3

soon after death – look at the staining on the left-hand side of her face and neck. Pass me the camera, I'll get a shot of that.' He took several pictures with a polaroid camera. The Sergeant asked him if he wanted the official police photographer back, but he said he did not and rose to his feet, brushing the knees of his trousers.

'Not much more I can do here. As far as I can judge she was interfered with, but I don't think that actual sexual intercourse took place. Mind you, decomposition is so far advanced that I may not be able to give you a definite answer. She might have been penetrated with a finger or some kind of instrument like a stick or a fountain pen.'

Sergeant Rosen did not blink, being used to the strange forms that lust can take. He asked, instead, whether great strength had been needed for the attack.

'Nothing exceptional. If you like to take a look, there is a fair amount of bruising on the chest.' The pathologist was on his knees again demonstrating, and the Sergeant found it necessary to bend forward to gaze at close quarters. 'It looks to me as if he knelt on her – so – and then, if he simply threw his weight over the head, like this, that would be enough. No, as far as strength goes anybody might have done it.'

The Sergeant signalled to the constables, who moved in with sheet and stretcher. The pathologist, he noticed, was amused by the evident distaste with which they approached their task. Gingerly, turning their heads away, they manoeuvred the corpse onto the stretcher and hastily drew the sheet over it. Then they stepped aside to gulp some fresh air before carrying it to the ambulance.

'It won't bite you,' the pathologist said as he picked up his case, 'it's quite harmless.' He grinned in the direction of Sergeant Rosen. 'I'll let you have my full report tomorrow, though I don't suppose there'll be much to add to what I've already told you. After that it's up to you.' He turned and set off to his car, his legs twinkling over the turf.

Sergeant Rosen followed slowly. He did not relish his task. The trail was already cold, twelve days cold. There had been a considerable hou-ha after the girl had been reported as a missing person and it had elicited precisely nothing. Her friend had waved goodbye to her at three-thirty in the afternoon in the centre of Abenbury, at which time she had been walking towards a spot favoured by hitch-hikers waiting for lifts, and then she had apparently vanished. It was one of those impossible cases. Short of some extraordinary stroke of luck there was no reason in the world why her killer should ever be caught.

The Sergeant reached his car and began to radio for assistance. He needed a team of men to comb these moors. He must find that skirt and brassière, and the haversack that the girl had been carrying. It was even possible that the murderer had obligingly left behind a monogrammed cigarette case, or a handkerchief with a laundry mark, but Rosen doubted it. And even if he had, looking at these moors, the chances of finding it were pretty slim. He posted his men to keep sightseers away, not that there were any, yet, and then sat in his car waiting, feeling sorry for himself.

It would have been nice, near the end of his career, to have got the promotion that had so far eluded him, it would have made a difference to his pension too; but a case like this was not likely to give it to him. He knew what was ahead – hours of routine questioning, tracing the drivers of cars, following up reports, house-to-house inquiries on the off chance that some lead would be fruitful. He had been through it all before – that business twelve years ago. He had had his knuckles rapped then. If he had been a little more meticulous he would probably have been more than a sergeant now. Once you got a mark like that against you in your record you never properly got rid of it. He would not make the same mistake twice, but he knew that, now, he could do himself little positive good. He wondered who would be put on the case

5

over him. He hoped it would be Chatterton; Chatterton was the sort of man you could get along with.

Sergeant Rosen sat contemplating the moor stretching away on each side. Bloody awful wilderness. Suppose the murderer did it again. You could leave a dozen bodies out there without being found out. Imagine another murder next week, the clamour in the papers, the pressure for results; and all the while you were helpless, without a single lead. What a way to end your professional life! A car drew up behind and he turned in surprise, not expecting his reinforcements to arrive so soon. Then he cursed. They hadn't sent Chatterton after all. It was Detective Inspector Nicholson, and behind him was another car, full of bloody reporters.

2

Miss Cranston was quite right – you could see Sandra Duckham's knickers. Conrad was sitting at the back of the class, wedged uncomfortably into a chair designed for a six-year-old, trying to concentrate on his job of assessing Sandra's teaching performance, and he would be distracted every so often when she bent languidly forward to speak to a child, and there the knickers were, plainly visible. They were white, dotted with tiny pale blue flowers and trimmed with a narrow embroidered border of the same colour. Perched on his inadequate seat Conrad found that his eyes were at just the right level for him to get the full effect. It was a beautiful spring day, and Sandra had celebrated by, apparently, leaving most of her clothing at home. She wore a cotton dress of ostentatious simplicity loosely gathered about her waist and coming about two-thirds of the way down her thigh. It had no sleeves and was cut low at the back and very low at the front. She had an excellent figure, it was a pleasure to watch her move about, but that, Conrad reflected, was not something you could put into your notes. Her teaching, what little he had seen of it, was deplorable.

She seemed to have no idea at all of what she had been put into the classroom to do. Conrad shifted his legs uncomfortably and surreptitiously scratched his groin. She was representative, he thought, of the new order, an order with which he had no sympathy. She belonged to a generation that had been encouraged to think only of itself, to whom ideas like discipline and self-control were foreign. Look at her now. A muffled roar, punctuated by screams, was rising from the

Wendy House in the corner. Did she investigate? Did she feel that she ought to be exerting some kind of control? Did she hell. But it was not her fault. She was a child of her time, a victim of the theorists. They called themselves left-wing and dangled their fancy ideas about. Conrad wriggled in his chair. The edge was cutting his bottom infernally.

His father had been left-wing, a disciple of people like Bernard Shaw and Keir Hardie, an austere man to whom socialism had meant disinterested fellowship, social justice, and dedicated work demanding its just reward and no more. He had been a man of high ideals and some innocence of character, who would have found the modern notions which masqueraded under the flag of socialism inexplicable and offensive. How on earth, Conrad asked himself, not for the first time, had those early high ideals degenerated so?

Sandra Duckham bent forward to examine the work of an infant on the front row. 'Ooh, that's lovely, Kevin,' she said.

'No it isn't,' said the young artist accurately, 'it's just scribble.'

Sandra smiled and moved on. She was a confirmed 'Ooh-er'. When she wished to indicate approval she invariably prefaced what she said with 'Ooh', fancying, Conrad imagined, that this conveyed winsome charm.

Of course the Alderman Robertson College of Education, where she, for want of a better word, studied, and Conrad taught, should have done something about her. Either she should have shaken her ideas up a bit or been kicked out, but the College was in the grip of this curious new idea that no unpleasant pressures should be permitted to spoil the students' enjoyment of life. It was Jacks's fault. Conrad briefly allowed his thoughts to settle on Milton Jacks, the Vice-Principal, the man whom he detested most. Jacks was young and bright, and had all the fashionably trendy educational ideas. Under Jacks's rule it was not possible to apply the rigorous standards which Conrad considered appropriate, and the result was this. Conrad looked round the classroom with hostile attention.

A little boy who had been drawing a picture of a dinosaur playfully jabbed the girl sitting next to him in the eye with a crayon, and she set up a howl.

'What's the matter, Debbie?' asked Sandra calmly. Conrad had to admit that her nerve was good. The yell had startled him, and he had been expecting it, but she had not turned a hair.

'Nigel poked me in the eye with his crayon,' the little girl explained tearfully.

'Oh, dear, naughty Nigel, what did you want to do that for?' Her tone did not suggest that she was pressingly interested in getting an answer, and Nigel, taking no notice of her whatsoever, turned away and seized a lump of plasticine off another boy's table. Sandra moved on with somnolent dignity.

'You have to remember,' Conrad wrote, 'that you are responsible for the safety of these children.' He looked up. Yes, you could certainly see her knickers. As she bent forward the embroidered hem could be seen to rise fractionally up her thigh.

Conrad resumed his meditations. His very presence in this room was a consequence of Jacks's actions. The tutor who had come down last year, Stan McHale, was a youngster, with virtually no experience, appointed because Jacks had a policy of appointing the young. The fact that they could not do the job they were supposed to do was neither here nor there. What had happened? Predictably he had been so slack in his approach that Miss Cranston had sent in a written complaint about it and, Miss Cranston being a woman of some force, with quite a lot of influence in local educational circles, Conrad had been sent down this year, because he was a reliable man who could be trusted not to make a mess of things. Jacks despised him, almost openly derided what he

9

called his 'somewhat reactionary attitudes', but when it suited him he made use of Conrad's skills.

Miss Cranston was a formidable woman, who had begun by eyeing him with suspicion, but he had brought her round. Conrad was quite proud of his ability to judge character and handle people, and he reckoned that he had handled her well. She had begun by attacking him.

'I am sorry, Mr Nield, that we did not manage to meet on the twenty-ninth.'

The twenty-ninth of April had been their visit day, when the students came to the schools to complete their preparations and the tutors came round to see that all was well.

'It was most unfortunate, Miss Cranston. I went to my other schools in the morning and by the time I reached here you had had to leave.'

'I had a meeting at the Education Offices, Mr Nield.'

'So I believe. I regretted missing you particularly, because I always find it so valuable to discuss with the head teacher, on these occasions, the placing of the students.' Conrad had leaned forward as he said this, and managed to infuse into his speech a note of such convincing regret that she almost visibly began to soften.

'It cannot be helped, Mr Nield, but it was particularly unfortunate in view of the experience I had with the man who was sent down to me last year.'

'There will be no repetition of that, Miss Cranston.'

'I sincerely hope not.'

She glared at him, to remind him that she was a person not to be trifled with, and Conrad put on an expression of anxious solicitude. She was an intimidating figure, if 'figure' was the correct word for that shapeless mass of flesh. She was wedged into a high, wooden, swivel chair and she bulged out from between the bars. Her head merged, with no neck to speak of, into formidable fat shoulders, and she held her jaw and its three chins aggressively high above the folds of her bosom. She sat with her legs splayed apart so that Conrad could, if he chose, see the swelling where the elastic pinched her flesh above the knee.

'Miss Grey has pleased me,' she stated. 'The extent and nature of her preparation shows, to my mind, a certain maturity; unfortunately I cannot say the same for the other student.'

Conrad bowed his head in sorrow at these words.

'I am bound to say, Mr Nield, that Miss Duckham seems to me quite deplorably ill-prepared for the task she has undertaken. If we are to make anything of her at all she will require the most careful supervision.'

'You can rely on me, Miss Cranston, to do my part of the work with every care, and of course I shall be grateful for all the help you can give me.'

She smiled. It was not a cordial smile but it was another step in the process of the thaw.

'I will be frank with you, Mr Nield. I had hoped, after the report I sent in, that Mr Penniman would be sent down here again. I got on very well with Mr Penniman when he came down a couple of years ago. He seemed to me a man with the right ideas.'

Conrad gnawed his lip at this. It did not please him to hear Penniman preferred to himself. He swallowed his annoyance and explained mildly that Penniman was no longer available.

'He is leaving us, you know, that's why he wasn't sent down.'

'Mr Penniman leaving you? What a tragedy for the College! I should say it could ill afford to lose such a first-class man.'

Again Conrad managed to show no emotion, but he marvelled, not for the first time, at the ability Penniman had to spread this notion that he was exceptionally brilliant. The only talent he had was the one which Conrad knew he himself conspicuously lacked: the talent to sell himself.

'He's been appointed vice-principal of a college in the south.'

If Miss Cranston had been sensitive to tones of voice she would have heard envy in Conrad's words. He listened quietly to her raptures at his news and, when pressed, promised to convey her warmest congratulations to the sod.

'It is a pity the College is so far away. Before he leaves do tell him that I would be delighted to see him if he is in this neighbourhood. When he was tutor here he brought his wife down, and the three little children. Are you married, Mr Nield?'

'Yes, I'm married.'

'And have you any children of your own?'

'No, no children of my own.' Conrad just stopped himself from adding, 'Nor of anyone else's.'

'How long have you been married, Mr Nield?'

'Er – nineteen years.'

'Nineteen years, and no children? How old are you, Mr Nield?'

'Forty-six.' He began to feel that she was going beyond the limits of good taste. What was she getting at? Suppose he opened his fly and laid his apparatus on the desk in front of her. 'There you are, Miss Cranston, I've got 'em, you see, all present and correct and in full working order; excuse me if I don't give you a demonstration.'

Possibly she read something of his feeling in his face, for she gave an artificial laugh and said, 'I always like to get on friendly terms with the tutors the College sends down. It is so much easier to work in friendship, don't you think?'

Conrad agreed, perforce, that it was.

'From what I have been hearing about the College recently, Mr Penniman is very wise to be leaving it. What exactly is the situation there now?'

'Confused, Miss Cranston, we are none of us sure where we are. As a matter of fact I am returning this afternoon so that I can attend a meeting about it tomorrow.'

'A number of the colleges have been closed already, is that likely to happen to the Alderman Robertson?' Her eyes sparkled with malicious pleasure as she asked this question.

'That is something we are waiting to be told tomorrow, Miss Cranston.'

'If they do close the Alderman Robertson down, Mr Nield, what will happen to people like you?'

'I can answer that one,' Conrad replied, attempting a laugh, 'we'll be out of a job.'

'It won't be easy to get another one, not in the present state of affairs.'

Conrad could have told her that. It was a thought that had been his constant companion for over a year now – it was the fate that Penniman had escaped from. 'Let us hope,' he said, 'that they will close Warley Hey instead.'

There were two colleges of education in Bickleton, the industrial town eighty miles away where he lived, and Warley Hey was the other, and older, one.

Miss Cranston looked sour at this. 'Warley Hey,' she said with some asperity, 'has a very fine tradition. I am an old Warley Hey girl myself and I have always been very proud of the fact.'

There was nothing Conrad could say to this that would help to cement relations between himself and Miss Cranston, so he said nothing and she continued.

'In my day, Mr Nield, and this was long before the Alderman Robertson had even been thought of, Warley Hey gave us a very fine grounding, a very fine grounding indeed. It had standards, but nobody talks about standards now, it is a dirty word, you are not supposed to use it. Students don't seem to be trained to teach children any longer. I blame all these new ideas about free expression and letting the children

13

do as they like. And what is the consequence, Mr Nield?'

Conrad begged to be told the consequence.

'The general laxity in society, the absence of any kind of moral discipline. Look at the way young people behave today.'

Conrad said that it was very true.

'That girl they found on the moors the other day. What was she doing? What were her parents thinking of? Off on her own, cadging lifts from total strangers, what did she expect?'

Conrad nodded. He had read something about the case. A body had been discovered on Tuesday, and yesterday and today, Thursday, the newspapers had been full of unpleasant details. He did not usually look at stories like that and had only briefly scanned this one because it had happened so close by.

'This Duckham girl is just that type, I would say, and she could very well end up the same way. Have you seen the clothes she is wearing? Her dress hardly covers possible, as my father used to say, and when she bends down you can see right into the middle distance. At her age I would not have been allowed to flaunt my knickers in everybody's face.'

At the very moment she said this Conrad caught one of those unavoidable glimpses up her legs, and he had to swallow a couple of times and clear his throat before promising to speak to Sandra about the matter.

'You have to think of the little boys, Mr Nield. I know you probably think they are only babies, but if you had had children of your own you would know that a five- or six-year-old mite is quite a little man in some ways, and sitting there in those tiny chairs of theirs they can look right up her legs: you can see them staring.'

Conrad, ensconced at the back of the class, thinking over the recent scene, found himself not blaming them. The temptation to stare was difficult to resist, and he busied himself with his notes to occupy his attention until the end of the lesson.

'You see, Sandra, what you've got to ask yourself is, "What is my role in the classroom supposed to be?"' The children had gone home, the classroom was empty, and Conrad was trying to tell Sandra what it was that he had found wanting in her performance. 'Did it matter to the children whether you were there or not?'

A large tear was gathering in the corner of Sandra's left eye.

'Let me put it this way,' said Conrad desperately. 'There were all sorts of things going on in that room that you weren't even aware of. There were two boys fighting behind your back, did you see them?'

'But, Mr Nield,' she said reasonably, 'if they were behind my back how could I see them?'

Conrad managed to suppress the remark which sprang to his lips. He had had a trying day and did not deserve this.

'You could have turned round, Sandra, you could have kept looking about you. It is a teacher's job to keep her eye on the whole class. There was that little boy who poked that girl in the eye.'

'Well, I spoke to him about that, Mr Nield.'

'A fat lot of good it is speaking to him about it. You should have stopped him before he did anything. Suppose he had put her eye out?'

The tear had formed and filled and was trickling down her face.

'But I can't be everywhere at once, I mean, it's just not possible.'

'If you hope to be an infant teacher, Sandra, that is exactly what you have to do. And your preparation is simply not good enough. I have been looking through your schemes of

15

work and they are seriously deficient. Did anybody in the College check them?'

'Yes, I had them all seen, every one of them.'

'Who looked at your English scheme, for instance?'

'Mr McHale.'

Ha, McHale, it figured!

'I am quite sure that Mr McHale did not approve this.' He was not by any means sure, but Conrad told himself that he must be loyal. 'Did he say that you should add anything to it?'

Sulkily Sandra agreed that he had made one or two suggestions.

'And did you add them?'

'I'm going to next week.'

'Next week isn't good enough, Sandra, you are in the classroom now.'

If Stan McHale had been doing his job properly, of course, he would have insisted on Sandra bringing back the revised work for him to see. A typical piece of slackness.

A cleaner started working in the corridor outside, and the whine of her machine irritated Conrad. He began to think that it was hopeless to try to get through to this girl.

'What are you going to do tomorrow morning?'

'Number.'

'What sort of thing in number?'

'Counting and sorting.'

'Let's have a look at your preparation.'

'I haven't done anything yet.'

'Leaving it a bit late, aren't you?'

'I'm going to do it tonight, that's in time for tomorrow, isn't it?'

Conrad gave up. He had no intention of watching her lesson. He would be eighty miles away in College. He would just give her a general warning and point out that Miss Cranston was already displeased with the quality of her work. At the mention of Miss Cranston's name Sandra wrinkled up her nose.

'Oh, by the way, Sandra, while I'm on the subject of Miss Cranston's criticism, she doesn't care for that dress you are wearing. She would prefer something a bit more – er – complete, longer in the skirt, for instance.'

'Is there anything else, Mr Nield?'

'No, Sandra, just work a bit harder, prepare a bit better, and change that frock, and we'll all be pleased.'

She picked up her bag and walked away without another word, like a princess who has been affronted by a peasant. Well, let the sulky bitch go hang. He had given her fair warning. If she didn't pull her socks up she would be chopped. Whatever Milton Jacks might think, he, Conrad Nield, was not going to carry any passengers.

He went out and got into his car and began the drive back to Bickleton. Anxiety about tomorrow's meeting gnawed at him. Suppose that the College was to be closed. Miss Cranston was quite right – he would not get another job, in teaching or anywhere else. He was just the wrong age, too old to be re-employed and too young to qualify for a worthwhile redundancy settlement. What a reward it would be for a life of dedicated work, finishing up in the dole queue. He tried to think what his father would say and failed. It was a good job he was dead. He had spent long enough in the dole queue himself, and thought that his son, at least, had lifted himself out of that pit. It was ironical. He remembered his father's pleasure when he had reached the unimaginable heights of becoming a teacher in a grammar school. It had been not only social respectability, it had been security, a job for life.

Conrad had left the village of Forton Cross, where Miss Cranston's school was situated, and was heading for the moorlands which separated it from the city of Abenbury. He had a headache coming on. He was liable to sudden, quite violent headaches, always on the left-hand side of his head –

he sometimes wondered if they were a preliminary symptom of a brain tumour – and he preferred not to drive while the pain lasted. There was a lay-by shortly, he remembered. He had stopped there on the day of his duty visit and climbed the hill and looked over the moorlands and blown away the cobwebs. He'd had a headache then too. He would stop there again. Yes, there it was. Conrad cursed. It was full of police vehicles, and he had the normal, law-abiding citizen's reluctance to mingle too freely with the constabulary, so he drove on. He would find somewhere on the moors – but when he reached them he understood the police presence at the lay-by.

There was some kind of search going on. It must be to do with that murdered girl. Conrad remembered reading in the paper that they were trying to find some of her articles of clothing, as they put it. Conrad slowed to a dawdle and watched. They were like black cattle, in long lines, all stooping low, carefully combing the grasses. What a job! Over there was what appeared to be a squad of soldiers helping the police out. A pretty forlorn hope. They could not realistically expect to find much on that ground, and after this length of time. It had been the twenty-ninth of April when the girl disappeared. The day of his last visit to Miss Cranston's school. He might have been quite near when it happened. The thought came to Conrad with a jolt. Then a policeman waved at him impatiently to move on, and Conrad, recollecting himself, wound his window up and drove past. He had always despised people who hung morbidly round the scenes of violent episodes. He put the matter out of his mind and concentrated on his own problems.

3

As Conrad drove homewards, sourly contemplating the unsatisfactory turn his life had taken, it would have surprised and irritated him to know that his wife, Stephanie, was engaged in a similarly gloomy review of her own. It would have irritated him because it was an article of his domestic faith that Stephanie was perfectly happy with the life he had made for her and still thought with wonder of the remarkable chance that had thrown him in her way.

Conrad's courtship of Stephanie had been quite a romance, the only romance Conrad had ever had, and he was still proud of it. It had been the romance of the penniless suitor who carries off the wealthy princess. Not that Stephanie had been a princess, though she had belonged to a social class that Conrad, when he was a boy, could never have dreamed of having contact with. Her father, Mr Kitchen, had been a financier, with a small mansion, standing in its own grounds, on the fashionable side of the city; the sort of place where you saw lines of limousines parked outside in the evening, and heard the muffled sound of music and glimpsed figures in evening dress through the long windows.

To Conrad's father, a man active in trade-union and socialist affairs, Mr Kitchen had been, simply, a crook and a rogue, and undoubtedly there had been stories about him and he had suffered the occasional bankruptcy, which had never, as far as any outsider could judge, in the slightest degree affected his style of living. When he had died it was noticeable that he left surprisingly little, in spite of which his widow and her daughter had continued to live in the mansion, with every appearance of comfort.

Conrad had never known Mr Kitchen, for he had died

when Stephanie was only twelve. He had met her at a tennis club dance, in itself a surprising detail in view of the fact that Conrad never played tennis, could not dance, and rather despised those who did. But the dance was for charity and Conrad, in those days a young and eager junior master at the local grammar school, had found himself roped in as secretary of the charity. Stephanie had been the tall, shy girl lurking behind the tea-urn, apparently knowing no more people than Conrad did himself. It had been quite a thrill to Conrad to discover that she was the daughter of the notorious Kitchen, and she had confounded his expectations. In so far as he had formed any mental picture at all of the daughter of the financier he had thought of somebody like a London model, beautiful, poised, hard as nails. Instead she had been almost agonizingly ill at ease, worse even than Conrad, who had spent most of his evening wondering how he ought to be behaving in the company of these hateful snobs. The two of them had drawn together, Conrad had made Stephanie laugh a number of times with the comments he had made on some of the other guests and, a week later, racked with nervousness, he had picked up the phone and suggested that the two of them should visit the cinema to see a recently released French film of some artistic interest, and Stephanie had accepted.

Part of the mystery of Stephanie's contradictory character had been solved when he met her mother. A romance needs a dragon of some kind, and, conventionally enough, Mrs Kitchen filled the role. She was a silent woman, silent to Conrad at least; tall and bony. At one time she had probably been handsome but by the time Conrad knew her she was beginning to look raddled. She had made it clear, without any need for words and with no departure from the highest standards of social politeness, that his attentions to her daughter were unwelcome. Gradually Conrad came to understand why.

Mr Kitchen's operations had left him no time to cultivate social graces. Such entertaining as he did was strictly in pursuit of his business interests, and all the friends he made were of that fragile nature that they might be converted into enemies in the twinkling of an eye. His wife and daughter were confined to the background, required to appear when it was conventionally necessary and keep out of the way otherwise. Stephanie was sent for long periods to a genteel private school for girls, which was short on intellectual stimulus and long on social training, where the only thing she learned efficiently was how to cook. On her husband's death Mrs Kitchen said goodbye, gratefully, to the entire set of people who had surrounded him when things were going well, and confined herself willingly to the society of three or four old school friends.

Stephanie had no friends. Conrad had naturally assumed that Mrs Kitchen did not like him because he was not a good enough match, and only gradually realized that she did not want her daughter to marry at all, intending to keep her as a companion in her old age. And so the romance had been played out, Mrs Kitchen incredulous and hostile.

'You can say what you like, Stephanie, but I think he's common. What does his father do?'

'He doesn't do anything now, Mother, he's got a disability, but he used to be a furnace-man in the iron foundry.'

Mrs Kitchen had stared ahead of her, her lips twisted into an expression of contempt. Later, when Stephanie had told her of the positive engagement, she had said, 'Well, all I can say is that I'm going to get Bangstetter to tie your money up so that he can't get his hands on it anyway.'

Bangstetter, the family lawyer, was a proven expert at tying up property so that nobody, however aggrieved or whatever their claims, could get their hands on it.

'Oh, Mother, you don't suppose he's marrying me for my money, do you?'

'I've never met anybody yet who didn't like all that he could get hold of.'

The young couple had bought a house, paid for by Stephanie, and furnished with the good, solid, expensive antique furniture from the small mansion. Mrs Kitchen had retired to a flat filled with glass cases holding her collection of silver, and solaced herself by drinking a bottle of sherry every day. The romance had thus been completed.

It is curious how things turn out, at least that was Stephanie's conclusion thinking over the events of her life. Conrad had come into her orbit with a refreshing unexpectedness and had awakened her to all sorts of latent possibilities. She had admired him because of his intellectual gifts, because he had had to make his own way up in the world, and because she thought him a sincere person, who was dedicated to his work, not in a vulgar or careerist sense but because he believed in its value. After they were married she had discovered that he was an unrelaxed man, who had difficulty in forming friendships. He had no hobbies and no vices. His nights were spent preparing lessons, or marking, or working for his second degree. After he got the degree he began immediately to prepare material for a book on the teaching of English Literature, and if ever this got finished, she began to realize, some other intellectual scheme would instantly be taken up. He conversed usually on serious topics, sport he considered childish and television he dismissed as rubbish. He had a theoretical interest in what he called the 'philosophy' of politics, but for all the practical aspects of the subject he had nothing but contempt.

Early on he had taken Stephanie in hand, culturally speaking, made out lists of books for her to read, taken her to the theatre when anything 'important' was being performed, encouraged her to listen to the best music. At first Stephanie had been glad of this, for she was deeply ashamed of her educational limitations, and was afraid of how much more fascinating Conrad must find all those immensely clever women teachers he consorted with every day. Later she noticed that Conrad did not care for these women at all and always spoke unkindly of them behind their backs, and she realized that part of her charm for him was that she would never challenge his intellectual superiority. It was her submissiveness that pleased him. She kept his house nice, she cooked for him, she provided an appreciative audience for his views on his colleagues and his students. In return he gave her security. She would never experience the wild uncertainties that had harassed her mother.

So why was she dissatisfied? Why was she not feeling more pleased that because of the meeting at College tomorrow Conrad was coming home a day earlier than he had intended? Why, more importantly, was she feeling guilty that she had been entertaining Stan McHale in her husband's absence?

Conrad did not like Stan McHale, but of course he would not have objected to a colleague, in the same department, visiting his wife. Stan had sat on the settee and she had sat in the armchair. Stan had had a whisky and she had had a sherry. They had discussed an Italian class of which they were both members. Stephanie's guilt, she knew, was because she had caught herself enjoying the conversation a good deal more than she had enjoyed any conversation with her husband in the last few years. Again she ran over all the excellent qualities Conrad possessed that ought to have made her thankful she had married him, and she experienced almost a sense of panic at finding one or two items missing. When he had rescued her from her mother she had had the sense of doors opening unexpectedly on limitless opportunities, now she felt like a convict who has tried to dig his way out of prison and found himself in the cell next door. She really must pull herself together.

She expiated her disloyalty in the kitchen and ran eagerly

to the door when she heard Conrad's key turn in the lock. A look at his face told her immediately that he was worried about the meeting tomorrow. There was an elaborate expression of unconcern about him which was quite transparent. Conrad was very dependent on her in some ways. He would want to share his anxieties, to get her reassurances and be comforted, but he hated to show this dependence. He would pretend that there was nothing wrong, that he was perfectly well able to cope, thank you very much. She would be expected to wheedle him, hide the fact that she had seen anything amiss, console him on the sly. So as they moved together into the living room she contented herself by saying that it was nice to see him back and asking if he had had a good week.

'About as bloody as usual. Any letters?'

'James rang, he wants you to get in touch.'

Conrad frowned – this was not pleasing to him. James was Penniman's Christian name, and he felt that he had heard quite enough about him from Miss Cranston without having him intruding upon his home life.

'He'll have to wait. I have absolutely no intention of dancing attendance on Jimmy Penniman the minute I get back from Abenbury.'

'Did you know that they are going to fill his job?'

This was a tit-bit Stephanie had been saving. She knew that it would please him, as, indeed, it did, though he was reluctant to show it. 'Brenda told me.'

This was not true. It was Stan who had told her, but she did not wish, in Conrad's present humour, to bring Stan's name into their conversation.

'It's on the notice board, Brenda said; they want the applications in as soon as possible. Perhaps that was why Jimmy phoned.'

'I doubt it, nothing to do with Jimmy how they fill the vacancy.'

24

But he did not say this in a snubbing way, he spoke slowly and thoughtfully, evidence that he was already feeling better. It was cheering news in two ways. If Penniman's job was to be filled after all, perhaps this meant that the College was not going to be closed down, though of course you could not place undue reliance on that argument. And, of course, Conrad must be regarded as a hot favourite to take over from Penniman; he had run him pretty close the last time the job had been on offer. Characteristically Conrad began to think of possible obstacles.

'I wonder if they're advertising it outside the College?'

'Brenda says not.'

'I suppose Cyril's already put in for it.' Cyril Davidson was Brenda's husband, and Conrad's great friend and rival.

'According to Brenda, Cyril said the job was probably yours.'

'Well, he would, wouldn't he? That isn't going to stop him doing his damnedest himself. It's a principal lectureship, you know. Even if the College does stay open it'll be a long time before another of those becomes vacant.'

But it was no use. In the face of this unexpected invitation to cheer up he could not maintain his gloom. He got himself a drink, he paced up and down his living room, taking in the antique solidity of the furniture, which always pleased him so much because it measured the distance he had come from his father's house, and his features gradually lost their pinched expression. He announced that they might as well crack a bottle of wine to have with their meal and bustled about getting the corkscrew and glasses. He kept popping in and out of the kitchen while Stephanie was finishing her preparations, and she was able to remark the gradual recovery of his spirits.

'Cyril won't be the only one, you know. Everybody will be after this.'

He held the bottle up to the light and peered anxiously into its depths.   .

'It would be a great mistake to think that it was going to be a walk-over.'

He opened the bottle with a flourish.

'It's about two thousand a year more, you know. I'd be getting very nearly ten thousand a year.'

What would his father have said to that – his own son a ten-thousand-a-year man – he would never have credited it.

'Did Cyril actually say that he thought the job was mine?'

Over the meal itself he became almost buoyant.

'I tell you one thing, I'm glad that I grabbed that course from Cyril.'

It was an old story, but Stephanie patiently listened to it all over again. It was Conrad's greatest success to date over his friend, and Cyril had neither forgiven nor forgotten it. The new BEd degree courses were widely recognized to be of the greatest importance in the future development of the College, and when the staff had been called together to consider how they were going to plan them there had been a keen interest in deciding who would be asked to chair the committee which would do the planning. Dr Gorning, the Principal, had asked for nominations, and Jacks had immediately proposed Cyril's name. 'I can't think of a man more capable of putting through the kind of scheme we need, one that will gain the approval of the University and that will attract the right calibre of student. I'd really be most grateful if we could prevail on Cyril to take on yet another onerous duty.' And Cyril had levered himself to his feet and protested his entire unworthiness for such work, and reminded the assembled gathering of the heavy burden which he was already carry-ing. And he had looked round in a pathetic humble way that had been maddening.

Conrad had jumped up. 'I think, Mr Chairman, that we

all have sympathy with Mr Davidson on this point. It is hardly fair to take advantage of his sense of duty in this way, he is already carrying far too great a load. I would like to propose that we look further afield.'

When Conrad reached this point in his story he took a mouthful of wine to savour along with his triumph, and went on to describe his rival's discomfiture.

'You should have seen his face when I said that.'

Stephanie said that it must have been worth looking at.

'He couldn't say a bloody thing, and neither could Jacks. And then Gorning turned to me and said, you know that way of his, all sheepish, not looking you in the face, "Perhaps we could persuade you, Mr Nield, to take on the responsibility yourself." Cyril looked as if he could have killed me.'

It had been a rich moment. At the time it had merely been a skirmish in the battle that the two of them were always fighting. Cyril had immediately got himself elected onto the committee and had kept up a constant sniping action at their meetings ever since. Now it assumed greater importance.

'Being Chairman of the BEd Committee is bound to be a help, Stephanie. After all, these are the courses that our whole future, if we have any, is bound up with.'

From this point onwards the meal ran merrily. Stephanie was even emboldened to make a proposal about her Italian class, a scheme which Stan had come round to discuss with her earlier. Conrad was not all that sympathetic to the Italian venture, in fact he did not favour any operation for the improvement of his wife's mind which did not begin and end with himself, so it was necessary for her to introduce the subject tactfully and gradually, and she began by talking about last Monday's lesson, and what Mr Burkinshaw, the class teacher, had said, and what her friend Margery had said, and how much better Margery had explained it than Mr Burkinshaw.

'She lived in Italy for two years, you know.'

27

'What's she taking the lessons for, then?'

'She wanted to brush it up.'

Conrad took a drink of wine and delivered his verdict. 'Can't be any fun for old Burkinshaw, having somebody like Margery in his class.'

'You'd think he'd be glad to have someone who knows the language.'

'Why should he? He's supposed to be teaching beginners. You don't want some damn know-all like Margery showing off and making you look small.'

Conrad disapproved of Margery, who seemed to him to typify a good deal of what was wrong with the world. She was a big, mannish woman, just coming through her second divorce, a strident activist for feminism who had a most unpleasant eleven-year-old daughter exactly like herself. Stephanie was impressionable enough, and foolish enough, to have been taken in by her completely.

Conrad interrupted the train of thought which the mention of Margery's name always induced in him to attend to what his wife was saying – something about a trip to Italy.

'I wouldn't mind going, Steph, I haven't been to Italy, but the idea of visiting Florence in the company of Margery doesn't exactly thrill.'

'Not you,' said Stephanie, nervously. 'It's only for members of the group. We thought that if husbands and wives went then we wouldn't speak the language. There's going to be a penalty for every word of English spoken.'

Stan had gone into it all that afternoon, he had made it sound very attractive.

'When was this thought up?'

'Oh, just recently. Mr Burkinshaw thought that it would be a good thing, and most of the others are quite keen.' She did not mention Stan's name, no reason to single him out more than anyone else.

Conrad pulled a face.

'Don't you like the idea? Don't you want me to go?'

'My dear Stephanie, the only question that matters is, do you want to go? It's your money. You're a perfectly free agent. Traipsing round North Italy with Margery and Mr Burkinshaw is something that I personally would go a long way to avoid, but every man to his taste. When is this jaunt planned for?'

'Next Easter.'

'Well, if I were you I'd hold my fire a bit. By the time next Easter comes you may have very different ideas about it.'

Stephanie waited, poised. How Margery would despise her. She was almost begging permission and had to stop herself asking, 'May I go?', substituting instead the words, 'You wouldn't mind, then?'

'I would mind in a way, of course. It would be nicer, surely, if you and I went somewhere on our own, but you do as you like.'

This was Conrad's philosophy; people were individuals, no one had a right to control another person; and he strove to live up to this in his private as well as public life. Stephanie eagerly accepted the gains she had made and hastily turned the conversation to the murder that had taken place near Abenbury, saying how dreadful it was about that poor girl. Conrad agreed that it was dreadful, but added that some of these young people asked for trouble.

'Every time I come through Abenbury there are always girls, on their own, at the side of the road, thumbing lifts. If you think about it it's surprising this sort of thing doesn't happen more often.'

'Of course, you go along that road, don't you?'

Conrad replied that it was the only road across the moors, and began telling her how he had seen the police that afternoon searching for something.

'They were all strung out, bending down. An impossible job, I'd say, on that ground.'

'It was the twenty-ninth she went missing, it says in the papers. Wasn't that the day of your last visit down there?'

This was tactless of Stephanie. They both had reason to remember the day of Conrad's visit to his schools in the Abenbury area. While he was away Margery had come, in great excitement, and proposed that Stephanie should join her at a meeting that evening. They were having a guest speaker to address them on the subject of battered wives, and there was even a chance that some of the victims themselves would be there. So Stephanie had put Conrad's dinner in the oven to keep warm, left a message for him, and gone off to enjoy herself. Conrad had returned, tired, worn-out by the effort of being pleasant to people all day, nursing a headache which his brief walk in the moorland air had only temporarily banished, and had had to find his own meal, which, when he finally sat down to it, had been dried up and lukewarm. He had been very reasonable about it afterwards. He had pointed out to Stephanie that he had no objection at all to her spending her evenings any way she chose but that it would be pleasant, courteous even, if she gave him prior warning.

'It would have been the easiest thing in the world for me to have stopped off somewhere on the way back for a meal.'

Since then the matter had come up once or twice in conversation, so her mention of the date made Conrad tense, and when she added that it was rather funny, he asked her what, exactly, she meant by that.

'Well, you being down there on the day she went missing, and then you seeing the police actually looking for her on the moors.'

'Funny isn't the word I'd choose. And they weren't looking for her, they'd already found her two days earlier.'

Stephanie persevered. 'The police say that they want everybody who went along the road on April the twenty-ninth to get in touch with them. Are you going to?'

'I shouldn't think so. I don't think I've got anything to say that would interest the police.'

'They want to know if anybody saw anything.'

'Yes, well I didn't, and I've got better things to do with my time than waste it in police stations. In fact I think I'll go upstairs now and make a start on drafting out my application. I suppose Brenda didn't tell you the actual date when they are due in, did she?'

No, Brenda had not told Stephanie this.

'I suppose,' she said, stopping Conrad as he was about to ascend the stairs, 'that if you're going to spend all the evening working I may as well go round to see Margery.'

Conrad indicated, with a wave of his hand, that she was free to visit whomsoever she wished, and he continued on his way upstairs.

In his study Conrad felt contented and secure. This was his spiritual home, surrounded by books, with the door shut, on his own, a manageable world. He settled down and began drafting out his application for Penniman's job. He put his date of birth, listed the schools he had attended, the University, his degrees, the jobs he had held. Even baldly set down like that they had a pretty impressive quality. It is not everybody who has a first-class degree from Bickleton. They were the record of a life of steady application, building on considerable natural ability. Look at that State Scholarship that had got him to the University in the first place, he had worked for that. On summer evenings, when other kids had been out playing in the streets, he had been stuck up in his little bedroom, at that desk that his father had made for him, swotting at his books. Modern children did not have to do that sort of thing. A State Scholarship had been a big thing in those days. He could remember that evening, when his father had got in from his work and he had told him about it, and his father had actually broken down and cried. There was a lump in Conrad's throat as he recalled the scene. A first-class degree – he had been offered the chance of research. His Professor had made the offer himself, but unfortunately, because of his father's chest trouble, he had not been able to accept. Nowadays every Tom, Dick and Harry was asked to do research, but at that time it had been a rarity. No, he could honestly say that if he did get this job of Penniman's he deserved it.

Conrad was so uplifted by the thought of possible promotion that he found the spirit to resume work on his book on the teaching of English Literature, an enterprise which went swiftly or slowly according to his fluctuating moods, and which had recently ground almost to a halt. Now he took it out and read approvingly the section which he had last written, dealing with the shortcomings of existing teaching: 'If the cultivation of pleasure in literature is our aim – and who is there to say that it should not be our aim? – then one turns from what goes on in far too many classrooms with something akin to stupefaction. In what way, one asks oneself, can this dull rote-learning of facts, this memorizing of plots, this stereotyped production of "character studies" contribute to enjoyment?'

Conrad smiled. It was well said, even finely said. Then he frowned and addressed himself to the task of describing what the teacher ought to be doing.

'The task facing the teacher of literature,' he wrote, 'is difficult indeed. For it is in literature, if anywhere, that the great humanizing influences are to be found. Contact with literature, rightly understood, is contact with the human mind and spirit at precisely those points where they are most sensitively displayed, and the child who is encouraged to make this contact will emerge from the experience more capable of responding in a human, sensitive, sympathetic manner to the demands made upon him by society and by his fellows. And this contact is especially needed in an age such as ours, where so many of the forces of mass culture seem combined to blunt sensibilities and coarsen our responses. It requires courage and steadfast purpose not to flinch in the face of such a challenge.'

Conrad paused to enjoy the savour of these words, their combination of classical balance and urgent force. This was the kind of thing that needed to be said.

Stephanie was not going round to see Margery, who, she knew, had gone with a group of women to picket a cinema which was showing pornographic films. To salve her conscience Stephanie took a route past Margery's door, but she went straight on until she came to Stan McHale's flat. Now that she had virtually got Conrad's permission to go there were one or two things she wanted to discuss with him about the Italian trip. It would be nice to have another chat with Stan. He might even take her for a drive into the country and they would have a drink at that remote pub they had found. Later they would sit in the car and talk. Nothing improper would take place. Stephanie had been strictly brought up. There was absolutely no harm in what she was doing.

4

At the murder headquarters Sergeant Rosen was working late, checking through his files and thinking of the meeting that had taken place earlier that day in Superintendent Pearce's room. It had not been pleasant. There had been criticism in the newspapers and the Superintendent, fresh from an encounter with a hostile group of reporters, had been in a mood to make things difficult.

It was the mother of the dead girl who had started it all, by complaining publicly of the lack of police response when she had reported her child missing. 'They didn't do anything at all. If those boys hadn't gone that way my poor girl would be still lying there.' That was how the newspapers had quoted her remarks, and when the Superintendent was tackled about it he had not had a convincing reply. Hence his indignation with his subordinate.

'I'm bound to say, Rosen, that you might have been a bit more energetic.'

'I took all the normal steps, sir. You get people reported missing every week. If we followed up every one of them in detail we'd get no other work done at all. Nine times out of ten, when it's a girl of this age, she turns up safe and sound in a few days. She was over eighteen, sir.'

'It's all very well to say all that, Rosen, but she didn't turn up safe and sound, did she? It puts us in a poor position.'

The Superintendent had scowled and fiddled with the papers on his desk and talked about the need to tighten up procedures, and Sergeant Rosen had squirmed like a rebuked schoolboy. Inspector Nicholson, stretching his legs on the other side of the room, had enjoyed his discomfiture.

What had prevented Rosen from defending himself more vigorously was the thought that this mother might have some truth on her side. He *had* been rather off-hand. She had come to see him and he had failed to see any urgency in the case at all. This daughter who had gone off was a young kid, on holiday, and was probably enjoying herself somewhere and had forgotten to get in touch with home. He had not been inclined to set the whole of the police machinery in motion over a thing like that. If a girl of eighteen chose to go off by herself who was to stop her? So he had spoken soothing words to the mother, expressing the belief that her child would soon turn up with a very simple explanation of her absence. When he had had to take the woman to identify the body these words had been flung back at him bitterly. Rosen knew that he could have done very little more than he had, and that whatever he had done would not have made any difference, but he felt guilty.

Even worse, this feeling of guilt had hurried him into an indiscretion at the meeting for which he was still kicking himself. Anxious to put himself right with the Superintendent he had suggested a reconstruction of the girl's movements. Dress a policewoman in the victim's clothes and walk her through the streets at the time when she was abducted to see if anybody recognized her. It might provide a useful lead, it would show that the police were active.

The Superintendent had been impressed and had even begun to nod his approval when Nicholson had put his oar in. He had been watching with a supercilious smile and turned and asked, in the gentlest way, 'What time was it when she was abducted, Jack?'

'She was last seen at half past three.'

'I know that, but when was she abducted? She could have been walking about the city for hours.'

'He's got a point there, Rosen.'

'You see, sir –' Nicholson turned and addressed the Superintendent directly – 'it's not only that. We don't know which way she went after she said goodbye to her friend. She could have been picked up anywhere in the city. Unless we know the time, and the route she took, it's no good putting on a show like that. We'd make ourselves look fools.'

The Superintendent's nod had become a shake, and he had muttered an acknowledgement of his Inspector's acuteness.

Nicholson had pressed his advantage. 'I think Jack's trouble is that he's jumped to the conclusion that the girl set out immediately for the road across the moors and was picked up almost as soon as she started. I think she'd be much more likely to stay in the city and that she met whoever it was in a pub or a dance hall or a club or something.'

Superintendent Pearce looked at Rosen, inviting comment.

'There's one thing against that, sir. According to the pathologist the dead girl had nothing to eat after she left her friend. They had a pork pie and a pint of bitter beer each at just after two o'clock. She wouldn't have hung about too long without having something else.'

Nicholson had had nothing to say about this except that you could not rely on it, but he had produced another, and disconcertingly novel, idea.

'How do we know, sir, that she hadn't arranged to meet someone in Abenbury? I mean, it seems a bit thin to me, the idea of two girls starting off on a holiday like this and then one of them just leaving the other in the lurch. Make much more sense if they'd come with the idea of splitting up.'

All that Rosen could say was that there was no evidence for this. He was annoyed. Nicholson seemed to be plucking theories out of the thin air just to embarrass him. He was convinced that he had some idea of his own which he was not prepared to reveal yet.

'That friend of hers, Denise Quilley, didn't say anything about it, and she ought to have known.'

36

'Not necessarily, and even if she did she might not have told you. Suppose they came away, both of them intending to meet boyfriends without letting their mothers know.'

The discussion had become theoretical and futile and eventually Rosen had hauled it back to immediate practicalities.

'We might get a photograph of the policewoman dressed in the dead girl's clothes, sir. Be useful to show people, help jog their memories.'

This had gained the Superintendent's grudging approval, but all he actually said was, 'I'm surprised you haven't had that done before, Rosen,' and the Sergeant had left the meeting feeling that his stock had fallen considerably.

Methodically he inspected the monstrous sheaf of reports which his men had already collected. He must get some more cardboard boxes to hold them. He was oppressed by the hopelessness of the task. Look at this, for instance. A sports car had been seen parked in a suspicious place, but the witness could not remember whether it was the twenty-ninth or the day after. Why was it suspicious? Because she could not remember seeing a car parked there before. Rosen dropped it into the box. Here was another. A van, travelling very slowly, 'as if he was looking for somebody' – was that important? At least the date was reasonably certain. Rosen read the description. The van was dark, and it was old. How very useful. The next one roused his interest more. A red Cortina had actually been seen to pick up a girl, on her own, at about twenty past four, on the road out to the moors. Rosen marked the card for high priority and continued with his work. Most of the reports were useless, or at least would only become useful if they could be collated with later sightings. In other words, what he was doing was collecting evidence for the time when there was another murder. This was the fear that haunted them all.

5

Conrad decided to walk into College on the following morning. He wanted time to think things over and the exercise
would soothe him.

The Alderman Robertson College of Education was situated in a fine eighteenth-century mansion which had been
built by the Potterton family on a hill overlooking the town.
Most of the landscaped parkland, with which they had
insulated themselves from the collieries and foundries and
mills that provided their wealth, still remained as a gracious
setting for the College buildings. To Conrad's father the
house had represented the tyranny of the capitalist bosses; to
Conrad it had represented the unreachable heights of wealth.
Generations of the Potterton family had controlled the des-
tinies of Bickleton from this house until finally the industrial
landscape they had created sickened them and they had left it
and it had fallen into decay. During the war it had been taken
over by one of the ministries and afterwards the Pottertons
had given the wreck to the city fathers, who had used it
gratefully for the new teacher training college they had
pledged themselves to found.

So when Conrad opened the small wrought-iron gate in
the high stone wall and took the path that wound upwards
through the trees he was entering, as lord and master,
territory that had been forbidden him as a boy, where his
father had gone only by permission, cap in hand.

Nearer the College the sight became impressive in another
way. Dotted about the park were elaborate structures of glass
and concrete: a sports hall, a library, student hostels, a
science block. A reassuring three-quarters of a million

pounds had been spent on that little lot. Surely no government would be insane enough to throw money away on that scale. Warley Hey, that Miss Cranston spoke so highly of, occupied a building which had once been a workhouse and was stuck behind the cattle market. Even the University, housed in a red brick Victorian monstrosity like a large public lavatory, envied them.

On his way up to his room Conrad heard steps following him and, turning, saw a tall, fat oaf of a student, wheezing asthmatically from the unaccustomed exercise, evidently trying to catch up with him.

'Mr Nield, it's about that assignment for C/P/12,' he gasped as soon as he got within range, 'will it be all right if I bring it in next week?'

Conrad gazed at him, outraged. 'No, I'm afraid it will not. The date is clearly stated on the assignment sheet. The work should have been handed in yesterday.'

'Yeah.' The student steadied himself against the wall to assist his breathing. 'But I've had a bit of trouble.'

'What sort of trouble?'

The student, Conrad wished he could think of his name, ducked and swayed his shoulders like an embarrassed child. 'Well, look, I don't want to talk about it really.'

A thought struck Conrad, he could not remember teaching this student.

'Whose group are you in?'

'Mr Milne's.'

'Have you asked Mr Milne?'

'Yeah, he told me to see you. He said you were the course director.'

This was a bit rich. Milne knew perfectly well that the date for completing the work had been decided by the Course Committee and was not on any account to be varied.

'Well, I'm very sorry but as course director it is my job to see that all the different groups are treated equally. If I gave you an extension then the other students would be entitled to ask for one also, wouldn't they?' This admirable logic left the student unimpressed.

'Yeah, but I thought, in the circumstances –'

'You don't tell me what the circumstances are. If you have a medical reason for failing to produce work then you should bring me a certificate from your doctor. I am bound by the regulations just as much as you are.'

The student gaped like a stranded fish. 'Yeah, but I mean, it's only a week.'

'What's that got to do with it? You are here to learn self-discipline. It will be no good, when you are teaching in a school, telling the headmaster that you're sorry but you can't take your class today because some private difficulty has come up, will it?'

Conrad waited for an answer but the student failed to produce one and, after a moment, turned away muttering. Conrad continued up the stairs springily and athletically, demonstrating that even at the advanced age of forty-six he was still in excellent shape. He wondered what was wrong with the student. Sex, or drugs, or both, no doubt. They were all the same, up till all hours drinking and fornicating like rabbits.

It was a pity that Milne had not been there to witness the scene. It would have taught him an important lesson about how to deal with students, if only he was willing to learn it. Milne was one of the younger men, a colourless, ingratiating person with a footling mind, who was anxious to be liked by everybody. A teacher should not, Conrad thought, shirk making himself unpopular at times. Look at this case. Unable to take a strong line with this student he had sent him along to Conrad. So now the student would be telling everybody how kind Mr Milne was, and that it was only that bastard Nield who had refused him an extension. And if it ever came to Milton Jacks's ears, Conrad reflected, reaching his room and opening the door, Jacks would be sure to support Milne and blame Conrad for his harshness. That was why it was so impossible to have standards in this bloody place.

On Conrad's desk was a note in Penniman's handwriting. He snatched it up, quickly hostile, but his hostility changed to amazement as he read it.

Dear Conrad,
Sorry I didn't get you at home yesterday but I assume you'll be at the meeting. I have suggested that you should take my place as examinations secretary. Perhaps we could have a chat about this some time.

J. T. P.

Conrad sat down to take in the implications of this. The invitation pleased him immensely. It was the duty of the examinations secretary to prepare for the University the lists of those students entered for the examinations. It carried no extra pay but it was important and it brought its holder into contact with the staff of the University, which Conrad considered a desirable thing. It was bound to strengthen his application. Coming at this time, in fact, it seemed almost a token. Penniman's post was open to competition and here was one of Penniman's most important subsidiary jobs handed to him as if by right. Penniman must have consulted the Principal about this, he could not have done it off his own bat. Some of the optimism of the previous evening, which had been chilled by Conrad's apprehension about the meeting this morning, returned to warm him, and he collected his papers and set off down the stairs again feeling almost cheerful.

Conrad's room was in one of the new blocks and the meeting was to take place in the old mansion, still the administrative centre of the College. As he started to cross the campus he saw Cyril Davidson ahead of him and called to him to wait. Cyril stood silently and made an elaborate pantomime of scrutinizing his friend, examining in particular his wrists. Conrad was puzzled and wary. Some kind of joke was clearly intended and he did not want to show that he could not see it.

'Handcuffs,' Davidson explained, 'I was looking for them. You mean the police haven't cottoned on to you yet?'

Conrad continued to look blank.

'What do you do when you go on these school visits? All these slaughtered girls littered about the moors. I'm surprised at you, driving a swathe through the local maidenry.'

Conrad smiled frostily. So that was it. The joke was not in the best of taste but delicacy had never been Cyril's strong suit.

'If it had been me,' his companion continued, 'I could have understood it. I was down in Abenbury a few years ago myself. Struck up quite a cordial relationship with the daughter of the Three Feathers.'

He smirked at Conrad, who recognized that his admiration was being sought for Casanova Davidson. He wondered what sort of a self-image his companion had. He must be in his fifties, he had a worn, leathery, blotched look, he hit the bottle more than a little, but he still fancied himself as the devil of a fellow with the ladies. He was contemptuous of Conrad's lack of ease with women, and it was a recurrent and tiresome joke of his to pretend that his friend shared his own prowess. It did seem, though, that his mind was not fully on what he was saying and he did not push the tease as relentlessly as he normally would. He was worried about the meeting, Conrad instantly concluded, and he became even more apprehensive himself.

'A surprise about this job of Penniman's,' Conrad ventured, 'I never thought they'd appoint in his place. You going to apply?'

Davidson assumed an expression of indifference. 'I doubt

it. It rather depends on what Gorning tells us today. We may all be applying for jobs elsewhere.'

'Why, what have you heard?'

Davidson spoke slowly and judiciously, spinning out the agony. 'The word is that they're just going to close us down and keep Warley Hey.' He turned and scrutinized his friend malevolently. 'Had you heard that Warley Hey have already got their BEd submission in to the University?'

'No.' Conrad was staggered.

'Absolutely cut and dried. Jacks is pretty livid about it, I may as well warn you. He seems to think that if you'd pulled your finger out we might have got our scheme in ahead of them and that would have improved our chances of surviving.'

The news affected Conrad like a blow to the stomach. They were blaming him for the College being closed down now, were they? What bloody cheek! It had been Davidson's constant obstructiveness at the meetings of the committee that had held them up. He had had a proposal ready months ago. He bit his lip and thought furiously. He did not believe for a minute that his friend was not going to apply for Penniman's job. A principal lectureship, and the extra two thousand a year it carried, were always worth having. There might be as little truth in everything else he had said. Cyril enjoyed spreading alarm, and missed no opportunity of getting at his friend about his handling of the BEd course. Neither man said another word until they entered the main building.

Conrad had always liked the room in the old mansion where the staff had their meetings. It was here that he felt most strongly the sense of the past. From the windows he could enjoy an uninterrupted view, across the parkland, to the distant, muted roofs of Bickleton. Somewhere among the huddle of terraced workers' dwellings, in the dip on the left-hand side, was the house where Conrad had been born.

43

He liked to give it a glance occasionally and measure the distance he had come. Today the spectacle was poignant.

The room was full and the staff were chattering nervously and loudly. They all seemed to have heard the rumour about the College closing and were anxious to cover their feelings by an almost hysterical jokiness. Several of them asked Conrad what he had been up to in Abenbury and it cost him an effort to keep civil. In the far corner, the only relaxed person in the room, was Penniman, who, since he clearly had no personal interest in the proceedings, must have come to enjoy the spectacle. He saw Conrad and waved, but Conrad made no attempt to reach him. Disconnected phrases came to his ears. 'Well, I'm old enough not to have to bother.' 'It's a Union matter, what do we pay our subs for?' 'I reckon it'll take at least four years to run this place down anyway.' Nobody seemed to be taking an optimistic view and Davidson turned to Conrad, spread his hands apart, and said, 'See, what did I tell you?' Then Dr Gorning, the Principal, entered, walked slowly to the front, and stood facing his audience.

The sight of him chilled the staff into silent immobility. His whole demeanour expressed the bearer of ill-tidings. Worse, he looked almost furtive, as though he had something shameful to say. He was a tall, diffident man, who writhed as he spoke and always tried to avoid looking his interlocutor in the eye. He was writhing excruciatingly now and directing his remarks at a picture of his predecessor which hung on the wall at the side of the room.

'I – er – it – er – falls to my lot – er – to make an announcement which some of you will find pleasing and – er – some of you will find – er – less pleasing.' He drew a deep, gasping breath and someone was heard to say, 'For Christ's sake, get on with it.'

'I won't beat about the bush,' continued Gorning. 'What is being proposed, not to put too fine a point on it, is a merger between the University and this College.' As soon as he had said this he started back, as if alarmed by the words that had come out of his own lips. There was a moment's stunned silence, and then somebody gave a nervous laugh, and a babble of conversation started. All over the room people were registering incredulous relief. No one had predicted such a glorious termination of the crisis. And then they gradually noticed that their Principal was standing with his head bowed and a look of sick anxiety on his face, and the chattering and the occasional spurt of laughter died away.

'Perhaps,' said Dr Gorning, 'you should hear the full story before making up your minds about it. As you all know the University is very cramped for space and the Education Department in particular has long been seeking ways to expand. Well, they have seen their opportunity, in these present difficulties, to take over our buildings for this purpose. In fact they want to move up here lock, stock and barrel.'

The spark of relief was quite extinguished. Dr Gorning's drift was unmistakable, but it was Tony Skillington, one of the more outspoken members of staff, who forced him to put it into words.

'We understand that the University is taking over the buildings and, presumably, the students, but what about us?'

Dr Gorning was glad that this point had been raised. It had formed the chief subject of many of the discussions they had had with the University authorities. What had finally been decided, after much soul-searching, was that all members of staff with the grade of principal lecturer and above would become members of the University staff. Dr Gorning took a long, sighing breath when he had got this out. 'As to the rest, there may be one or two places available, and I can give you my personal assurance that applications from you will receive the most careful consideration.'

It was Tony Skillington who, in the storm of abuse and

45

protest that followed this, made the neatest demonstration. He rose to his feet, eyes ablaze, quietened his infuriated colleagues, and said, 'I would like to propose a motion congratulating the senior staff of this College on the truly excellent way in which they have looked after their own interests, and add a rider expressing regret that there was no one present at these meetings to look after ours.'

Dr Gorning smiled foolishly and stood before them like a Christian martyr trying to take his stoning in good part.

Throughout this demonstration Conrad remained quiet. He was as lividly angry and as achingly disappointed as the rest of them, but a voice was whispering prudence in his ear. This job of Penniman's was at the principal lecturer grade. If he got that he would be safe, he would have entered paradise, he would become a University don. Silly to be seen making a fuss in these circumstances.

6

Conrad returned to Abenbury on the following Tuesday morning in a divided state of mind. There was considerable relief in putting eighty miles between himself and the irritations both of the College and of his home, but he was also aware that it might be dangerous. On the Monday he had called a meeting of the committee which was planning the important new BEd courses, and Davidson had made it plain straight away that the knives were out. Conrad still felt furious about it. It should have been such a simple meeting. Conrad had produced his draft of the proposals which, in nearly four months of bickering, they had finally agreed together, and when he had dropped Davidson's copy on the table in front of him the man had shied away from it as though it was infected.

'I am not at all sure, Conrad,' he had said, leaving it lying there, 'that we shouldn't re-think this in the light of last Friday's announcement.'

Conrad had almost snarled at him. The only difference which last Friday's announcement had made was that Davidson had woken up to the fact that he had been a fool to let this chairman's job slip through his fingers.

Conrad had argued, he had threatened, he had pleaded. Davidson had lounged back in his chair, sticking his legs out in front of him, his voice the reverse of apologetic as he had said, 'I'm sorry, Conrad, but I didn't think we had come to any decision.' It had all been very trying and unpleasant.

Davidson had become confidential and solemn. Among his many vanities was that of thinking, on any issue, that he was on the inside, privy to information denied to ordinary mortals. 'The fact is, Conrad, that I was having a chat about this with Jacks last Friday, and he's got a pretty shrewd idea who the chairman of the assessors is going to be. He thinks it will be Professor Carnaby, and if it is then the sort of scheme you've got here will be no good at all.' And he had looked at Conrad as if he had just trumped his ace, which, in a way, he had done. Professor Carnaby was one of these modern, unsound men, who would eagerly support the sort of loose, trendy, sociological mish-mash that Jacks and Davidson had been proposing.

Conrad had begun to feel desperate. They were not arguing about trivialities. There would be almost no teaching for Conrad under the sort of scheme Davidson was proposing. Also, it was becoming obvious that he was aiming to snatch the chairmanship of the committee off him.

Davidson had fished in his case and brought out a sheaf of cyclostyled documents. 'I did this over the weekend and had them run off this morning. I think it's more likely to be the sort of thing Carnaby would go for.'

'This is quite unauthorized, Cyril,' Conrad had said. 'The committee hasn't approved it or anything.'

'Want to put it to the vote?'

Conrad looked about him. The meeting had been called at short notice and two of the members who normally supported him had failed to turn up.

'I don't think we're all here, Cyril.'

'Too bloody bad. You said yourself that it was urgent. If they can't be bothered to attend we must get on without them. You'll be in Abenbury for the rest of the week.'

'Perhaps,' suggested Wymark, one of Davidson's closest friends, 'Cyril could take over the committee temporarily, while you're away.'

'I'd be prepared to, to help out.'

Driving now through the outskirts of Bickleton Conrad frowned as he remembered how coolly his friend had tried to

48

steal the show. But he was not going to be edged out of this job, not he. He had made a strong point in his application of the fact that he was chairman of this committee. And it would not have escaped Cyril's attention that, if they were going to be merged with the University, the man who was in charge of their only degree course would be in a strong position. He had thanked Wymark for his suggestion and declined Cyril's offer, but from this point of view it was a nuisance being down in Abenbury.

On the other hand it had its points. The weekend had been unpleasant, culminating in a row with Stephanie, and it was not a bad thing to get away for a few days. It was the fault of that bloody party at the Hallidays'.

Conrad did not like parties. He pretended that this was because they were trivial occasions and he preferred to be doing something more constructively useful with his time, but the fact was that meeting people socially made him uneasy and consequently depressed him. If he had a job to do which brought him into contact with others then he was all right, because their relative positions were clearly defined and their conversation had a focus; but a merely social occasion, where responses had to be gauged according to complicated rules of human relationships, baffled him. The Hallidays' party had justified him totally, it had been dreadful. Where, for instance, was the pleasure in standing pinned against a wall while that bloody woman, Margery, yakked at you at the top of her considerable voice about women's rights, and a picket which she had organized of some cinema that was showing blue films? And it was not much fun watching Cyril Davidson making an exhibition of himself dancing with Angela Brown of the Modern Languages Department, or Stephanie, come to that, in the arms of that little shit McHale.

'Disgraceful exploitation.' 'Degrading to womanhood.' 'Typical male contempt.' 'A symbol of the domination of

49

masculine values in a male-orientated society.' Margery had hissed her shrill complaints at him, and over her shoulder he could see Cyril and Angela, jigging up and down in the delusion that they were bright teenagers. Did Cyril realize that the bags under his eyes were bouncing up and down in time to the music? And why had Angela not continued that plaster stuff, which she had so liberally applied to her face, down as far as her neck, to cover a betraying scrawniness there?

'What exactly did you do at this cinema of yours, Margery?'

'We took photographs of all the men as they came out, wasn't that superb? We're going to put them in the windows of our headquarters in Brunt Street with a big heading: "Come and find out if your husband visited the porno-film." Why should they get away with it? Don't you think that's a good idea?'

Stephanie and McHale had danced past. The young creep was actually fondling Stephanie's shoulders and playing about with her hair.

'No, Margery, I don't think that it is a good idea. It seems to me an essentially fascist idea, an attempt to force your ideas on other people by violence and blackmail.'

What had followed would have been comic if it had not been embarrassing. Her face distorted by hatred, her voice stuttering with the vehemence of her speech, Margery had denied that she was violent. At the top of her voice she had denounced Conrad as a reactionary shit – she thought that it was manly to use expressions like that – she had called on the assembled company to observe that he was a prissy, pompous prig. Every attempt he had made to answer calmly, to pursue a rational discussion, she had shouted down. Finally, it was Stephanie, actually running across, her face showing her alarm, who had led her away and released him.

Later on his host had joined him and Conrad had had the

sensation of being got at in a different way. Charles Halliday
was not a bad old stick. He was a bit pious, there was too
much of the conscious Christian about him for Conrad's
liking, added to which he was rather stingy and had a sharp
eye to his own advantage. He was a dull, ponderous speaker
at College meetings, reflecting there the dullness of his mind.
Naturally, with these advantages, he had done well, and was
a principal lecturer, with a secure future as a University don
ahead of him. Still, there were worse people than Charles
Halliday about, and Conrad did his best to be civil to the
man.

'A very pleasant occasion, Charles.'

'Glad you're enjoying yourself, Conrad. Let me top you
up. What's your tipple?'

Conrad said that he was drinking whisky, and Charles's
face fell. There were more economical drinks on offer.

'There's some of the fruit-cup left, Conrad.'

Conrad was firm. Damn it, the man was a principal
lecturer, his wife was a headmistress, there must be pots of
money coming into that house, he could afford another
whisky. 'I'd love that, Charles, but, to tell you the truth, I've
got a bit of an upset tummy. I think I'd better not risk mixing
them.'

And Charles had got him his whisky, and then Conrad had
realized that there was a price to be paid.

'I just wanted to have a word with you,' Charles had said,
handing over the glass, 'about young Matthews.'

With a prodigious effort of memory Conrad identified
young Matthews as the lout who had accosted him on the
stairs the day before.

'What about him?'

'There is some trouble there, Conrad. I think he is a young
man who deserves every consideration at the moment.'

Conrad rolled a morsel of whisky round his gums and
considered this. It sounded a typical Hallidayism. He asked

51

what sort of trouble Matthews was in, but Charles had been evasive.

'I think, if you don't mind, Conrad, I'd rather not be too specific. I just want to say that if you find that he's late with his work you'll make allowances, won't you?'

'It would be easier to make allowances, Charles, if I knew what I was supposed to allow for.'

'Things can always be stretched, Conrad. We must remember that we're human beings first and educators second. I was sure that you'd understand if I put it to you. And now,' said Charles, 'I suppose I'd better go and play the perfect host again. Enjoy yourself, Conrad.'

Conrad looked after him with indignation. He did not take kindly to being told by anybody what he should do, and he certainly did not need Charles Halliday's instructions in humane behaviour. What was involved here was a basic principle of fairness to the other students. He was damned if he was going to relax his standards to suit the vagaries of a lout like Matthews, just because Charles Halliday told him to.

The whole evening had continued like that; Conrad had had a constant sense of being got at. At one point he had been watching Cyril, dancing this time with one of the prettiest of the third year students, when a voice had interrupted him.

'Old Cyril's well away.'

Conrad had spun round sharply. It was young Aspinall. Conrad was not aware that his acquaintance with Barry Aspinall was intimate enough to justify that young man using this sort of tone about his friends. Aspinall was another of Milton Jacks's new recruits, cosseted through University, given grants to stay on for research, and now, with no classroom experience to speak of, walking into a job at the Alderman Robertson.

'We old fellows,' Conrad had replied with pointed irony, 'like to let our hair down occasionally.'

'I don't know what you mean by occasionally. He was exactly the same last Tuesday at the Barracloughs'. I didn't see you there. I saw Steph and Stan.'

Steph and Stan, by God! What gave the cheeky young sod the right to call his wife by her nickname, and why had she said nothing about going to the Barracloughs' on Tuesday? And how did Stan come into it?

'I couldn't go. I was carrying the flag in darkest Abenbury.'

'Abenbury? Isn't that where that girl was murdered?'

Conrad said that it was.

'Is that why Cyril called you Jack the Ripper when you came in?'

Conrad said that Cyril had a peculiar sense of humour.

'He's a lad is Cyril,' Aspinall agreed appreciatively. 'Look at that girl he's dancing with. How does he do it? I hope I'm half as good at his age.'

This was what Conrad could not understand, the tone of indulgent approval. What was so admirable about a disgusting old satyr cavorting with a girl young enough to be his daughter? Afterwards, if Cyril's own testimony was anything to go by, he would take the girl away and 'screw her arse off'. Was that the kind of thing one ought to applaud? Somebody, down in Abenbury, had taken another young girl out onto the moors, presumably with the same idea in mind, and things had gone dreadfully wrong. Why could people not see the uncomfortable parallel with Cyril's casual treatment of the girls he abused?

Conrad forced his thoughts onto another subject. 'Bad news for us all at the meeting yesterday.'

'Pretty bad,' Aspinall replied, 'but I expect I'll be all right. Jacks seems to think I'll have a very good chance of a University post if we merge.'

This youthful confidence impressed Conrad unfavourably and he said, 'I suppose you'll be putting in for this new job, then?' The question was intended ironically – so new a member of staff could hardly thrust himself forward in this way – but Aspinall took him seriously.

'I hadn't thought of it. Everybody I've spoken to seems to think that it's yours.'

Conrad tried not to show that this gave him pleasure. 'If you knew them a bit better,' he said, 'you'd understand that they're just covering up. I daresay, if the truth were told, that most of them got their own applications in on the way down this evening.'

'Do you think so?' Aspinall seemed impressed by this mature wisdom. 'In that case I may as well have a go myself.'

Fortunately Conrad had been too chagrined to reply.

More distasteful than anything about the evening had been the behaviour of Stephanie. She had danced almost the whole evening with McHale. Conrad did not, it goes without saying, object to her having a good time in her own way, but that she should enjoy so obviously and so publicly the company of a squirt like McHale showed a strange weakness of character. McHale was shallow, slack, and unpunctual. Did she realize that the reason why Conrad was down in Abenbury was that he was picking up the pieces after McHale? He was popular with the sillier young girls among the students because he made juvenile jokes, gave them high marks, and was lax about handing-in dates. He was a conceited young man, quite capable of making fun of Conrad's ideas at departmental meetings, and here he was, actually fondling Stephanie's arm, running his fingers through her hair, cradling her neck in his arms. Conrad was not jealous. Stephanie was not such a fool as to mean anything by all this, but he was irritated that his wife should be making an exhibition of herself. She ought to be aware that conduct which is fetching in a sixteen-year-old is less attractive in a woman of thirty-seven. Presumably she was flattered that a younger man should be making up to her. Look at them now. The way they were staring at one another was quite distasteful. Conrad strolled over towards the couple, and, as he passed near to Stephanie he asked her in a loud voice if she was having a good time.

'Yes, thank you, Conrad,' she answered. They did not spring apart guiltily, they did not even stop swaying in time to the music. McHale continued to cup his hands round her neck. Conrad walked firmly past them, and had a sudden feeling, very strong but incapable of proof, that McHale had made some kind of derogatory gesture. It was like the sensation that he got sometimes in the classroom, when writing on the board, that a boy was playing the fool behind him. Conrad exerted his will power to appear as though he was unaware of anything wrong. He turned in a deliberately slow fashion and leaned against the wall and watched Stephanie again. McHale was nuzzling her left ear, and she was giggling and slapping at him playfully. Whatever McHale had done behind his back, all the others must have seen it. Conrad eyed them covertly. They weren't giving anything away, but were they deliberately avoiding looking at him? Had Stephanie seen whatever it was that McHale had done? If she had it was very disloyal of her to be giggling with the fellow.

When Conrad reached this point in his meditations on the weekend's events he discovered that he was driving too fast and carefully corrected the fault. He had shaved that corner rather close. He was out in the countryside now and the road was narrow and winding. He brought his mind back to concentrate on the road. It was absurd to get so worked up about trivial matters, but the McHale business had spoiled his Sunday. He had felt obliged to comment to Stephanie on her behaviour at the party, and she had not liked it. Yet he had done it gently.

'After all, Steph, we've always laughed at Angela Brown

and her rather desperate attempts to prolong her youth, haven't we?'

'What's that supposed to mean?'

'I was able to see how other people were looking at you. You don't want to attract that sort of attention, do you?'

What less could he have said? What was there in a hint like that to justify the spoilt, petulant sulks that Stephanie had indulged in? The trouble was that he and Stephanie had so little in common. She was not intellectually in his class, so there were few interests they could share. It was not a case for blaming anybody, it was as much Stephanie's misfortune as his own, but the fact was there. Perhaps he should make a greater effort, as one would with a child. Some of the things Stephanie had said had been hurtful, but they had sprung from wounded vanity and perhaps, in an oblique way, expressed a truth about their relationship. No doubt Stephanie was sometimes bored, probably she did occasionally find him cold. It was difficult for her to comprehend his intellectual isolation or to appreciate the strains of his position. As he drove further from his wife Conrad began to feel quite noble. He must do better. His was the more powerful personality, more capable of disinterested generosity. He would make things up next weekend.

Conrad drove on slowly and carefully, hugging his problems, gradually giving them all a turn that was comforting to himself, and had at last achieved a kind of tranquillity when an unfortunate incident occurred. He had just passed through a village and was approaching a sharp double bend where the road crossed a bridge over a stream. It was narrow, and there were no pavements, and on Conrad's side there was a woman, walking in the direction of the village, pushing a perambulator. Conrad swung out to avoid her. And then, over the bridge, suddenly, an enormous articulated lorry appeared, carrying what looked like a complete and spacious bungalow, which jutted several feet on either side of the trailer. On the window of this residence was a notice: 'Another of Houlihan's Happy Homes.' Fortunately both Conrad and the Happy Home were able to stop, the bungalow with considerable wheezing noises from its air-brakes. Conrad leaned back in his seat and breathed heavily; that had been a close thing. He stared up at the driver of the bungalow, and the driver stared down at him. Then the driver wound down his window, poked his head through, and addressed Conrad: 'Why the fucking hell don't you leave enough room on the fucking road, mate?'

Conrad wound his own window down. It was the man's manner that irritated him. Of course, as a civilized person he could see things from the lorry driver's point of view. A man who had to earn his living by piloting a monstrosity like that about the country was entitled to expect a measure of co-operation from other road users, and in normal circumstances Conrad would have been quite happy to offer that co-operation, but the chap did not have to be rude. Why, Conrad thought, did not he ask nicely? Conrad had to spend most of his life keeping his temper bottled up, pretending to be civil to people he did not like or be diplomatic with people who were being difficult; he could not for the life of him see why he had to be mild to this artisan.

'Normally,' he said, looking up to the window of the cab, 'I do, but, you see, my road was blocked. There was a woman, pushing a perambulator, and I had to move out to make way for her. I don't know about you –' Conrad pushed his head a little further through the window of his car – 'but I make it an absolute rule when I am driving not to run over women pushing perambulators. I'm not entirely certain, but I've even got an idea that there is something about it in the Highway Code.'

The driver looked down, he appeared to be considering

how to deal with this irony, then he spoke: 'Get out of the fucking road, you fucking cunt.'

'Strictly speaking,' said Conrad primly, 'you are the one who should move. I am still on my own side of the road, it is your vehicle that is occupying almost the entire width of the carriageway.'

There was a short pause after this speech. Conrad continued to look up at the driver, and the driver continued to look down at Conrad. Then the door of the cab opened and the driver clambered down onto the road. He was a young man, about twenty-eight Conrad guessed, and he appeared to be in prime physical condition. His face was burned a deep red by the sun, he wore a thin, short-sleeved shirt which fitted him like a skin and showed off his sinewy arms and broad chest. The top four buttons of the shirt were undone and displayed a thick mat of black hair extending up to the man's throat. He walked slowly across to Conrad's car and leaned against it with his arms outstretched, his hands resting on the roof. Conrad felt the car quiver as he touched it. He leaned down so that his face was on a level with Conrad's, and perhaps six inches away from it.

'You going to fucking well back up?' he asked, without raising his voice.

'Why can't you be a bit more civil?' said Conrad. His mouth was dry and he had a pain at the pit of his stomach, but he was not going to knuckle under tamely. A van had drawn up behind him, and now its driver began impatiently sounding his horn. Conrad looked into his enemy's face. He had black eyebrows and narrow eyes set rather too closely together, and his mouth had a bitter droop at the corners. He rocked the car gently.

'What the fucking hell are you talking about?' he said, still speaking with a deadly calm. 'You don't think I could bloody move, do you? Have you seen it?' He nodded towards his own vehicle. 'You don't expect me to go back with that, do you?

What do you want me to do, touch me fucking cap to you and jump in the fucking river? Do you think I'm going to reverse a fucking load like that into the fucking hedge just to please you? Do you think I'm going to get into my cab and drive backwards simply because you open your great big twatting mouth? Do you know what you are? You're a fucking bag of wind and piss, that's what you are. Now, what are you going to do about that?'

He kept his face six inches from Conrad's as he said this, and spoke venomously but quietly, odd specks of spittle falling on Conrad's cheeks. With every question he gave Conrad's car another slight shove to make it rock again.

'I'm simply asking you to be more civil,' said Conrad.

'Do you know what I'm going to do?' asked the man. 'I'm going to go back and get into my cab. Then I'm going to start driving that fucking lot forward, and if you're still in the fucking way you'll land up in the fucking hedge.' The man stood away from Conrad's car at last and looked down at him witheringly. 'Fucking civil!' he said. It was his parting shot, then he turned and went back to his cab and climbed in.

Conrad's mind was in a turmoil. The driver behind him was hooting monotonously and shouting obscenities out of his window. Conrad was lividly angry and cravenly afraid. He had felt sick with fear when that man's face had been inches from his and the spit was falling all over him, and he had been furious with himself for this fear. People just did not behave like this. He tried to tell himself that he had nothing actually to be afraid of. The man could not touch him, he was only bluffing; but then it was difficult to be quite sure of this. People were assaulted, and property was damaged. One read of such things. This man was scarcely sane, with his drearily monotonous profanity and his hypnotic stare and his spittle. Conrad heard the sound of the engine starting up. Why the devil should he give way? He would stay where he was, and to hell with the consequences. He saw the lorry start moving

59

forward. The driver behind had stopped hooting. The Happy Home inched its way forward and then began to gather speed. It was moving quite quickly, it was moving very quickly, in fact, even if it was all a bluff the man had miscalculated and would not be able to stop in time. Conrad switched on his engine in a panic, put his car into reverse, and executed a poorly controlled swerve back. There was a nerve-wrenching hooting from the van behind. He put his car into first gear and swerved forward, pulling strongly to the side in order to get out of the way of this monstrous pantechnicon and its maniac driver. There was an opening on the left for the entrance to a field, and there should be just enough room to squeeze his car in there between the road and the gate. Another swerve brought the rear of the car out of the way. It bounced over the grass verge and the shallow ditch, and his near-side wing thumped into the gatepost.

Without any pause in its acceleration the Happy Home swept past. Conrad glimpsed a notice announcing that Houlihan's apologized for any inconvenience that he might have been caused before the bungalow disappeared round the corner into the village. The driver of the van behind him exchanged a congratulatory wave with the Happy Home before drawing out to pass Conrad, tooting and gesturing obscenely. As the van passed Conrad saw that its rear numberplate was loose and hung down in a highly illegal fashion.

Conrad switched off his engine and climbed out to inspect the damage. It was not extensive. There was a dent in the wing, but that was all. Conrad found that he was shaking. He felt humiliated. He had been so helpless, so feeble, he had been simply ridiculous. And it had not been his fault. Not a shadow of it had been his fault.

7

It was on this same Tuesday morning that Rosen got his first real lead, and it came as a result of the photograph that had been circulated of the policewoman dressed in the dead girl's clothes. Many sightings were reported but one of them seemed to Rosen very promising. A man called Tapscott came forward to say that he had seen a girl exactly like the one in the picture walking along a road that led out of Abenbury in the direction of the moors at ten past four in the afternoon. The story fitted the evidence that Rosen had already collected so neatly that he was inclined to doubt his luck, but when he saw Tapscott his doubts vanished. Here was an honest man if ever there was one. He was elderly, on his pension, he was quiet, and uncomfortable at thrusting himself forward in this way. He called Rosen 'sir' and held his cap in his hands and his Adam's apple jerked nervously up and down as he spoke. He supplemented his income by doing odd gardening jobs, and it was when he was just starting for home after finishing the last of these that he had seen the girl. That was why he could be so exact about the time. When the widow for whom he had been working had paid him he had checked his watch. He had come out of the house immediately and it was when he was getting on his bicycle that he had seen the girl.

'That's her, I'm pretty sure it's the same one, sir,' he had said, squinting at the full-colour print Rosen had handed him. 'She was just walking along,' he added in reply to a question. 'No, she wasn't waiting for a lift. I didn't notice her particularly. It was only when I saw the picture in the paper that I remembered. No, she was all by herself.'

'You didn't see a car pick her up, or anything like that?' asked Rosen hopefully, but Tapscott shook his head.

'There was a car there, parked by the road, I noticed that.'

Rosen demanded details.

'It was one of those estate cars with small wheels, Minis. Colour of mustard.'

'Fawn Mini estate car,' Rosen wrote down. 'Anybody in it?' he asked.

'Just the driver, nobody else.'

'Which way was the car facing?'

'Same way as the girl was going.'

'So the driver would be looking down the road at the girl as she passed him?'

Tapscott agreed, adding that the girl was already in front of the car when he saw her.

'The car wasn't following her? I mean, was it moving slowly along behind her?'

'No, it was standing still. No, I didn't see it move at all. Mind you, I didn't wait, I was on my bicycle and off home.'

Rosen did not press him further. He was convinced that this must have been the murdered girl, in spite of minor discrepancies in the man's story. He had got the colour of her sweater wrong, for instance, until he saw the colour picture, and he did not remember that she was carrying a knapsack, but no experienced policeman expects perfection in these matters. The whole story held together in a way that carried conviction. Rosen could picture the driver of that car sizing up his victim, waiting for her to get further along the road, out of view of the houses perhaps, before he tried to pick her up. He wondered if there was another sighting of a fawn Mini estate car in the files at the headquarters.

He took Tapscott out to the road where he had seen the girl and made him go over his story again, and it seemed even more plausible. It was a broad, tree-lined thoroughfare passing through one of the most select residential districts of

62

Abenbury. The large, detached houses were set well back from the road behind high hedges which effectually concealed them. At ten past four it would have been pretty quiet. In one respect Rosen modified his speculations. The driver would not have needed to wait until he was out in the country before picking up the girl, he could have done it here in perfect safety, except – Rosen clicked his fingers excitedly – for Tapscott. Suppose he had been about to, and Tapscott had suddenly appeared. That would have made him careful. Finally, Rosen called at the house where Tapscott had been doing his bit of gardening, and the widow confirmed his story.

Rosen sent his witness home in the police car and walked slowly back to the spot in Abenbury where the dead girl had parted from her friend. It took him thirty-six minutes. Half past three to ten past four, that was how long it had taken the girl, it was a perfect fit. Rosen went back to the station feeling almost light-hearted. It was a treat to have a definite course of action to follow instead of just casting about in blind hope. He must go through those files again, then he must get his men in and check all the cars on that estate. Finally, and most important, he must go back to the Superintendent to bring up that plan again about reconstructing the girl's last walk.

'We know where we are now, sir. We've got the times exactly, and the route she must have taken. It goes through a shopping area, there are two schools there and they would be coming out at that time. Lots of people must have seen her. And if there are any sightings of that fawn estate then we're really beginning to get somewhere.'

This time the response was cheering. The Superintendent, seeing in his mind's eye headlines like 'Promising lead' and 'Police get valuable clue' almost patted his Sergeant on the head. At the very least the newspapers and television news would be able to show that the police were doing something purposeful.

It was Nicholson who struck the sour note.

'Even if we do get people saying that they saw the girl I don't see that it'll take us any further. We already know that she was there. What we don't know is whether it was the same girl that was killed out on the moors.'

'Bit of a coincidence if it wasn't,' Rosen said.

'Not at all. Lots of youngsters use that route out of the city, you know. My patrols have to keep an eye on it right through the summer. The identification's very doubtful. This witness of yours got the sweater wrong, didn't he? And the girl he saw wasn't carrying a knapsack.'

'We still haven't found that knapsack, sir. Perhaps she lost it before she went out there.'

Nicholson made a peculiar noise with his mouth indicating scorn. 'Between leaving her friend and reaching that road? Come off it. No, what I'm afraid of, sir, is that we may find ourselves concentrating on this lead and let the real one slip through our fingers.'

It seemed to both Rosen and Superintendent Pearce that Nicholson had some idea of his own that he wanted to follow up, but whether he had or not the Superintendent was bound to admit the soundness of the general observation. He thought that Sergeant Rosen's lead was a very promising one, but he knew perfectly well that it could easily fizzle out. Behind all his thinking there was a nightmare. There would be other murders, they would be unsolved, questions would be asked in the House, the Home Secretary would make himself unpleasant. And if he could be shown not to have done something that he ought to have done, then he would be in the soup. So he fixed his eyes on the Inspector and asked him what he had in mind.

'I still feel, sir, that we ought to keep a constant patrol on that road across the moors. Look at it this way, sir. If this chap's going to do it again then he's likely to use the same method. He'll pick a girl up somewhere, take her out to the moors and do what he wants with her when he gets there. We've got to be ready for him. And it does seem to me, sir, very unlikely that he'd strangle a lass in broad daylight.'

Rosen moved to speak at this, but Nicholson silenced him. 'I know what Jack's going to say, she hadn't had a meal, and all that. Well, perhaps he kept her shut up somewhere. I still think he'd wait until after dark.'

'Lighting-up time,' Rosen said heavily, 'was about quarter to nine. He'd have to have kept her shut up for quite a long time, sir. And the pathologist didn't think it was that long since her last meal.'

There was a pause. The Superintendent screwed up his face in thought.

'Let's face it, sir,' said Nicholson. 'Our best chance of getting this bloke is when he does it again. What I want to do is to increase our patrols along that road across the moors. Get regular trips going, day and night, but especially from about an hour before sunset to about five hours after. If they see anything suspicious, parked cars, people wandering about even, they get out and check up discreetly. One thing is for sure, sir. If there is another girl missing and we don't find her quicker than we did this one, then we're in trouble.'

Nicholson was an acute practical psychologist, and although Rosen did not like him he had to admire his technique. The Superintendent visibly shuddered at these last words and almost cravenly agreed to the request, although it would use valuable manpower from a force that was already becoming over-stretched. As they left their chief's office Nicholson grinned at his colleague and winked.

8

By the end of that Tuesday afternoon Conrad was in a state of depression that was low even by his standards. Still smarting from the humiliation of his encounter with the lorry driver he had gone to the first school on his schedule for the day. It was a pretty little junior school in an idyllic country setting, and the Headmaster was a cheerful man, totally wrapped up in his job and happy with it. After his previous visit Conrad had envied him, so it was unsettling to enter his room and discover him seated at his desk, with his head in his hands, scarcely offering his visitor the courtesy of an upward glance, and with an expression of misery on his face. For the want of anything better to say Conrad had made a remark about the beauty of the area and added that he always enjoyed visiting the school, at which Mr Buick, the Headmaster, had groaned.

'You'd better make the most of it, then. We're being closed, you know.'

Conrad took a seat, recognizing high tragedy when he saw it, and braced himself to receive Buick's confidences. He was told how unexpectedly the news had come: 'I was called to the Offices, I thought they wanted to talk about furniture,' and how thunderstruck Buick had been: 'I just sat there, I couldn't take it in.' For three quarters of an hour Buick explained all that he had done for the school. 'If I was to tell you, Mr Nield, how many times I've sat at this desk until nine and ten at night, you wouldn't believe me. And now this happens.'

'What will you do?'

'There's nothing for me round here, Mr Nield, and I'm too

old to move away. They're putting me out to grass.'

Conrad struggled to find words, but there was nothing that he could say. Buick had put the whole of his life into his work and when his work came to an end his life would be a morose void. Conrad had seen it happen often enough and, listening to this wretched man's complaints, wondered how he himself would react if the same thing happened to him. He was in danger, he saw it now, of focusing his interests too exclusively on the College. In fact, as he thought of it, he realized that his own position was worse than Buick's. The Headmaster was eligible for a pension, but he was too young. What the devil could he do? In clearer, more concrete terms than ever before the desperate plight he would be in if he failed to get that job was brought home to him, and by the time Buick had finished, although he did not know it, his visitor's misery was as great as his own, and it required a positive effort of will on Conrad's part not to walk straight out of the school again, so futile suddenly did everything seem. Instead he inquired dully how his students were faring, and Buick answered, with equal lack of interest, that they were excellent boys, and that he was very pleased with them. Conrad forced himself to his feet and went down the corridor to watch the first of them, Andrew Carney.

Sitting on the bed in his hotel room later Conrad wondered what he had done to deserve having a student like Carney thrust on him. He had not attached much importance to Buick's tribute, but he had not expected to find a youth so little prepared, so nervous and hesitant, so stupid, and so downright ill-educated. The presence of such a student in the school surely pointed to something radically at fault in the system which had produced him and reinforced the sense of futility which had swept over him in Buick's room. The best years of his life had gone to the production of louts like this. Firmly, for the sixth or seventh time since he had stormed out of the classroom, Conrad tried to put the depressing image of

67

Andrew Carney out of his mind. He would sally forth, that was what he would do, and seek entertainment in the great city.

When Conrad spoke of himself as being in Abenbury for his school practice he spoke loosely. His students were actually in schools scattered about the countryside to the south-west, and he preferred to put up in a small village called Long Moreton, nearly twenty miles from Abenbury, on the road across the moors. Normally this arrangement suited him because he was by nature a solitary person, but today, contemplating an evening spent catching up on his marking or wrestling with a book which he had brought with him on curriculum development, Conrad felt like a change. Abenbury was not very large but it surely had possibilities. Perhaps it was time to begin living the larger life which, he had seen in Buick's room, was eluding him. He had a quick shower and followed it with a liberal application of some scented talc that Stephanie had given him. Then he shaved and brushed his teeth and put on the second-best suit that he always brought and seldom used, and his best shoes. Finally he left a message that he would not be in for the evening meal and set off.

As he drove he kept going back to the thoughts that were troubling him, like a dog that is fascinated by some filth on the ground. Milton Jacks, Cyril Davidson, the row about the BEd course, the chances that he would not get that job, redundancy, Stephanie's behaviour, Buick's dolorous tones, jostled unpleasantly in his head. Finally, to get relief from these ideas he deliberately fixed his attention on Andrew Carney and the scene he had had with him after that disastrous lesson. He had bent over backwards to be kind to the lad. 'You've got a good, clear voice, Andrew,' he had said, picking on the only thing that he could, without too much damage to the truth, praise. But as soon as he offered criticism Carney had bridled, that was the only way to describe it.

'The purpose of your lesson was to stimulate creative writing, Andrew, by talking about their hobbies, but even though they all denied that they had any hobbies you still insisted that they should write about them.'

He had flared up like a peevish girl. 'Oh, well, Mr Nield, it's all very well saying that. That was your fault.'

Conrad had kept his temper admirably. Looking back now, taking into account what he had already been through that day, he could still say that. Quietly he asked in what way he had been to blame.

'I was going to prepare them more but you stopped me. I was in the middle of what I'd got ready and you told me to stop.'

'I did not tell you to stop, Andrew. I told you not to write the word "philanthropist" on the board.'

'It's the same thing, isn't it? I mean, it just left me looking like a fool. How could I go on after that?'

'The word that you were looking for, Andrew, was "philatelist". A person who collects stamps is a philatelist, a philanthropist is a different kind of man entirely. And, incidentally, neither word is spelt with a double "l".'

Carney had looked taken aback at this, but he soon rallied.

'I still think, Mr Nield, that you could have done it in some other way. You just made me look small in front of the whole class. I mixed up the words – all right – I freely admit it, but anybody could do a thing like that. What troubles me, Mr Nield, is that I've got to work with that class. I've got to have their respect. How am I going to get that back, Mr Nield?'

It was at this point that Conrad had to admit, also freely, that his self-control had wavered.

'You might try earning their respect by doing your preparation a bit bloody better, Andrew.'

Thinking it over Conrad regretted that he had spoken

quite so strongly. He had made the mistake of becoming sarcastic. He had asked Andrew how far he wanted him to go in covering up his mistakes. He had suggested that they ought to work out a code of signals so that he could warn Andrew about his grosser solecisms without diminishing the children's admiration for him.

'You see, Andrew, look at it from my point of view. Every dozen or so mistakes that you make I may find one that I really think ought to be corrected. In the normal way, of course, it doesn't matter what you tell them as long as they respect you, but I'd still like to be able to do something. I tell you what, Andrew, suppose I carry a large, spotted handkerchief, and then whenever you make a really important mistake I can wipe my brow with it, how would that be?'

Carney had stood before him as he said this, and his face had crumpled, as though he was on the verge of tears.

'This is very humiliating, Mr Nield. All you're doing is making fun of me. I don't understand you, Mr Nield. I thought that you were here to help me.'

'I can't be helpful to you, Andrew, if you flare up at the first word of criticism. I am trying to point out what is wrong with your work, and you behave like a great baby.'

'I don't think that this is a useful relationship, Mr Nield. I think I ought to ask for a different tutor. Obviously, you and me, we don't share the same philosophy about things like this.'

It was at this point that Conrad had abandoned him. 'Different philosophies', ye gods. What drivel they did talk! And yet Conrad regretted some of the things that he had said. He should have remembered that Carney was a young man of enormous limitations.

Lads like Carney were a standing wonder to Conrad. He was a long, stringy, anaemic youth, with a suspicion of a stutter. He had no personality, he wasn't clever or athletic, yet he was never to be seen on the campus save in the company of some girl or other of exceptional beauty. Conrad could find no originality in the thought that women were unaccountable creatures, but it was true. He was not exactly being conceited if he thought that when he was Carney's age he had been more attractive, more intelligent, more amusing, but no girl had ever looked at him as he had seen girls looking at Carney. It was not just a fault of taste in this particular instance, it seemed to be a general rule. There was all this talk about equality between the sexes, girls being treated like men, but nowadays, as far as Conrad could judge from his own observations, they were a lot more abject than they had been in his own youth. In Conrad's day the girls had not been liberated; they had been bloody careful instead. If they had had any feelings then they had kept a tight control over them, and had not been in the habit of giving themselves away in any sense of that term. When Conrad had taken a girl out she had made a favour of it; she had not clung onto his arm and looked up at him with adoring eyes. They were lucky bastards these modern young men. An ineffectual booby like Andrew Carney had it made. He was engaged, so Conrad understood, to a quite gorgeous young thing in the second year. No doubt, in this new freedom of theirs, she gave herself up to him freely and frequently. There he would be, night after night, pale and stringy, with bad breath and pimples, jerking away on top of her like the frogs Conrad had kept when he was a boy. Carney would do it very like a frog. Conrad remembered them, with their impassive industrious faces, pushing in and out like squat piston engines. All over the campus Conrad could imagine them doing it, all jerking away, in and out, frogs. That was the modern ethos, the liberated society; there had been nothing like that in Conrad's day.

And it was not only the youngsters. Conrad carefully negotiated a bend as he made this qualification. Plenty of those on the staff kept their end up, so to speak, judging by the way they talked. Cyril Davidson was only one of the more notorious. Conrad had a sudden mental picture of Davidson in conversation, as he so often was, with one of the prettier students, and touching her. He had a vast repertoire of touches. He did not seem to know that it was possible to talk to a woman without pawing her, and breathing over her, and sliding his face close to hers. And his talk was intimate and whispering, words that no one else could hear. If he was interrupted he would look round lazily, with a kind of leer, as if to say, 'How clever I am, what a devil of a fellow.' And he got away with it. Cyril was not attractive, he was a senile satyr, but he could get away with murder. If Conrad had so much as laid a finger on a girl he was sure she would have backed away indignantly, but Davidson could stroke their knees and pat their arms unrebuked. It was depressing.

Every newspaper and magazine spoke of sexual freedom. Grave counsellors instructed couples in how to make their sex lives more adventurous. Wives boasted of the number and intensity of their orgasms. Stephanie never did this. Perhaps that was what was wrong. Conrad remembered reading, in one of Stephanie's magazines, a letter from a young lady outlining an especially peculiar variation on the sex act that she and her husband performed, and asking if it was 'all right'. The doctor's answer had been firm. 'Yes,' he had said, 'it is perfectly all right. It is not even unusual, as you seem to think. Every week I receive letters exactly like yours. All that matters in such cases is that both the partners should find the act aesthetically acceptable.' That was it, that was the magic formula. If you could only get the threshold of aesthetic acceptability low enough, it appeared, there was no limit to what you could do. That was the trouble with Stephanie: she had too limited an aesthetic sense. He wondered if she had read the letter, and, if so, what she had thought of it. Conrad could well imagine the sort of reception he would get if he should try out with Stephanie what was suggested in that letter. 'Most wives,' the doctor said, 'enjoy such experiments.' He did not know Stephanie. Somewhere outside was a world of exciting lingerie and curious sexual aids, and he, Conrad, was missing out on it. By the time he reached Abenbury he was in a sombre mood.

He parked in the 'Trust the Motorist' car park. How many of the cars had been honestly paid for? he wondered, as he drove into an empty space. Not many, he dared say, if the truth were known. It really was too bad. It did seem to Conrad that if society could not trust people to pay honestly for something like this without being supervised and badgered, then it did not have much chance. Civilization was a complicated concept, but at root it depended on quite simple things like this. Conrad pressed two tenpenny pieces into the slot of the machine and placed the ticket carefully in the ashtray of his vehicle. Then, with a virtuous sense that he had saved the world from chaos and old night, he went forth.

He carried his disaffected mood into the town with him. It took him only ten minutes to decide that Abenbury was smug. It had the air of an overgrown market town, full of gentleman farmers in tweed jackets and corduroys, and horsey-looking women with haw-haw voices. The shops reflected the world they served. There were gunsmiths, jewellers, leather and harness shops, retailers of furs, all the flunkeydom necessary to a pampered minority. Conrad pressed his nose, metaphorically speaking, against the glass and examined the prices. You could say what you liked, there was a lot of money about in some people's pockets – and he felt an upsurge of his old, socialist puritanism.

The shops and business premises were emptying, and the streets were full of people hurrying home. Young girls in light summer frocks swung past him in pairs chattering together, and he eyed them covertly. Conrad's spirits began to lift slightly. He found himself relishing his freedom. He was in a place where he was not known and where, consequently,

73

he could do as he liked and nobody would know anything about it. The dashing thing to do would be to pick up a girl. If Davidson had been in Conrad's position he would probably already have done it. How, Conrad wondered, would he have gone about it? Those girls ahead, now suppose that you wanted to pick up the one on the left, what would you do? Conrad followed at a distance which enabled him to take her in. A classy sort of girl. Walked with a self-confident swing, expensively dressed, looked as if she might have been getting herself measured for a new pair of jodhpurs. Conrad could not hear her voice, but he had no doubt that it was plummy. Suddenly her companion turned away and disappeared down a side street with a wave of the hand. Now, presumably, was his chance.

Just suppose he did it, what would her reaction be? She was tip-tupping along very attractively, you could see the movement of the buttocks under the dress. She looked the sort of girl one saw in television plays who is longing to give herself to a sweaty mechanic, somebody like that lorry driver this morning. A vivid picture came into Conrad's mind of the man leaning against his car, his arms brown and sinewy, the hair showing on his chest and up his throat, beads of sweat on his upper lip as he mouthed his obscenities and sprayed saliva over him. Was that the sort of man she would go for? He had a rough, brutal strength that probably attracted the women. No finesse, just direct action. Conrad increased his speed to keep up with her, she was walking at quite a pace, and took in her figure with what he fancied was the eye of connoisseurship. She had good legs, and a good bum. He thought, and even spoke of himself in conversation with the boys, as a leg man – legs and bums. There was a chance that she was the sort of girl who is looking for an older man, a father figure. You used to see them in old-fashioned films. That would be more of a chance for him. He could play the role of the sophisticated man of the world rather well. The girl reached an intersection and stopped suddenly, so Conrad began to examine some tins of udder wash in an ironmonger's window. Out of the corner of his eye he watched the girl standing there. He had just turned his head sideways to examine a horrific looking instrument used for castrating bulls when a Bentley drew up and the girl got in. Daddy, no doubt, on his way home from the office. As the car drew away from the kerb Conrad received the impression of an indignant look directed towards him. He sighed and turned away to find somewhere to eat. There was a steak bar, he had noticed, near the cathedral.

Conrad bought himself a local paper, which was full of details of the recent murder, and, on an impulse, confident that he was far away from prying eyes, succumbing to a natural curiosity, he also purchased one of those naughty magazines. It had a picture of a well-built young lady on its cover. She had no clothes on except a straw boater, and she was leaning nonchalantly on a bicycle. When he entered the restaurant he hid this under his coat and read the newspaper, which was concerned, as far as he could make out, to extract as much gruesome entertainment out of the killing as possible and to give as little real information as it could. The police were being very active, he learned – well, he had not noticed them being active – and were appealing for members of the public to come forward if they had seen anything suspicious. Special patrols, the newspaper said, were being organized, and the whole district was in a state of terror. That was a laugh. Precious little terror about that he could see. The police, he read on, were not releasing details of the injuries the girl had received, but it was understood that these had been horrific. Conrad flicked through the rest of the report and then turned to find something more savoury. How curiously morbid the public taste was. Failing to find more agreeable entertainment he folded the paper up, with the magazine inside it, and gave his attention to the femininity

75

about him. The restaurant seemed to be run by a gaggle of extremely good-looking girls, and he found this disturbing. The one who had met him at the door was a decidedly superior sort of person, tall, jet-black hair, a rather olive skin. There was a real beauty at the cash desk, and a pretty, smaller, plump, blonde young thing was waiting on him. He decided that he would chat this last one up. That was the term, wasn't it? He would chat her up.

'Lovely day,' he said when she brought him his bill.

'You don't see much of it in here,' she replied absently, as she scribbled on her pad.

'What do you do when you finish here?' he asked.

'Go to bed usually, we don't close until eleven.'

'That's a very long day.'

'Well, I don't come on until half past four, that's when me husband gets in.'

So she had a husband.

'Hard work for you.'

'It's not so bad. It gets me away from the kids. Ta.' She took the money he offered her, stacked his dishes on her tray, and swung off towards the door leading into the kitchens. She was only young, yet she had a husband and children. And a funny sort of life. As soon as the husband was in she was out. Conrad thought that if he was married to her he would want to see more of her than that. Perhaps the husband had a bit on the side; perhaps she had. Did they know about one another? Did they mind? Possibly not. That would be the modern way of things; people respected one another's inde-pendence, they did not think of themselves as owning one another. It was a healthier society, you had to admit that. Healthier and saner, more adult, not to say adulterous. The girl brought his change and Conrad left a generous tip.

'You don't get out much, then?'

'We don't do so bad,' she said, whisking over the table with a cloth.

She went to the cashier's desk, and he saw her talking to the girl behind it. He wondered if they were talking about him, and what they were saying. A dirty old man, something like that, was that what she was saying? Probably they were laughing at him.

'Do you know what that old bugger did? He made a pass at me.'

'What, him?'

Conrad watched them to see if they looked in his direction, but they were too sly for that. He stood up and prepared to go. As he passed the cashier's desk he glanced at her with studied casualness and nodded. Outside, on the pavement, he breathed easily again.

He opened his paper to see what entertainment Abenbury offered of an evening. There was a Young Farmers' Dance at the Jubilee Hall, he noticed. Could he pass as a Young Farmer? The Abenbury Amateur Operatic and Dramatic Society were giving a performance of *My Fair Lady* in the main hall of the Abenbury Comprehensive School. There were two cinemas. The Ritz was showing *Nicholas and Alexandra*, and the Lido was showing something called *Sex Confessions of a Nymphomaniac*. That was it. After seven centuries of western culture that was the best that a city of the size and wealth of Abenbury could offer. Conrad folded his paper again and put it under his arm. The spirit of romance still flickered fitfully in his bosom. What he wanted to do, face it frankly, was to pick up a woman. As much as anything else, he wanted to prove to himself that he was capable of picking up a woman. He decided that he would walk boldly up to the next girl he saw, the next girl who caught his fancy, and engage her in conversation. He looked around. That girl there, at the corner of the street, she was a nice looking thing as far as he could judge; she had her back half turned to him.

Conrad took his spectacles off and put them in his pocket, then he walked over to her.

'Hullo there,' he said, jovially, 'how are things?'

She turned to face him.

'Oh, hullo, Mr Nield,' she said, 'fancy seeing you.'

Conrad reorganized his conversational strategy in a flash. It was – he could not think of her name – she had been in one of his professional groups – Cathy, that was it, Cathy Winters. He dipped into his repertoire of chatty openings.

'How's it going, then?'

'Not bad, now I've got settled in.'

'Yes,' Conrad said wisely, 'that's the important thing – getting settled in. Who's looking after you?'

'Mr Milne.'

Conrad was surprised. He had not known that Philip Milne was down here; he must remember to avoid him. He racked his brains for something else to say.

'You waiting for somebody?' he asked, at last.

'Yes, I'm waiting for Wally.'

Wally was her young man. A powerfully built thick-head in the PE Department, or, as he really must remember to call it, The Sphere of Active Expression. He decided to make a joke.

'Not very gallant of Wally to keep you waiting.'

'Oh, he's helping them put the stage up. He's at the Comprehensive School. They're doing *My Fair Lady* there tonight.'

'Yes,' said Conrad, 'I saw that it was on.'

'Aren't you going to see it, Mr Nield?'

'No, thank you very much. It's not quite in my line. In fact I was just thinking that there isn't a great deal going on in Abenbury of an evening, is there?'

'You could go to the pictures.'

'It's *Nicholas and Alexandra*, which I would define as marginally worse than *My Fair Lady*. I shall probably

78

toddle back to my hotel and read an improving book.'

Over her shoulder he saw Wally approaching and made his farewells. She turned from him, doubtless with relief.

It was beginning to grow chilly, and Conrad decided to return to the car park to fetch his coat. The park was nearly deserted and as he made his way to his car Conrad noticed a large, dark-blue van that seemed familiar. Then he saw that the rear numberplate was hanging down, held, apparently, by a single bolt. It was that bastard who had been behind him this morning. The memory of its triumphant tooting and the derisive wave of the hand came to him acutely. He strolled across to take a closer look. The van was empty. Conrad looked round, nobody was within sight. He bent down and studied the numberplate. Yes, it was almost off, hanging virtually by a thread. Conrad looked around him again and then tentatively touched the plate, which swung freely. He seized it between his finger and thumb and pulled it towards him. The metal bent but it did not break. Conrad looked round again, but the area was still deserted. He grasped the plate firmly and worked it vigorously from side to side until the metal snapped and he stood up with the plate in his hand. Disgraceful to have a vehicle in that condition. The car park was bounded by a fence which, at one point, ran alongside the wall of a laundry. Conrad carried the plate across and dropped it between the fence and the wall, then he took his handkerchief out of his pocket and wiped his hands. That would teach the sod.

Twenty minutes after this Conrad was leaning against the bar of the King William, one of the two really first-class hotels in Abenbury, gathering courage for a final attempt to pick up a girl. There was one all on her own at a table in the corner. She was not exactly a girl either, but perhaps an interesting, mature woman would be a more agreeable companion, more likely to meet him half way. He picked up his

79

whisky and, slowly, trying to make it look as if he was approaching her table by accident, went over.

'Nice evening,' he said. She did not reply.

'It's been a beautiful day,' he continued, 'really hot for the time of the year.' Still she said nothing. He sat down, near, but not exactly at, her table.

'Rather quiet this evening.' He made a great play of turning round and looking about the room. 'There's not a lot to do in Abenbury, is there?'

She took a sip of her drink.

'I've just come in for the evening to sample the night life,' said Conrad, 'but it's a bit dull on your own, isn't it? I always think it's easier to enjoy yourself with someone else, don't you?'

He noticed that her glass was empty.

'Can I get you a drink? What are you having?'

She stared at him, and finally she spoke.

'If you don't stop annoying me I shall send for the manager.'

Conrad drank the rest of his whisky and left, hoping that nobody else had witnessed his discomfiture. You could say what you liked. There might be a new, liberated society, but he could not get into it. He could not even persuade a woman to let him buy her a drink in a public house.

He wandered aimlessly through the streets. Abenbury had been a wash-out. He would have felt less lonely in his hotel room in Long Moreton. He even began to think about implementing the policy he had outlined to Cathy Winters, going home and reading his book, when he found himself outside a cinema, and paused listlessly to look at the stills displayed on the façade. Then he looked closer. There was a picture of a young man without any clothes being fondled by a number of naked ladies. Conrad stepped back to get a look at the title of the film: it was *Sex Confessions of a Nymphomaniac*. Conrad moved forward to examine the pictures again. What was the young man doing to the girl in that one up there? They weren't actually showing that sort of thing in the film, were they? Conrad drifted towards the box-office.

9

The cinema show ended at about ten past ten, and the audience filed out into the foyer. Each one walked sedately, his eyes directed downwards, and if two of them by accident exchanged a glance, they looked hurriedly away again. On reaching the publicity of the open street each gave a quick, nervous look up and down, and then scuttled hastily to the obscurity of the shadows. Conrad performed this ritual and maintained a brisk pace until he had put a couple of hundred yards between himself and the cinema, then breathed more easily. It had been a curious experience, he thought, making towards the car park, not without a certain sociological interest. Actual girls had actually taken off all their clothes and consented to behave like that. What an odd way of earning your living! Some of the older ones at any rate must have been professional actors and actresses, who had begun their careers full of artistic ambition. No doubt they were the products of some foreign equivalent of RADA and had mastered the classical repertoire. What curious turn of fate had led to their stripping off and touching one another up in public? What would Dame Lilian say, or Stanislavski?

The younger ones had been guilty of no artistic betrayal. They had had no professional training, not on the stage at any rate. What puzzled Conrad was how they had been chosen for their roles, since the ability to act did not come into it. A minimum qualification ought to have been good looks and a good figure, but some of the girls had not even possessed these. There had been fat, flabby girls and thin, stringy girls and lank, spotty girls on display, probably, if you thought about it, with a view to providing for all tastes. And the thing had been so badly done that it had been positively infantile: banal dialogue, naïve motivation, everything just cobbled together in a hurry and photographed any old how. It had been just an excuse to get couples to take their clothes off and simulate sex unconvincingly while the camera zoomed in on their arses. The only imagination shown had been that expended on finding novel angles from which to shoot these heavings. Not so much, Conrad thought, the beast with two backs as the beast with about fourteen backsides. Of course the whole thing had been richly and unintentionally comic, and an interesting example of the kind of thing which a permissive society had brought forward.

Conrad had read about pornography, but he had seen few specimens of it, and it was interesting now to judge its effect in the light of his new experience. He speculated on the pinched and starved emotional lives of the men who needed stimulation of this sort. Surely the existence of such a craving represented an educational failure. Conrad began to wonder if he could work this into one of the chapters of his book. If the schools had nourished the full life of the spirit, as they ought to have done, then everybody would bring to films such as this the adult, and critical, and therefore destructive response which he had brought himself, and they would cease to exist because they would no longer serve a need.

Of course if he put this into his book he would have to talk in a general way, he could not very well use the actual film as an example. That girl on the rocking-horse, for instance, what an extraordinary thing to allow to be done to one. It must have hurt quite a bit, that. Conrad analysed his own emotions. At first – he must be quite honest about this – he had been a little excited, there had been an erotic thrill, but it had worn off very quickly. By the end one had become almost indifferent to the sight of naked flesh. Except, possibly, for that rocking-horse scene. Conrad glimpsed again the girl swinging backwards and forwards, her breasts flopping about, and that chap creeping up behind her . . . No, it had been the unexpectedness that had done it, all the rest had been so dreary. After an evening of films like that, he decided, one could happily devote one's time to pigeon racing or constructing model railways. Perhaps there was some substance in the claim that pornography had a useful social function. Possibly rapists and sexual offenders ought to be sentenced to so many hours of these films according to the heinousness of their offences. Conrad imagined the judge's voice intoning the words: 'Twenty-seven hours of the *Sex Confessions of a Nymphomaniac*, and may the Lord have mercy on your soul.' He pictured crazed malefactors beating at the doors of the cinema, pleading to be let out, and flint-hard warders, made merciless by years of exposure to the films, shooting the bolts on them and laughing sadistically.

He amused himself with these fancies until he reached the car park where he noticed that the blue van had left. It was entertaining to think of retribution awaiting the driver in the form of a stern-faced policeman.

He drove carefully through the town centre, being uncertain of his route, but as he reached the suburbs, and found the road which went unmistakably towards Long Moreton, he settled down to enjoy the drive. This was the posh quarter of Abenbury, full of large detached houses, each set in a fair-sized garden, well back from the road. There was money round here. It was to a house like this that the girl in the Bentley had gone with Daddy. Conrad took in the details resentfully. Wrought iron house names, glimpses of private tennis courts, three garages to every residence, stockbroker's tudor all over the place. Elderly ladies and gentlemen abroad exercising their dogs. Last walkies, no doubt, before beddy-byes. All that sniffing about the trees that lined the road, cocking their legs, fouling the pavements. Well, so long as they didn't do it in the garden.

Ahead of him, trudging along at the side of the road, Conrad saw a figure. It was a girl. She had on one of those long, shapeless frocks that swept the ground. She walked with a slouch and trailed a duffel bag in her left hand. She did not look up, or betray any other awareness of his existence, but Conrad just managed to make out a barely discernible twitch of her right thumb which hinted that she requested a lift. Conrad drew to a halt a few yards ahead of her. She did not hurry, he noticed. Maintaining the same shamble she drew alongside and peered in through the window.

'I'm going to Long Moreton,' he said, 'any good?'

She weighed this offer. 'I'm going to Bristol,' she said, at last.

'I'm not going quite that far,' said Conrad, 'just to Long Moreton.'

'Got anyone with you?' she asked.

'No, all alone.'

She considered for a moment or two. It could not possibly be, thought Conrad, that she was afraid for her virtue. She was probably trying to decide whether it was worth her while to accept a lift for so short a distance. But the road was empty, there was very little traffic, and finally she did him the favour of opening the door and getting in beside him. She swung her duffel bag onto the floor behind the front seats and lit a cigarette-end without asking if he minded. Conrad opened the window beside him in a marked manner which was completely lost on her, and started the car.

She was not a chatty companion. She slumped on the seat and fixed her gaze on the glove compartment in front of her and drew fiercely at her cigarette.

'You're going to Bristol, then?' said Conrad.

'Yeah.'

'It's a long way. You're not hoping to get there tonight?'

She shrugged her shoulders; tonight, next week, next year, it was all one to her she implied.

'What'll you do if you don't get a lift?'

'I'll make out.'

'You in college in Bristol?'

'No.'

'Visiting a friend?'

She shook her head indifferently.

Conrad gave up. He felt annoyed. It was a bit thick. After all, there was a certain code. He had taken the trouble to stop and give her a lift, the least she could do was to be a bit civil in return.

He glanced at her. Her dress was a dingy brown colour, with a denim jacket over it. At some time in the past she had had her hair treated in that curious style that caused it to frizz out and stand up from her head in a great golliwog mass. The effects of the treatment were beginning to wear off and she had a bedraggled look. She must be quite young, nineteen or twenty, and probably, under that shapeless, trailing, Victorian dress, she had quite a good figure. Anyway, there she was. He was driving along in his car all alone with a young girl. It was a classic situation. In the films, in books, in magazine and newspaper articles, it led automatically to one thing. There had been a hitch-hiker in the film that he had just seen. It had taken her and the driver about thirty seconds to get their clothes off and to get down to it. This one probably hitch-hiked all over the place. She must quite often receive attentions from the men who picked her up.

He stole another look at her. She was either lost in her thoughts or sunk in a stupor, he could not make out which. How would a driver make a start? This was where the film had not been helpful. The driver had taken the girl aboard, reached out his hand and yanked off her blouse, and she had responded by starting to unzip his trousers. Obviously it needed leading up to a bit more carefully than that. Conrad was sure that if Davidson gave a lift to a girl like this he would not leave matters there, but what would he do? Engage her

86

in conversation? Conrad had tried that. Still, remember Bruce and the spider.

'I'm just going as far as Long Moreton.'

She blew out a cloud of smoke through her nostrils and shifted slightly in her seat.

'I'm a representative, for a firm.'

This was clever. Conrad had no intention of giving himself away.

'Electronics,' he explained, 'I travel over the country selling electronic equipment, computers, that sort of thing.'

'Yeah.'

'It means that I'm on my own quite a lot.'

She was looking at him, not with interest but with a wary speculation; then she looked back at the glove compartment again. Conrad wondered what she would do if he put his hand on her knee. He did. She shifted it irritably.

'Do you mind?'

He put his hand back on the steering wheel. He was furious, with himself and with her. The bloody little slut. Who did she think she was? She had not been frightened, she had not been indignant, her tone had expressed a horrible, worldly-wise, weary contempt. She had marked him down in her mind as a squalid nuisance; he had made the expected pass and she had dealt with him and she could go back to staring at the glove compartment and dismiss him from her mind. Of course he ought not to leave it like that, he ought to take the offensive. What the bloody hell was she doing cadging lifts at this time of night? What did she expect to happen to her? What right had she to put on her prissy airs? Conrad looked at her reflection in his mirror. She was not over clean. He wondered when she had last had a bath. Her jacket was stained and spotted, the cuffs of her dress, which showed at her wrists beyond the sleeves of the jacket, were soiled, her feet were filthy. She wore no stockings or socks; her bare feet were stuck into sandals, and they were filthy.

She was on her third cigarette now, puffing deeply at it, and her fingers were stained with the nicotine. She was an unwholesome object. Frankly, even if she had made a more positive response to his advances Conrad was not sure that he would have been pleased. The sooner he got her out of his car the better. He put his foot on the accelerator and began to speed.

It was not a road made for speeding. They were in the country now and on each side the ground rose sharply to the moorland which stretched for miles in every direction. The road had become quite narrow and it wound about so that Conrad had to keep braking sharply to avoid running into the verges. From time to time sheep loomed out of the darkness at him. They were wandering about quite freely, loitering on the road, cropping the grass at the edges. Conrad had to give all his attention to his driving and had no time to spare for the little tramp next to him. Once or twice, as the car swerved sharply, she was flung sideways against him and he caught a whiff of cheap scent and body odour. Each time she straightened herself without comment, without even looking at him. He hoped that she did not think that he was doing it deliberately. Once he had to push her knee aside in order to manipulate the gear lever. It occurred to him that he might make a sarcastic apology, but he thought better of it. He opened the window wider to get rid of some of the cigarette smoke which was beginning to make his eyes smart. Conrad did not smoke himself and preferred his air to be fresh. It was really a bit thick. To cadge a lift like that, smoke cigarette after cigarette without so much as a by your leave, sit huddled in a sulk without uttering a word; it was simply bloody cheek. The car swerved round another bend and a sheep jumped down from the bank right in front of it. Conrad braked violently and twisted the steering wheel, the girl was flung against him once more and knocked his arm, the near wing of the car hit the sheep squarely in the middle and it went into the verge with a surprised bleat. Conrad drew into the side of the road and got out. The sheep was lying very still. The girl got out and joined him and they stood looking down at the body.

'Bloody hell,' said Conrad, feeling that this was the bitter end, 'I shall have to report this. If you hadn't knocked my arm I could have avoided it.'

'Yeah,' said the girl unrepentantly, 'too bad.'

'It just jumped right in front of me, I didn't have a chance.'

They stood looking down at the body. Conrad felt as though he ought to do something more, examine it, see if he could help it, but he was not a damned vet. How did you take a sheep's pulse?

'I suppose we ought to do something,' he said.

'Give it a nice funeral,' said the girl, and suddenly, unexpectedly, she giggled.

Conrad looked at her with loathing. 'You're not much help,' he said, 'don't you know anything about animals?'

'Not much. I had a hamster when I was a kid.'

The sheep stirred and raised its head. Then it rose unsteadily to its feet, gave Conrad an indignant look, and tottered off into the night. Conrad and the girl just stood and watched it go.

'There y'are,' said the girl, 'now you won't have to report it.'

'It might be injured,' said Conrad, 'we ought to get the farmer to have a look at it.'

'Yeah,' said the girl, 'if you could tell him which one.'

All around, dimly in the darkness, sheep could be seen cropping the grass. The girl spoke again.

'I'm going to have a pee,' she said.

For one dreadful moment Conrad thought that she was just going to squat down where she was and do it in front of him. It would be like her. But she retained some vestige of maiden modesty and wandered off out of sight over a slight rise on the left-hand side of the road. Conrad stood waiting for her, jigging from one foot to the other, marvelling at her crudity.

'I'm going to have a pee,' she had said. Well, why not? This was the new, liberated age. By all means spell it out. 'Going to have a pee' – he should be thankful she had not wanted a shit. He ought to have told her that he was going to puke. He moved towards the car. The door on the near side was open, the passenger light was on, and he saw the girl's duffel bag on the floor. The rage which had been smouldering within him for a long time suddenly burst into flame. He looked quickly round to make sure that there was no sign of her, and then he sprang upon the bag, tore it open, and began scattering its contents over the grass. Almost hysterically, and in dead silence, he ran up and down, skipping over the heather and the wiry turf, flinging blouses and knickers and brassières and tights to the right and left. When it was empty he flung the bag as far from him as he could and jumped into his car. Fortunately the engine started immediately and he let in the clutch and drove off. As the car pulled away he thought he heard behind him an angry cry. He smiled. His heart was pounding and his hands trembled, but he smiled. At last he had got a positive response from her.

Once he got round the bend he relaxed a little. He was sweating, and the pain in the left side of his groin was making itself felt. Also he noticed that the passenger door was rattling. In his haste he had failed to shut it properly. He leaned over, but the car swerved dangerously. He would wait. There was a lay-by a short distance ahead. He remembered it because he had stopped there when he was on his way home after making his duty visits in April. It was on his left, in the shadow of a hill, he could get out there, walk about, calm himself down. He saw the sign and pulled in, switching off his headlights. But he was out of luck. There was another vehicle already there, almost lost in the darkness, parked with its lights off. A couple, no doubt, snogging, resenting his intrusion. He opened the near-side door, bringing the passenger light on, and picked up the cigarette ends which littered the floor, fastidiously dropping them into the ashtray. She had not left anything else, had she? No. He decided against getting out. Better not hang around with that other car there. He slammed the door and started his engine. When his headlights came on he saw the vehicle ahead of him clearly for the first time. It was familiar. It was a van, dark blue, rather dirty, and it had no numberplate at the rear. Hastily, hiding himself from possible identification, Conrad drove away.

10

The next morning, Wednesday, Conrad set off early. He was anxious to be in time for the start of the first lesson. He would not be expected then, and he particularly wanted to see how Denise Shotter approached the task of setting up an experiment with Class Three A. She was not getting on very well with Class Three A, and Conrad suspected that if she thought that he was not going to come in she would just do the experiment herself while Class Three A watched her. She had said in her preparation that she intended the class to do it for themselves. Well, he would give her a little surprise, and see what he would see. He turned the nose of his car in the direction of Abenbury and began to retrace his route of the previous evening.

What had happened to that dreadful girl? He did not want to meet her suddenly, still trudging along on her way to Bristol. He was slightly ashamed of the way he had abandoned her, but really he had not left her any worse off than she would have been if he had put her down in Long Moreton itself. She would simply have been flagging the same cars a few miles further down the road, that was all. It should have taught her a bit of a lesson in manners. Next time she might be a bit more civil.

Conrad glanced at his watch. He ought to be in school by about ten past nine, which would just be in time to catch Denise on her way to her class. Conrad turned a corner and cursed under his breath. Ahead of him was a policeman, hand up, directing him into the near-side lay-by. A traffic census, he supposed. There was another queue of vehicles on the opposite side of the road. It was really too bad at this time of the morning, when people were bound to be in a hurry. He drew up behind a line of cars and stopped his engine.

Conrad sat there for several minutes, fidgeting and looking at his watch. It was taking a long time for a census. He decided to get out and stretch his legs, and had walked a few yards when he heard his name called, turned, and saw a vision across the road waving to him. It was Sandra Duckham. Conrad had time for a momentary twitch of irritation. These bloody students with cars of their own. He had been nearly thirty before he had been able to afford one, but Sandra preferred to stay in Abenbury forsooth, and drove to school every day.

She presented a startling spectacle as she minced her way across the road. She had followed to the letter his instructions about covering up, and had adopted a figure-hugging costume of some stockinette material, which clung to her like a second skin. The skirt was below the knee, the neck was throat high, the sleeves were long: but it was the most provocative dress Conrad had ever seen. It was nearly flesh-coloured. It showed every curve of her body. In the slightly misty morning air, at a short distance, she looked naked. Conrad wondered what Miss Cranston would make of it. It was a calculated act of defiance, he was sure.

'Hullo, Sandra,' he said as she got near. 'You're going to be late this morning. Miss Cranston won't be very pleased about that.'

Miss Cranston had expressed herself twice already on the undesirability of Sandra Duckham's being allowed to lodge away from the village, and Conrad could already hear her saying, 'If that girl had been told she had to live near the school this would never have happened.'

'You'll have to speak up for me, Mr Nield, tell her it wasn't my fault.'

'Whose fault is it? What are we stopped for? Any idea?'

Sandra was wiggling her body about in a singularly

attractive way, as young girls sometimes do when they are in the grip of excitement. She was experiencing the pleasure that comes to people who have sensational news to impart.

'Don't you know, then? I asked one of the policemen and he told me all about it.' Conrad had a brief vision of a poor sod of a young policeman being wrapped round this gorgeous creature's little finger.

'It's awful. There's been another murder. They've found a girl's body up on the moors.'

It was fortunate that Sandra was in no mood to observe other people's reactions closely or she would have seen that this news affected Conrad powerfully. He had to catch hold of his car to steady himself, and he was sure that he must have turned pale. He just managed to check an exclamation and turn it into a cough, and he had difficulty in controlling his voice to ask the question.

'Where – where did they find it? Where was it?'

'On the tops, he said, where the road goes over. It was a policeman who found it, he said, they had special patrols out. He said they saw some clothing scattered by the side of the road and got out to investigate.'

Oh, God, this was terrible. Conrad began to feel that he would have difficulty in getting through this without giving himself away. His heart was going again, and there was a churning at the pit of his stomach.

Sandra, however, was not looking at him. She chattered on, excited, animated, and as she spoke her eyes were roving about, eyeing the men who were standing near, and she smiled, automatically, unconsciously, if one of them looked in her direction. Conrad gathered his wits.

'He said she'd been strangled, with her own tights, just like the other one.'

'It doesn't do to talk too much about such things, Sandra.' His voice, he was glad to note, sounded reasonably normal.

'No, but it's awful to think about it, isn't it?' said Sandra happily, squirming in sheer pleasure. The idea of the crime seemed, Conrad noticed, to give her an actual, sexual thrill. 'I mean, happening so near, and all that. Me and my boyfriend were driving along this road last night. We might have been right by when it happened.'

'In that case, Sandra, the police will want to have a good talk with you, and you must remember to tell them clearly what you saw.'

'We didn't see anything, Mr Nield.'

Thank God for that.

Conrad was feeling better now, he had got over the first shock.

'Hadn't you better get back to your car, Sandra? You'll be holding all the others up.'

'There's loads of time. They can go first for all I care. It's Wednesday. Miss Cranston always has a long assembly on Wednesdays, telling the children Bible stories. If she says anything to me I can say the police kept me, can't I?'

Conrad preferred not to comment on this, either officially or unofficially, so he said, austerely, that he was going back to his own car.

'I'll tell Miss Cranston I saw you, shall I?'

'Just tell her the truth, Sandra; but I really think you ought to get back to your car.'

She wiggled her way across the road and Conrad got back into the driving seat and drew up behind the vehicle in front of him. He had still not fully assimilated the news. In a few minutes he would reach the head of the queue and the police would be asking him questions. How was he to answer them?

As a citizen his duty was clear. Perfect honesty, that was the ticket. It was a precondition of civilized society that in an inquiry of this kind every citizen told frankly all that he knew. An innocent man had nothing to fear from a police investigation. When they asked him he would, quite simply, tell them what had happened. He had picked this girl up, out of a

95

desire to do her a kindness, and driven up to the moors, where the road goes over. They had hit a sheep and got out to see if they could render it any assistance. She had decided to have a pee, and, on a sudden impulse, he had driven off leaving her stranded, alone, at getting on for midnight, in that desolate place. That was what he must tell them.

The car in front of him moved forward, and Conrad let in his clutch and followed. It would not do; it would not do at all. He reviewed the likely consequences of telling this story. The police would have to follow it up. They would take him away and ask awkward questions. Just at this time it would be an especially bad thing for him to get unpleasant publicity. It was easy to imagine a sensational headline in the *Bickleton Herald*. Suppose the police did not believe his story about driving off, suppose they thought he had more sinister reasons for leaving her there? A gap appeared ahead of him and Conrad drove up to a police officer with a notebook in his hand, who guided him into place.

'We're sorry to delay you, sir –' he poked his head in through the open window and took a good quiz round the interior of the car – 'but we'd just like to ask you a few questions.'

'Of course, officer.' Conrad put on the voice he used to reassure students. 'Anything I can do.'

He gave his name and address.

'Are you staying in the vicinity, sir?'

'Yes, in Long Moreton, at the Red Lion.'

'Did you travel into Abenbury at all yesterday?'

'No. Er, no, I didn't.'

'You weren't travelling along this road, between here and Abenbury, at any time from about half past nine to midnight, sir?'

'No, officer, I'm afraid I can't help you.'

'Do you mind showing me your licence, sir?'

Conrad produced it and the constable examined it and

handed it back. Then he went to the front of the car and made a note of the number. Then he thanked Conrad, and told him he was free to leave. It was as easy as that.

Conrad drove slowly. There was no longer any hurry; he had no chance of catching Denise Shotter out now. His sense of relief was enormous. He realized that, although he had answered on the spur of the moment, without adequate reflection, he would have been a fool to have acted in any other way. The general rule that one should speak the truth breaks down in exceptional circumstances. There are occasions when the truth is inconvenient, not merely to oneself but to other people. The truth in this case would have been a red herring, wasting the time of the police and drawing them away from their real business. If the truth could have been helpful to the investigation then Conrad was quite sure that he would have told it, but it would not have been helpful, quite the reverse. The wise policy, in the situation in which Conrad had found himself, had been to tell a judicious lie. Now it was all over, there would be no more fuss, and the police were free to get on with their inquiries. Yes, Conrad was quite satisfied with himself, quite satisfied. He preferred not to think about the girl. He pushed the thought of her out of his mind.

That afternoon Conrad visited Miss Cranston's school again. He was unlucky. The Headmistress was standing in the corridor when he arrived and swept him into her study.

'That Miss Duckham was very late this morning,' she said, wasting no time on a preamble.

'Yes, as it happens, Miss Cranston, I do know about that. She ought to have told you that she had seen me at the police roadblock.'

'She did tell me. One never knows whether to believe these girls or not. I suppose that she did not happen to mention, when she saw you, that she had already been late on Monday and Tuesday?'

'No, Miss Cranston, she didn't say anything about that.'

'I thought at the time that it was very unwise to allow a girl like Sandra Duckham to live away from the village. She is the sort of student who ought to be very closely supervised. Miss Grey lodges with my sister and devotes every evening to the most careful preparation.'

Conrad nodded. Sandra had been offered this accommodation also, and he had a clear memory of the terms in which she had rejected it.

'I think there is a good deal in what you say, Miss Cranston.'

'Young people these days are spoiled. Have you seen the clothes she is wearing today? And she has a car of her own. I had been working for fifteen years before I was able to afford such a thing. Everything has just dropped into her lap. The result is that she has no sense of values.'

Conrad murmured that it was true.

'People like that think that the entire world exists just for their pleasure. I told her. I said, "This business of that girl they have found on the moors, it ought to be a warning to you." They say that she was trying to get a lift. At that time of night! I ask you.

'You know as well as I do, Mr Nield, what kind of a girl it is who goes round taking lifts from perfect strangers late at night. Some of these young women are sex mad. Sow the wind and reap the whirlwind, that's what I say. If you flaunt yourself at a man and drive him wild, you have only yourself to blame for the consequences.' As she said the words 'flaunt yourself', Miss Cranston, in her excitement, rose on tip-toe and bounced her monstrous bosom towards Conrad, who retreated a step in alarm.

Her diagnosis failed to agree with his own recollection of what had actually happened, but he did not say anything. He preferred not to think about the girl at all, he had spent the day suppressing her troubling image, and he brought the conversation to a halt as soon as he could and got himself out of the study and into Sandra Duckham's room. Here he had a pleasant surprise. The children were all actually engaged in doing something which appeared to have been designed for them to do. He must make encouraging noises about this.

'Well, Sandra, congratulations. There is certainly more of a sense of purpose than when I was last here. What are they doing?'

'Finger-painting,' she replied. 'It's Miss Williamson; she's been giving me a bit of help.'

Conrad felt rebuffed. This was one in the eye for him. As her tutor he should have been giving help himself, not leaving it to the class teacher. That was what she meant. Well, he had tried to be pleasant. If that was how she chose to take it, bad cess to her.

'Good,' he said, 'I'm very glad. She didn't happen to say anything about not making a mess, did she? Haven't these children got any smocks, for instance?'

'They don't use smocks, Mr Nield.'

'I can see they don't, Sandra. What I am asking is, shouldn't they? And these tables, oughtn't you to have covered them with something? I mean, if I've read Miss Cranston's character aright, she won't take too kindly to having a slop like this in one of her rooms.'

'I haven't got any papers,' she said, on the point of bursting into tears. 'I can't give them papers if I don't have any, can I? I'm trying to do my best and all you do is to shout at me. I can't make papers out of nothing.'

Conrad stopped himself saying, 'No, but you could bloody well think ahead and bring some in.' He did not want a weeping girl on his hands, he must try to be kind and constructive. 'Hang on,' he said, and went out to his car.

Newspapers were a weakness of his. When he was away

99

from home he was in the habit of buying two or three a day, and these, since he was unwilling to litter the countryside, accumulated in the back of his car. He could do Sandra a good turn, raise his stock in the eyes of a student, and have a good clear-out, all at the same time. It struck him that it was rather decent of him to do this. Lots of his colleagues would have resented being spoken to as Sandra had just spoken to him, but he was ruled by a wise magnanimity. This, damn it, was turning the other cheek if anything was.

He returned to the classroom and flung the papers on a table with the careless negligence of a king in a fairy story tossing a peasant a purse of gold. 'There you are, Sandra. These any use to you?'

'Ooh, thank you, Mr Nield.'

It occurred to Conrad, taking his cue from the intensity of her tone, that she had probably been warned not to make a mess and had simply forgotten. Well, she was learning.

They both bustled about in a companionable fashion, lifting up the paint pots and spreading the news sheets under them, and Conrad began to feel that he was breaking down some of her hostility towards him. She would see that he was not such a bad stick, after all. When the class had settled to its painting again she even became ponderously whimsical.

'You didn't get arrested then, Mr Nield?'

'Arrested?'

'This morning, at the roadblock. I noticed that they let you go straight away. They kept me for hours, kept asking questions over and over again.'

'That's because you were along that road last night. I told you how it would be. If you'd been like me and stayed at home working, you'd have been all right.'

She sighed and turned away from him, pretending to attend to a small girl who had upset a pot of water. But the subject appealed so much to her morbid imagination that she could not resist opening it again.

'I can't stop thinking about it,' she said. 'That poor girl, all alone in the middle of those moors at that time of night. It makes you wonder who'd do a thing like that, doesn't it?'

'I prefer not to think about it, Sandra.'

'Keith and me must have been going back to Abenbury just about the time when it happened. It makes you wonder, doesn't it, whether you could have done anything to stop it.'

'I don't suppose you could, Sandra, and I think it is much better not to speculate about these things. If I were you I would just concentrate on trying to teach these children.' That would switch her off. Conrad had decided that if that was the best she could do, conversationally, when she was being friendly, he preferred her hostile. He went down the corridor to have a look at Toni Grey.

Aesthetically it was a change for the worse. Toni Grey was an immensely fat girl, afflicted with spots and adenoids, and with a surprisingly good opinion of herself. She was conducting a class in 'Music and Movement', which involved her in skipping ponderously round the floor and ever and anon telling the children to curl up into tiny balls.

'Make yourselves as tiny as possible, children,' she kept saying. 'Teensy weensy balls, that's what I want to see. You can do better than that, Deirdre. I want you all to look at Simon and see the balls he makes.'

From time to time she would fatly demonstrate the feat herself, like an elephant trying to clamber through a hoop. When Conrad had got as much entertainment from this as he could stand he decided to call it a day. As he walked down the corridor he glanced through the window into Sandra's classroom. She was leaning against the wall, oblivious of the children, reading one of the newspapers.

While he was enjoying his meal in the hotel that evening the waitress came to his table to tell him that there was a phone call for him. Puzzled, he asked who it was and was told merely that it was a gentleman's voice. He experienced a stab at the pit of his stomach. It could not possibly be the police, could it? His conscience, or his fear of being found out, had been troubling him ever since he had left the roadblock that morning. He could think of nobody else who would be likely to want to speak to him, but why, oh God, why should the police want a word? He picked up the receiver and said guardedly: 'Conrad Nield here, who is that, please?' and felt a mixture of relief and chagrin when he heard Philip Milne's unmistakable voice.

'It's me, Conrad, I thought I'd give you a ring because I understand that you're having some sort of trouble with Andrew Carney.'

Conrad drew in his breath with annoyance. For this his meal was getting cold!

'It would be more correct, Philip, to say that Carney is having trouble with me.'

'I wondered, Conrad, if I could be of any use. I feel a bit responsible. Andrew is one of my "pastorals". I've always found him a well-meaning sort of lad.'

This was one of Milton Jacks's schemes. A few years earlier he had attended a conference somewhere and returned full of ideas about pastoral responsibility, and as a result of this each tutor had been given the care of a small group of students. People like Milne and Charles Halliday tended to take their pastoral duties with dramatic seriousness.

'I don't really think that there is anything you can do, Philip. I'm quite capable of supervising my students adequately.'

'I am sure that you are, Conrad. I just thought that I'd offer. Andrew came over to see me last night in Abenbury. He seemed quite upset. He rather had the idea that you had not been fair to him.'

Conrad again drew in a long, sighing breath, and this time he made no attempt to conceal it.

'Well, I can hardly go into it now, Philip. You've called me in the middle of my meal. I've got a duckling going cold. If you want to help Carney tell him to get down to a bit of proper preparation. His lessons are no good because he's not working at them hard enough.'

'Sorry if I've called at a bad time, Conrad. We'll have a chat about it, shall we, when we get back to College? Carney told me that his Headmaster was quite pleased with him. I just think he needs a little help, you know. I tried to ring you this morning but you'd already left.'

'Yes, I believe in getting into school pretty early, Philip, and in the meantime I'll treat Carney as I treat all my students and give whatever assistance is needed.'

Conrad hung up in a temper and went back to lukewarm duckling and cold sprouts. Milne was a bloody nuisance. It all stemmed from a vanity he had that nobody else was as caring or could handle the students as well as he could. It was fundamentally wrong, thought Conrad, chewing at a piece of meat which had the consistency of india-rubber, because it encouraged the students to be soft and to lean on others instead of cultivating self-reliance. Anybody could molly-coddle a student like Carney through a teaching practice, but what he ought to be learning was to stand on his own two feet, to think for himself, and to discipline himself to put in a good performance even when nobody was watching him. Conrad rehearsed phrases that he would use when he did speak to Milne about it at College.

'Didn't you like your duck?' asked the waitress when she came to clear his plate.

11

If Conrad had needed any examples of the imperfections of the popular press for the book that he was writing, they were readily to hand in the accounts of the second murder. Here, in supreme degree, was the de-sensitizing sensationalism which so worked against the efforts of the preachers of culture whom Matthew Arnold had so warmly recommended. 'Flower child strangled on the moor' a headline screamed. 'Unidentified waif victim of sex maniac' shouted another. The parallels between the two murders were heavily under-scored and the details of the injuries inflicted on the bodies were hinted at with a reticence which was surely worse than direct statement would have been.

He thought that a close examination of the language used might yield useful results. 'Fear stalks the moors.' Look at that word 'stalks', consider its overtones. How many synonyms for 'crazy' had been found? How often was the word 'sex' used? The whole impulse of these pieces was to generate an atmosphere of unhealthy sexual excitement. Beneath it all the ostensible purpose, the dissemination of accurate information, had not been fulfilled. Few details were given, and these were confused and contradictory. There was not even agreement about the description of the dead girl and some of the facts stated certainly did not correspond with what Conrad remembered of her. In fact Conrad found it comforting that the police evidently knew so little because it seemed to offer security against his tiny prevarication being found out. There was an appeal to members of the public to come forward with information, but he stifled any impulse he might have had to act on it. If he had been an ideal person then he supposed he would have spoken, but Conrad had never claimed to be ideal. He was human, with ordinary human failings. Indeed, as he came to think of it, there would be an almost exaggerated idealism about trotting along to the police station and telling his story. He tried to imagine the expression on the faces of the officers, and failed. So he went about his normal business, and when his duties took him past two large police vans, prominently labelled Murder Inquiry, parked in the village of Forton Cross, he drove with unusual care, but he did not stop and go inside.

That evening something absolutely characteristic took place. Conrad had foreseen it and taken precautions against it, but he still had not quite believed that it would happen. Just as he was settling down to enjoy his meal Philip Milne had rung again. Conrad had warned the waitress to ask any caller his name, and he had given appropriate instructions if that name should be Milne, but it was still a bit thick.

'You told him that I was out?'

'Yes, sir.'

'And that I would not be back till late?'

She nodded, and Conrad went on with his braised steak. What a cheek! It must have been deliberate. He had chosen that time knowing that he was likely to interrupt Conrad's meal. This was not just lack of consideration, it was active malice. Well, it had not worked. Conrad took a sip of wine – he had treated himself to a half bottle feeling that he deserved a little cosseting – and congratulated himself on his foresight.

On the Friday morning, just as he was finishing breakfast, an elderly chambermaid put her head round the door and told him that there was a gentleman at the reception desk wanting to see him. Conrad rose grimly. This was the last straw. This was bloody persecution. Milne must actually, at this absurdly early time, have come all the way out from Abenbury just to talk about Andrew Carney. Clearly he needed a lesson, his perspectives ought to be adjusted. Conrad strode down the corridor rehearsing a few terse phrases with which he would open his campaign, turned the corner into reception, and found himself confronting a total stranger. He was tall, he was burly, he had a weather-beaten face, and the hands which stuck awkwardly out of a cheap-looking blue suit were large and red and hairy.

'Mr Nield?'

Conrad agreed that that was his name.

'Rosen, Detective Sergeant Rosen.' He flashed a card in front of Conrad's nose. 'I wonder if you'd mind answering a few questions, sir? Is there anywhere where we could talk in private?'

Conrad had difficulty in controlling his voice to make a reply, and was immediately afraid that this vocal failure would be noticed by the policeman and marked down against him. He led the way to the lounge, which was empty at that time of the morning, and they sat in a corner by the dead ashes of a fire. Common sense told him that he had nothing to fear, but common sense failed to reassure him.

'It is only a small matter, sir,' the Sergeant spoke affably enough, 'but we'd just like to clear it up. It should only take a moment of your time.'

Conrad cleared his throat again and said that he would be happy to help.

'You always stay here, do you, sir?'

Conrad said that he did, adding idiotically, 'When I'm in the neighbourhood, that is.'

'When did you arrive, sir?'

'Er – Tuesday – Tuesday afternoon. I'd booked by tele-phone.'

'That would be from Bickleton, I take it, sir?' The Sergeant consulted a notebook as he asked this question. 'I under-stand, sir, that you were detained at a roadblock on the Abenbury road on Wednesday morning?'

'Yes, that's right.'

'You were asked if you had travelled into Abenbury on the previous day?'

Conrad nodded. The Sergeant had a country slowness that was beginning to get on his nerves. He left massive pauses before every speech, and in these pauses the slow tick of a clock on the mantelpiece seemed to fill the room. There was something the matter. They had found out something.

'In reply,' said the Sergeant in his unemotional, official, sing-song voice, 'you stated, "I did not." Is that right, sir?'

'Well, I suppose so, if you say so.'

'Did you go into Abenbury on Tuesday, sir?'

'Let me see.' Conrad made a face-saving pretence of thinking hard; he must try to leave his options open. 'I don't think I did.'

The Sergeant did not say anything. He was a jolly-looking family man, he could have been mistaken for a farmer. Not a subtle person, not a giant intelligence, but a slight movement of his lips expressed very clearly his impatience with what Conrad had said. 'Come now,' he seemed to be saying, 'it is not too difficult to remember what you were doing three nights ago, I'm only a simple sort of chap but I can do that at least.' What he actually said was subtle enough in its way.

'I think you told me that you came down here on Tuesday, sir?'

Conrad took his point. He must make a decision. Surely the police could not really know anything. The best thing he could do was to stick to his guns.

'No,' he said firmly, 'I didn't go into Abenbury.'

The Sergeant received this stolidly, opening the case he was carrying and peering inside it before drawing out a newspaper, folded, as Conrad sickeningly remembered, very small so that it would fit into a coat pocket. Conrad could recollect the moment when, the paper having become tiresome to him, he had looked around for a litter bin and, not finding one, had folded it thus because, like a good citizen, he had not wished to litter the Abenbury streets with it.

'This newspaper has come into our possession, sir, and we understand that it was yours.'

He unfolded it in a splendidly unhurried fashion and passed it across to Conrad, who took it helplessly, and observed an infant handprint in emerald green paint on the lower corner.

'Was it?' he said. 'I don't know about that.'

'It is the *Abenbury Courier*, sir.'

'I can see that.'

'Dated Tuesday. Did you buy a copy of the *Abenbury Courier* on Tuesday?'

'I bought one. I don't know whether this is it. You can get the *Abenbury Courier* at all the villages round here. You can get it in Long Moreton.'

'Is that where you got it, sir, Long Moreton?'

Conrad was not to be taken in that easily. He had recognized the Sergeant's tone. It was the tone of a schoolteacher who says, 'You came the shortest way then, Tomkins?' when he has three unimpeachable witnesses that Tomkins took several unnecessary detours.

'To be absolutely frank,' he said, 'I can't remember where I bought it.'

'The fact is, sir,' said the Sergeant, speaking slowly, almost dreamily, like an adult explaining a point to a rather backward child, 'that there are different editions for different parts of the country. We can identify them by the different numbers at the top of the page. And it is possible to say that this particular copy would only have been on sale in Abenbury itself.'

There was a long pause after this. Conrad was thinking very hard, but he tried to give the impression of a man who is racking his brains to recollect imperfectly-stored impressions. He was aware that he was being watched with an acuteness that belied the Sergeant's simple, farmer's face.

'I suppose, Sergeant, that in that case I must have got it in Abenbury. I'm trying to think – don't hurry me. I could have passed through on the Tuesday afternoon.'

The Sergeant made a note. 'Any idea of the time, sir?'

'I've got a shocking memory, Sergeant. I'm not even absolutely sure that I was there at all.'

'I think I ought to tell you, sir, that you were seen in Abenbury on Tuesday evening.'

Conrad made a great show of striking his forehead and flicking his fingers in the air.

'Of course. I was getting the weeks muddled up. I'm down here each week, Sergeant, and it is very easy to mix one week up with another. As a matter of fact I keep forgetting what day of the week it is.'

The Sergeant agreed that it must be very confusing and added, 'But you were in Abenbury on Tuesday evening?'

'Yes, I remember now. Silly of me.'

'Perhaps, sir, you would give me an account of what you did in Abenbury that evening?'

The farmer-sergeant had a fountain pen, and apparently took shorthand. He smoothed out his notebook on his knee and waited for Conrad to begin. Conrad thought furiously, trying to piece together the story. He had been reported seen in Abenbury. Now, unless one assumed that the statement was a trick by the Sergeant, and this seemed unlikely, that could only have been by Cathy Winters. It began to make sense. Sandra Duckham shared a flat in Abenbury and it was quite likely that she would meet Cathy there. It was easy to imagine her telling Cathy about the newspaper and Cathy, in return, saying how she had met him in the town itself. He could picture those two girls gossiping together, magnifying the discovery they had made, in glee at the prospect of going to the police. It would be all over the campus this weekend.

He addressed himself to the problem of answering the

Sergeant. It should not be too difficult. He began to explain about his sudden fit of boredom, his decision, on the spur of the moment, to go into the big city – he waxed quite comic on the subject of the big city, but the Sergeant was not a responsive audience. 'I just mooched about, you know. I looked at the sights, went round the cathedral. Then I had a meal.'

The Sergeant was interested in this and asked for details. What was the name of the restaurant? What time was this? When did he leave? Conrad found it difficult to remember the name, and this was quite genuine. He was pleased, because he was anxious to establish a reputation for being an habitually vague, feather-headed sort of chap. He was most eager to help, he told the Sergeant exactly where to find the restaurant: 'Near the cathedral; a little street almost opposite the front of the cathedral. There's a typewriter shop on the corner.'

The Sergeant knew it, he even knew its name, The Lantern Grill, but then the Sergeant was the reverse of feather-headed, his mind functioned simply, in an orderly fashion. He remembered details.

'What did you do after the meal, sir?'

'Walked about again. Oh, and I went to the pictures.'

Conrad deliberately chose this way of putting it: 'went to the pictures', better than saying 'went to the cinema', more homely, more what the sergeant-farmer would expect. The sergeant-farmer became interested.

'What was the name of the cinema, sir?'

Again Conrad had to confess his innocence. He had a positively abominable memory for names, though, mind you, he was not even sure that he had looked at the name of the cinema.

'Well, what was the film, sir?'

Conrad hesitated. It was impossible to tell this man, whose broad, red face would have been so perfectly at home looking round the backside of a cow, that he had been to witness an entertainment called *Sex Confessions of a Nymphomaniac*. The incongruity was too great. Fortunately Conrad's memory proved strong enough to offer him the name of the other film which had been on show that night.

'It was called *Nicholas and Alexandra*,' he said, 'one of those historical epic things.'

'That was on at the Ritz,' said the Sergeant, like a walking information bureau. He made a note. Then he asked Conrad a series of other questions. When had he arrived at the cinema, when had he left, what had he done after leaving, what route had he taken out of the city, about what time would Conrad say that was?

'Just about the time we were inquiring about, in fact, sir?' he said in response to Conrad's last answer.

Conrad felt a return of his earlier discomfort, which had worn off in the course of the benevolent chat he had been having.

'Tell me, sir, and please think very hard about this, on your way out of the city did you see anybody?'

Conrad demurred. Of course he had seen people, the city had not been exactly deserted.

'Quite so, sir, but on the road out did you see anybody hitching a lift?'

'No, Sergeant, nobody like that. It was pretty late you know.'

'The girl we are inquiring about was on the road pretty late, sir. You didn't see her?'

'I didn't see anybody like that, Sergeant.'

'You didn't give anybody a lift yourself?'

'I don't often give lifts, Sergeant.'

The sergeant-farmer refused to let him get away with this prevarication. 'You did not give a lift to anybody on this occasion, sir?'

'No, I didn't. I already said so.'

The Sergeant wrote it down in his book and Conrad watched him do it with a sense of doom. It was a foolish act, and Conrad knew that it was a foolish act, but he had no intention of not committing it. In the circumstances, it seemed to him, he had left himself no option. His conduct at the roadblock determined his behaviour now, and his reason for keeping quiet and hoping that this would all blow over was just the same. Of course, if Sandra Duckham had not been there to see him, or if he had not out of a totally mistaken sense of kindness given her those papers, or chatted with her so incautiously, he would have been all right. He was certainly paying for that piece of amiability.

He wondered about Sandra Duckham. She had been curiously sharp to catch him out in his little untruth. Her dislike of him must have concentrated her mind wonderfully. No, it was all a bit of a mess, but there was no point in making it any worse than it was. If he stuck to the story he was telling now then he would be pretty safe. If he made the mistake of blurting out the truth the consequences would be appalling. This Sergeant was a straightforward, practical man, with the capacity to see simple, obvious facts and to act on them in the most direct way; certainly not the person to trust with the truth in a matter as delicate as this. In the important sense, in the only sense that mattered, he was not deceiving anybody. He was completely innocent because he had done nothing at all. There had been a crime, and the police were interested in finding the culprit. Telling them his story would not help them – it would hinder them. They would waste their time and resources chasing a red herring, and meanwhile the trail would go cold and the real criminal would get off scot-free. No, it would be much the best that he sat tight and kept his mouth shut. It was stupid to lie to the police, but in these special circumstances it was probably the most sensible thing to do. So Conrad watched the Sergeant write his words down in his notebook and felt, helplessly, that he had cast his die.

'Do you mind telling me, sir, where you were on April the twenty-ninth? It was a Thursday. Were you in this vicinity?' He asked the question with the air of a man who knows the answer. Again Conrad pretended to search his memory, and even took out his pocket diary to check the date, though he knew perfectly well, unaided.

'Yes, I thought so, that was the day of our duty visit – the day we visit the schools where we are to have a practice in order to make the final arrangements.'

'So you were down here, sir?'

'Yes, Sergeant.'

'Do you mind telling me which schools you visited that day, and the order in which you visited them?'

Conrad obliged.

'So St Luke's Infants was the last school you went to?'

'That's right, Sergeant. Where, I suppose, you got that newspaper from.'

Conrad could not resist this dig, but Sergeant Rosen ignored it.

'What time did you leave the school, sir?'

'Just before half past three. I like to get away before the kids are let loose.'

'And you drove back to Bickleton through Abenbury?'

'Of course.'

'So you were driving along the road between Forton Cross and Abenbury, over the moors, between half past three and half past four?'

'That's right, Sergeant.'

'I don't know if you remember it, sir, but April the twenty-ninth was the day the first of these girls who have been murdered went missing. We have put out quite a lot of publicity asking any motorist who was along the road at that time to come forward. Do you mind telling me why you haven't done so, sir?'

'To tell you the truth, Sergeant, it just never occurred to

me. I didn't see anything along that road, I couldn't tell you anything that would be useful, so I didn't bother.'

'Why don't you let us be the judge of that, sir? You drove straight back?'

Conrad said that he had driven straight back. No, he had not stopped in Abenbury. No, he had not seen anything suspicious. No, he had not noticed anybody walking on the moors nor seen a car parked up there. He felt relaxed. This was easy. It was all true. There was no need to wonder if he was contradicting himself. It was obviously disappointing to the Sergeant, but he could not help that.

'I warned you that I had nothing useful to say.'

Those unexpectedly shrewd eyes were again fixed on Conrad. 'Is that your car outside, sir? The fawn Mini Clubman estate?'

'Antique gold,' said Conrad.

'I beg your pardon, sir?'

'The manufacturer prefers to call it "antique gold", not fawn. Quaint isn't it?'

'Do you mind if we take a look at it, sir?'

'By all means.' Conrad positively bounded to his feet.

In the hotel car park, alongside his own vehicle, was a police car, its driver elaborately looking at nothing in particular. As the Sergeant appeared he straightened himself up smartly.

'There it is,' said Conrad amiably, 'not much to look at but she carries me from A to B.'

'Have a bit of an accident, sir?'

'Eh?'

'Your near-side wing – you seem to have had an accident.'

Conrad laughed merrily and explained about his encounter with the lorry driver. This enormous transporter-contraption had swung rather quickly round the bend and forced him into the side. He put on his best isn't it amusing, social chatter voice, but the Sergeant remained stolid.

'You should have reported that, sir – dangerous driving. Where did you say it happened?'

His notebook was out again, but once more Conrad had an atrocious memory for names. It was that little village, he explained, just this side of Wearmark, did the Sergeant know it? Where the road bends over the river.

'You didn't get his number, I suppose, sir?'

'Didn't think of it. Could have kicked myself afterwards. There was a name on the side – "Happy Homes" – something like that.'

The Sergeant insisted on all the details that Conrad could remember. What time was it, was there anybody about, any other vehicle involved? Conrad mentioned the woman with the perambulator. 'I'd had to pull into the middle of the road to avoid her. The lorry driver cursed me a bit but I told him I thought there was something in the Highway Code about not hitting women with perambulators.' He failed to say anything about the dark-blue van with the loose numberplate. It had not strictly been involved, and he was not anxious to establish, before the police, any connection with that vehicle.

'Do you mind if I take your keys, sir?'

The Sergeant held out his hand for them and Conrad, not quite understanding, handed them over. The Sergeant tossed them to the constable, who opened the door and got in.

'We'll bring it back as soon as possible, sir.'

This was more than Conrad had bargained for. He felt a return of the earlier, unpleasant sensation, and asked the Sergeant what he meant.

'We'll just take it to the station to get it looked at. We should have it back by the beginning of the afternoon.'

Conrad felt that he could risk some indignation. This was a bit thick. He needed his car for his work, he had an important job to do.

The Sergeant remained tranquil. 'It's up to you, sir. I can't take your car without your permission. Of course I could get a warrant, but I understood that you were willing to help us.'

Good heavens! Naturally he was willing to help them. But he could not see what they wanted it for, and what was he to do without it?

'It's pure routine, sir. The more people we can eliminate from the inquiry the more we narrow it down. If your work is urgent I could get a police car to take you round.'

Conrad declined this offer hastily. He had no desire at all to arrive at his schools in a police car. Ungraciously he gave his permission and, at a nod from the Sergeant, the constable revved up the engine, shot spectacularly out of the car park, and vanished down the road.

'I hope he's going to be careful with it,' said Conrad peevishly.

'We'll get it back as fast as possible, sir.' And the Sergeant lowered himself into the police car and departed in a more stately fashion.

The car was not back by the beginning of the afternoon. Conrad abandoned all hope of getting into his schools that day. It was a nuisance. He had wanted to see Carney again – just to forestall awkward inquiries from Milne. 'Naturally, Philip,' he had wanted to be able to say, 'I looked in on Friday. He needs all the help he can get.' Now he would have to give that up. When his car came back he would drive straight home to Bickleton.

It was returned just before four o'clock. Conrad commented on the delay.

'Yes, sir, Sergeant Rosen sent his apologies, sir, and said that they did it as quickly as possible.'

'This isn't what I call the beginning of the afternoon.'

'No, sir. And Sergeant Rosen told me to tell you that your front, near-side parking light isn't working. He says it's probably the result of that bang you had, and if he were you he'd get it fixed.'

He was a jaunty young man. He looked Conrad straight in the eye. He did not exactly smile but there was a merry turn to the corners of his lips. Conrad peered into his car. It was very clean and neat, unnaturally tidy, and there was a silver-grey powder on the door handles and other exposed parts. They had been dusting his car for fingerprints. He opened the door and got in. It had all been cleaned. How very kind of them. It had been gone over, if not with a fine-tooth comb, with a vacuum cleaner. Again Conrad had that uneasy sensation.

12

Sergeant Rosen had driven slowly back to the police station after his interview with Conrad. He wanted to think. Conrad had not impressed him favourably, but then he had approached the interview with a degree of prejudice which, he recognized, must be allowed for. He felt that he knew Conrad's type, and his reintroduction to it had stirred unpleasant memories. One of his daughters had studied briefly at a training college near London, and he had had the job of going down there and arguing her case when the college had wanted to get rid of her on the grounds of academic unsuitability. The youngish man who had dealt with him had been very like this Nield person, plausible, full of clever talk and professions of friendliness and concern, and, in Sergeant Rosen's view, not to be trusted. He had muddled up Janet's marks with those of some other student and then, instead of frankly confessing the slip, had thrown an elaborate smoke-screen of words round it. He had simply refused to listen to the points the Sergeant had wanted to make.

'She's very good with children.'

'I am afraid, Mr Rosen, that more, much more, is required in modern teaching than a good heart and a good manner with children.'

'I mean, I know she's not a high-flyer –'

'I am afraid not, Mr Rosen. Unfortunately, in the modern world of education, we have to fix our standards pretty high. Janet, I am sorry to have to say this, simply does not measure up to it.'

And he had smiled a sneer and jingled his money in his

pocket and looked at the Sergeant as if to say, 'What are you wasting my time for? Take your thick-headed daughter out of this and get home.' Janet had sobbed all the way back, and he had been left with an abiding distaste for academics.

Well, it was all water under the bridge now. Janet was married, with two lovely children, and very happy, but it was this memory that had been awakened when that pretty little girl and her friend had walked into the station in Abenbury with their story. She had reminded him of Janet. Not that Janet was pretty, bless her, she took after her father too much for that, but because of her youthful vulnerability. Reading between the lines this Nield person seemed to be making things difficult for her, and Sergeant Rosen knew whose side he was on. And then the story that she and her friend had told was an odd one. At the very least, unless they were telling deliberate lies, Nield had been in Abenbury on that evening, whereas he had said at the roadblock that he had not. A glance at the card-index confirmed this. Questioning the girls further Rosen had discovered that Nield had also been in the neighbourhood on April the twenty-ninth, which quickened his interest considerably. Then he had seen his car and found that it was a fawn Mini estate. All this was circumstantial, Rosen did not need to be told that, but if you collect enough details of this sort they acquire an impressive appearance. The Sergeant worked it out again in his head. Nield had left that school at just before half past three. By his own admission he had driven straight to Abenbury along the road across the moors. He would be entering the city at about four o'clock. Tapscott had seen that girl at ten past four, on the same road, walking towards the moors. A fawn Mini estate had been parked behind her. The question now remaining was, what had Nield been up to in Abenbury last Tuesday?

With considerably uplifted spirits Rosen entered the police station in Abenbury, confident of being able to wipe the smile off Nicholson's face at last. It needed wiping off. Since the time when they had sighted the body of the second victim, just after dawn on Wednesday, he had gone round suffused in smiles. Nicholson had always been lucky. He had been made a sergeant when most men were still in panda cars, and he owed his present rank to a monstrous stroke of good fortune. And now this. 'Let me put patrols along the road,' he had said. 'If we don't find the next missing girl quicker than the last one then we're in trouble,' he had said. So what happens? He puts his patrols on the road and that very night one of them picks out, in their headlights, a pair of knickers caught on a tuft of heather. They get out and search and find nothing, but when the dawn breaks and reinforcements are brought in the body is located three-quarters of a mile away, in a place where it could have lain hidden for months.

Rosen began to write his report and thought about Nield again. A nasty piece of work. His flippancy had irritated the Sergeant. Murder is not a thing to make jokes about. The Sergeant recalled his first glimpse of the second victim's face, hideous, purple and swollen. Through all Nield's jocularities the image had been at the back of his mind, souring his reception of them. The fellow would not have been so comic if he had been there when the mother identified her child. It had been a painful scene. Rosen and Nicholson had met her at the station and shown her the knickers which the patrol had picked up and she had not recognized them as her daughter's. This had given her false hope. When she had seen the body itself she had broken down completely, becoming hysterical and blaming the policemen for misleading her. Afterwards Nicholson had been scathing.

'It's obvious. The poor kid left home weeks ago. She didn't give a piss for her. She was putting on a show for our benefit. You'd think a mother would know her own daughter's knickers.'

But Nicholson was a bachelor, and Rosen thought the

woman was genuinely distressed. His own wife was as good a mother as one could wish to meet, but she had been heard to say more than once that daughters' knickers were unaccountable.

He was just finishing writing his report when Nicholson came in and asked what was cooking, so he had pleasure in silently handing him the typed sheets to read while he completed the last page. Nicholson's smile did not diminish, though Rosen thought that it became a trifle fixed.

'Interesting,' he said, 'well worth following up.'

Rosen understood from his tone that he had some news of his own, but he did not immediately reveal it. Nicholson had been going through Rosen's files on the first murder, and proceeded to bring his colleague up to date.

'They've traced that red Cortina. The girl the driver picked up was the daughter of a friend of his, so that's no good. No news about the white Citroën. We've found the van driver that woman said she saw. According to him he wasn't looking for anybody and he thinks she must have seen him earlier in the afternoon when he was trying to find an address. We've checked the address and he was there all right. At half past three he wasn't in Abenbury, he was in a lay-by near Forton Cross changing his wheel.'

'Anybody back him up?'

'No, he was alone, but he left his jack handle there and we picked it up. And they found that lorry driver. The girl in the car was his friend. We've seen her and she confirms his story. They haven't found that sports car, if it ever existed.'

He dropped the record cards on the desk and looked at Rosen as if to say, 'So much for your system,' but instead, after a pause, he added: 'I can tell you one person who was along that road on the twenty-ninth and who isn't in your files. And, what's more, he was along last Tuesday as well.'

The Sergeant braced himself for a triumphant announcement and obediently asked, 'Who?'

'What do you say to Bronniford?'

Sergeant Rosen did not say anything, remaining absolutely impassive, but he suddenly understood a good deal. That was what Nicholson had been keeping up his sleeve. Bronniford had been one of his earliest successes and if he was a genuine suspect now then he was undoubtedly a convenient one.

'A man like Bronniford,' said the Inspector, 'is a damn sight more likely to have done something like this than that bloke you're chasing.'

'I didn't think murder was in his line. He was done for mucking about with a little girl, wasn't he?'

Bronniford had been shopped by one of his pals to whom, in his cups, he had blabbed about what he had done. Nicholson's role had been limited to taking down the statement. That was what Rosen meant by considering him to have been lucky. He had got a lot of kudos out of the case.

'She wasn't so little. She was fourteen, and when she was dolled up for the evening you'd have taken her for twenty. And there were a few details about that case that never came out in court. He was a nasty bloke, was Bronniford, that's why his pal turned against him.'

'How do you know he was on that road on the twenty-ninth?' asked Rosen.

'He works for Cross's. They gave him a job as a lorry driver under the rehabilitation scheme. He's often on that road. I looked up their schedules. Tuesday and Thursday are his regular days.'

Rosen swallowed. April the twenty-ninth had been a Thursday. He began to understand Nicholson's confidence.

'What time was he along there? On the twenty-ninth, I mean.'

'Just after eleven.'

Rosen relaxed a little. It wouldn't work. The timing was wrong. The girl had had her last meal just after two o'clock.

She wouldn't have gone nearly nine hours without taking anything else. He reminded Nicholson of this objection and received a lecture on his own blinkered vision.

'He could have picked her up earlier, Jack. He could have killed her much earlier in Abenbury and then driven the body out later when he went on duty. You're still thinking in terms of a motorist stopping and picking up a girl on the road, but it might not have happened like that at all. He uses a car to get rid of the body, that's my idea.'

The Sergeant sighed. It was ingenious and, for the moment, unprovable. They knew so little. There was no real case against Bronniford, but he was a useful sort of card, and the Inspector would play him to his own best advantage in talking to the Superintendent: 'We've got a very strong lead, sir. He's known to us – did a stretch for a sex offence a few years ago. We've got him under surveillance.'

'You rather fancy this man of yours, don't you?' Nicholson asked.

Rosen shrugged his shoulders.

'You haven't got much on him yet.'

'Why did he tell that lie at the roadblock about not going in to Abenbury?'

'There could be a dozen reasons. He's got a woman there and doesn't want it made known. He went gambling. He's got a fondness for small boys. My money's on Bronniford.'

Late that afternoon Sergeant Rosen received the report from the laboratory on Nield's car. It was disappointingly negative. He accepted this set-back philosophically. All that it showed was that Nield, if he was guilty, had had the wit to clean up after himself. But one item which the constable handed to him made Sergeant Rosen grin.

'We found this tucked away under the carpet at the back, sir.'

It was a magazine. On the cover was a picture of a naked girl leaning on a bicycle and sticking her bum out towards the reader. Inside there were many more, similar photographs. So that was what those academic chappies studied in their spare time.

'I thought we ought to keep hold of it, sir.'

'Yes, quite right. We'll keep it safe. If he wants it he can always ask for it.'

The centre page was a double spread and Rosen turned the magazine on its side to examine it. As he did so he heard again Conrad's voice protesting about the confiscation of his car and urging the importance of his work. 'I have a job of my own to do, Sergeant, trying to ensure that the students we train make competent teachers. It has some small import-ance, you probably do not realize this, not least to the students themselves.'

The Sergeant put the magazine away in the file marked 'Nield'. It was harmless in itself, but it pointed in a certain direction. What mattered was what it told you about the man's mind. Perhaps he had others like it at home. Perhaps he had worse. Perhaps he had other things. It would be nice to have a chance to find out.

13

Not even bothering to dust the fingerprint powder off his door handles, Conrad loaded his cases and drove home, trying to pull himself together after the interview with Sergeant Rosen. He thought that he had acquitted himself well and that he would probably hear no more of the matter, but it had been an ordeal and his stomach churned each time he remembered it. He needed a tranquil weekend to restore his nerves, so it was typical of his rotten luck that no sooner had he got his foot through his front door than Davidson was on the phone to him bringing fresh trouble.

'It's about that in-service course tomorrow. Porter can't take his class.'

Conrad swore. It was an important course, for the teachers in the area, and if anything went wrong he, as Director, would get the blame.

'What's the matter with him?'

'He says he's got a cold.'

'Cold my arse. He never intended to take that class, Cyril. Porter's always doing this. I only gave it him because Jacks insisted. He did exactly the same thing last year only then it was a bilious attack.'

'I know, Conrad, don't blame me. All I'm saying is that we've got to find a substitute.'

'How can I do that at such short notice? I can't even contact the class to cancel it.'

'Rearrange the programme,' suggested Davidson breezily, 'do your session on literature in the classroom, that'll have them queueing three deep outside the lecture theatre.'

Conrad was not amused by this. 'I haven't got it ready, it isn't due for another month. Could Pomeroy fill in?'

'He's doing the school management course.'

So there it was. He would have to spend the rest of the evening preparing, inadequately, the lecture he had been intending to give, brilliantly, in a month's time.

'It's really too bad, Cyril. We none of us like Saturday work, why should Porter always get out of it? I could have done with a good rest this weekend.'

'I bet you could, Conrad. It must be exhausting, all these girls you're getting through. I can never open a paper without reading about it.'

This was tiresome and childish and ill-timed.

'A man's got to have a hobby, Cyril. Mine is assaulting young girls.'

It was the best he could do on the spur of the moment. He supposed that he would have a lot of this sort of thing to put up with.

Preparing the lecture probably did him more good than loafing about all evening would have done. He might make it into a criticism of the mass media, contrasting the debased values which they offer with the real values of genuine literature. 'The great writer does not flatter us or offer easy solutions. He places squarely on our shoulders the responsibility for our own conduct and forces us to accept the full responsibility for what we do.' How about that for an opening?

As Conrad worked he became happier, gradually losing himself in the pleasure of what he was doing. Taking down the volumes he intended to refer to and selecting the most effective passages, he often indulged the luxury of reading on for several pages. Sincerely he hoped to communicate his pleasure in reading, and the profit that he felt he himself got from these books. When he came downstairs to supper he surprised Stephanie by his affability.

Conrad walked into College the next morning, taking his private path and concentrating his mind only on positive and helpful thoughts. He reflected, as he did this, that he ought to practise mental control more often, but he did succeed, by the time he reached his room, in establishing a tranquil, if not optimistic, frame of mind. He made a final check of his notes and set out for the lecture theatre, rehearsing his opening words and going over the main headings of his talk. He was absorbed in this task when he was accosted by a young man in a loud sports jacket with a puffy, dissipated face. Conrad had not caught what he said so he endeavoured to look pleasant and asked him to repeat it.

'You are Mr Nield, aren't you?'

'That's right, what can I do for you?'

'I wondered,' said the man, drawing a notebook out of his pocket and licking a pencil, 'if you'd answer a few questions on this business down in Abenbury?'

Conrad gaped. It took a full ten seconds for the penny to drop and then he remembered. The last time he had seen this awful fellow was when the students were organizing their occupation of the administrative block and he had been asking Dr Gorning if he would care to make a statement. He started back as though the interloper was an adder.

'Who are you?'

'I represent the *Bickleton Herald* –'

He was about to add more when Conrad stopped him.

'What are you doing here? Are you aware that this is private property?'

'There is a good deal of public interest in this case, Mr Nield, and I wondered if you'd like to answer a few questions.'

'Has anybody given you permission to be here? If not I must ask you to leave at once.'

'I believe the police interviewed you yesterday, can you –'

'I'll give you,' said Conrad, 'two minutes to get off this

campus. If you are not gone by then I shall have you ejected.'

'Is it a fact that they took your car away to examine it?'

Conrad gazed helplessly round. He was at a complete disadvantage. Already a few curious students were drifting towards them, attracted by his raised voice. The man from the newspaper, indifferent both to threats and to the arrival of an audience, stolidly continued to put his questions.

'We understand that you were in Abenbury last Tuesday evening –'

Conrad fled. He tried to do it in a dignified manner, walking very fast but not actually breaking into a run, and holding his head up in the air as though there was nothing strange about being pursued by news-writing hacks.

The reporter loped behind him. 'Am I to understand that you don't wish to answer my questions, Mr Nield?'

Conrad reached the security of the main building and breathlessly instructed the porter to keep that man out. Then he went to the cool of the cloakroom, where he splashed water over his face and tried to calm his nerves.

He had handled that badly, hadn't he? It must have been the unexpectedness that had unmanned him. What stupid things he had said – 'have you ejected' indeed. Why hadn't he remained calm? Why not stop and have a quiet word with the man, answer his questions instead of putting his back up? Conrad peeped out. The porter was holding the glass door shut. On the other side of it was the reporter, mouthing something, and behind him a group of students laughed and jostled. Conrad would have paid a month's salary for the chance of living the last five minutes over again.

After his lecture Conrad walked over to the staff room and pitched his papers into his pigeonhole, because he could not be bothered to take them back to his room. Alec Stewart was there standing before the notice board, and he looked round as Conrad entered.

'Hullo,' he said, 'anything wrong? How did your lecture go?'

'Bloody awful.' Conrad's face looked drawn, and twitched spasmodically as he spoke. 'Sodding teachers. You pull your guts out trying to give them just a few fresh ideas and they don't want to know.'

'As bad as that, was it?'

'One of them had the cheek to tell me that I didn't know what I was talking about.' He looked such a tragic figure as he said this that Alec was hard put to it not to laugh. 'I told him, "When you've had as much time in the classroom as I've had you'll be entitled to speak."'

'Never mind.' Alec waved a soothing hand towards the notice board. 'Have you seen that?'

Conrad blinked suspiciously, breathing heavily through his nose. The failure of his lecture had deeply wounded his pride and, he suspected, might have a damaging effect on his prospects. There would be at least one teachers' representative on the appointment board for that job, and news of his humiliation would be sure to travel. He peered forward at the paper which Alec was indicating. It was the short list. There were six names on it: Aspinall, Davidson, Milne, Nield, Porter and Skillington. Oddly, Conrad did not even feel particularly pleased at seeing his name, because he had expected it. If it had not been there, that would have been devastating. Alec was watching him closely so he tried to whip up a spurious reaction.

'So far, so good. That's a relief anyway.' Then, for want of anything better to say, he added, 'I didn't expect to see Aspinall's name. He's only been here two minutes.'

'You know what Jacks is like, all his talk about youth.'

Conrad leaned forward again. At last something had registered. What was that fifth name? Porter – he had never even thought of Porter. There was something monstrous about the idea of Porter putting in for a job like this. Porter was seen in College so seldom that it was a joke. If you saw Porter on the campus you wrote a letter to *The Times* about it.

'What the hell is Porter doing there?'

'He looks good on paper,' said Alec, 'he's a Cambridge double first.'

Conrad made an uncomplimentary remark about Cambridge.

'Besides,' Alec continued, 'he's a pal of Milton Jacks.'

This was a surprise.

'They went on holiday together in Brittany last year.'

'Fancy taking a holiday with Milton Jacks,' mused Conrad, 'what shocking taste. On the other hand, fancy taking a holiday with Porter.'

The news disturbed him. It began to sound as though Porter was a serious threat, and it seemed ludicrously unfair.

'Be absolutely typical if Porter got it. He's notoriously the most unreliable man on the campus. It's entirely because of him that I've just had that set-to with my class. He let us down and I had to take it at the last moment. If I'd had time to prepare properly, of course, they'd never have reacted like that.'

At this moment the door opened and Davidson came in.

'Hullo, Conrad, how did the class go? Did they carry you shoulder high round the room?'

'It was pretty bloody awful,' said Conrad frigidly.

'Not exactly been your week, has it?' Davidson asked. 'Did you know there was a chap outside from the *Bickleton Herald* earlier on trying to find you? There was quite a crowd by the door.'

'I saw him. I told him that I had nothing to say.'

The door opened again. This time it was Milne.

'Conrad,' he said, 'just the man I was looking for. Weren't we supposed to get together about Andrew Carney?'

'Oh, Christ,' said Conrad, 'this is all I want.'

'What's the matter with him?' asked Milne.

'He's had a bad time,' explained Alec. 'He's been filling in for Porter and the class did not respond too well.'

'So, if you don't mind, Philip,' said Conrad, 'perhaps we could postpone the discussion.'

'On your head be it,' said Milne. 'I mean, I tried to get in touch last week, and you weren't all that co-operative.'

'If you will insist on phoning me in the middle of a meal.'

'All I'm saying, Conrad, is that young Carney needs help. You've only seen him once this week.'

'I know, Philip. The fact is things have been difficult. I did intend seeing him on Friday –'

'But you had to see the police. Well, it can't be helped, but if you are otherwise engaged then someone else ought to get in to Andrew. I offered to go myself.'

Conrad was too astonished by the first half of Milne's speech to react properly to the second half. Alec and David-son, who had begun to drift away, stayed their ground instead.

'How did you know that I had to see the police, Philip?'

'I didn't know, but I took it for granted, after what Sandra and Cathy told me, that they would want to see you straight away.'

You could not tell, with Milne, whether it was malice or simple obtuseness. He just stood there looking bleached, with no particular expression on his face, and blurted out these things without seeming to realize how embarrassing they were.

'What do you know about Sandra and Cathy?'

'They came to see me.' Milne gazed solemnly at Alec and Davidson. 'They couldn't understand it. Sandra had picked up that paper you left in her classroom.'

Davidson begged somebody to explain to him what this was all about, and Conrad tersely obliged.

'I suppose it's a lesson to me, Cyril, not to be so bloody obliging. She was doing some art-work and, like the damn fool she is, had forgotten to protect the tables, so, out of the kindness of my heart, I got some old newspapers out of my car and gave them to her.'

'That's right,' said Milne, 'and she saw this one that you'd bought in Abenbury, and naturally she was a bit worried.'

'Isn't Conrad supposed to buy papers in Abenbury?' asked Davidson.

'He told her that he hadn't been in.'

'I didn't exactly say that, Philip. What I said was that I had not been there at the time the police were asking about.'

'She was worried anyway. It seems that she met Cathy Winters – they're friends, you know – and Cathy told her that she'd seen you in Abenbury that evening, so they both came over to have a word with me.'

Things were a good deal clearer to Conrad now. Sandra had not been as cute as he had thought, it was just his bad luck that she had run into Cathy Winters like that. Milne's role, on the other hand, had been decidedly questionable.

'It was by your advice then, Philip, that they went to the police?'

'It was the only thing I could do, Conrad. It seemed to me that it was my duty.'

'I'm not blaming you, Philip. Of course it was the only thing you could do. You might have warned me, though.'

'I tried, Conrad. I rang your hotel on the Thursday evening, but they told me you were out. I was quite certain, in any case, that it was some little thing that you'd be able to explain quite easily. It was, wasn't it? The police must have kept you a long time if you didn't manage to get to Andrew at all.'

'It was my car,' explained Conrad, 'they didn't bring it back until four o'clock.'

'Good heavens, Conrad, "bring it back"? What were the police doing taking your car away in the first place?'

'They wanted to examine it.'

132

He was surprised at the effect this had on the three of them.
Instead of making jokes about it, which was what he had
expected, they fell silent, avoided his gaze, and remained
carefully expressionless. 'With a bit of luck I'll get in to
Andrew on Monday, Philip.'

'Good, good. I've advised him to see somebody in the
English Department about his schemes because you said you
were not satisfied with his preparation.'

'Why doesn't he see me?'

'He'd love to, Conrad, but he doesn't find it too easy to get
hold of you. Anyway, if you have any more problems with the
police don't hesitate to call on me.'

Conrad was trying to find an answer to this when he was
interrupted by Cyril Davidson, who said, 'You haven't
forgotten, have you, Conrad, that we've got another meeting
of your BEd committee on Monday?'

Conrad had forgotten; with all the harassment he had been
subjected to recently it would have been a miracle if he had
remembered, and he cut Philip Milne's protests short by
pointing out that he had better be there as well.

'Carney will just have to wait until Tuesday, Philip. This
BEd course is vital to all of us, and you missed the last
meeting altogether.'

'We have a duty to our students, Conrad.'

'We've got a duty, Philip, to produce a decent course, one
that is academically sound and that the University will
accept.'

Didn't the fool understand that if he did not turn up for the
meetings Davidson and his group would foist their ridiculous
shambles of a scheme on them? It was a waste of time talking
any further and Conrad cut the discussion short by walking
out of the room. He noticed that both Davidson and Alec
were looking at him in a peculiar way and that neither spoke
as he left them.

14

'I just don't see what it was that the police wanted to see you about.'

Stephanie was getting tiresome. This was the fourth time she had said this or something like it. She had been bad enough on the Friday evening when she had started off, as soon as he got through his own front door, by throwing the newspaper article in his face.

'But it says here a college lecturer has been helping them.'

'Oh, for God's sake, Stephanie,' he had said, 'it was at a roadblock. They must have stopped hundreds of people.'

Now she was at it again.

'But Margery says that the police went round to your hotel, Brenda told her. Everyone's talking about it.'

'I made a mistake, I just made a small mistake, and they came round to check on it. I set it straight in about five minutes.'

'Brenda says that they took away your car.'

'It was routine. My car had been along that road, at about the time they were trying to check, so it had to be examined.'

At about the fourth repetition this began to wear on Conrad's nerves. Stephanie would sit there with her mouth slightly open pondering what he had said, and then she would come back to it: 'I still don't see . . .' Sunday was not being the restful change he had hoped for. All around him were the newspapers, every one of them a prime example of the corrupting influence of mass culture.

He had spent the morning comparing one account with another. The business troubled him. His contact with the girl had been fleeting and unfriendly, but it troubled him; and now, here she was, spread out for the entertainment of the Sabbath public. Conrad learned that her name was Dixon, Fiona Dixon, and that she came from Birmingham. There was a photograph of her, a very bad one, apparently the only one – it appeared in all the papers. Conrad would never have recognized her. It showed a schoolgirl, in a gymslip, squinting awkwardly into the camera through a straggle of hair. It was blurred, the photograph of a mousy little kid. He marvelled at the change from this naïve, pathetically vulnerable child, to the morose, prematurely worldly person he had picked up. And this false impression was reinforced by the text. Her mother, 'stony-faced with grief' according to one sheet, 'fighting back her tears' according to another, said that Fiona had always been a good girl. 'She was quiet and shy and afraid of strangers,' the mother had said, 'she would never have got into that car of her own accord.' That was what they had said about the first girl, wasn't it? Of course you could not judge anything from that. The newspapers had edited out the true person and substituted clichés.

It was the same throughout. None of the people interviewed spoke like human beings. A friend said that she was 'a merry, fun-loving girl, a simple, trusting kid', a neighbour said that she was 'not at all the sort of girl to do anything wrong'. Did the papers have these phrases permanently in type? The solid fact in all this was that this quiet, good, fun-loving girl had left her home, where she was said to be so happy, three weeks before the murder, without saying a word to anybody. Conrad tossed a paper aside.

Then there were the articles. 'How can we help these girls?' asked one lady columnist, as she painted a picture of a world full of unhappy, wandering victims, all seeking a life of glamour but doomed to be exploited. Well, that was rich. You could help them, Conrad thought, by not actually glamourizing these things. The same paper that contained this article had, on an earlier page, an explicitly illustrated account of the doings at a topless bar. 'How have we failed these girls?' the lady columnist asked. We have failed them by filling the pages of our news sheets with tits and bums, we have failed them by describing in detail the doings of silly society people, by offering for their admiration the trashiest standards.

Another paper had the headline: 'What happened to Fiona?' so he picked it up and read the article underneath. 'How did she get to the desolate moorland hollow where she met her death, and what happened to her on the way?' Well, he knew, Conrad knew. What had happened to her was that he had put his hand on her knee, and she had knocked it off again. If she had not done that then presumably she would be still alive. The question was, would it help the police to know this? Conrad did not see that it would, and the longer he read these newspapers the more impossible became the idea of telling them. That police sergeant chappie had seemed an amiable enough turnip, but suppose that Conrad went up to him and said, 'Look, I gave that girl a lift out to the moors and left her there.' What would he think? More important, what would he do? Conrad lacked that confidence in his police which the ideal citizen should have. He knew, he had read, that they were capable of making ghastly mistakes, and it seemed to him that there was a particularly ghastly one here, waiting to be made.

He turned back to the papers. Several of them reported the words of the police superintendent in charge of the case, a man who had caught the journalistic tone with remarkable fidelity. 'I tell you,' he was reported as saying, 'when something like this happens it sickens every policeman engaged on the case. You see experienced officers, hardened to the job, and they look down at a poor little kid like this one, and there are tears in their eyes, and you know what they are thinking. Come hell and high water they are going to get this man.' There was a photograph of the Superintendent next to this article, over the caption: 'Come hell and high water.' The Superintendent had a wooden look, like a poor amateur actor expressing determination.

At this point Stephanie spoke again. 'It says here that the police want to know how the girl got to the place where she died. Is that what they were asking you about?'

'They wished to know,' he replied, adopting the tight-lipped voice he used for replying to a tiresome child in class, 'if I had seen anybody hitching a lift, anything like that, yes.'

'Had you?'

'Some, yes, you know what it is like.'

'You mean you might actually have seen her, you might have passed her?'

'I suppose I might.'

'It's an awful thought, isn't it? Just think, if you'd stopped to give her a lift then she would still be alive now.'

Stephanie said this quite casually, without really thinking what she was saying, and was surprised to see an expression of something like pain pass fleetingly across Conrad's face.

'That's not a very useful thing to say, Stephanie.'

She was disturbed. There was something the matter with him. He had been nervy and edgy all weekend, and he was taking an unusual interest in this murder, buying all these popular newspapers for instance. Normally he liked to consider such sensational items as beneath his notice. Was he feeling guilty? Was that it? Had he recognized the photo in the newspaper as that of a girl to whom he had refused a lift? If so her words must have flicked a very raw nerve. Conrad tended to take a high and censorious line about young people who went about, as he put it, cadging lifts. It might be that he was experiencing remorse, or it might be something else, something deeper.

Stephanie had spent a miserable week. Always anxious to be fair and honest with herself, she had recognized that the quarrel with Conrad after the Hallidays' party had been mostly her own fault. She had danced with Stan almost the whole evening. She had observed her husband standing alone, leaning against a wall, looking thoroughly unhappy, and she had ignored him completely. Well, not completely. Stephanie could still go hot with shame when she remembered the moment when she had seen him in conversation with Margery and overheard her friend beginning to tell him about that picket of the cinema she had organized. She had been very lucky there. It was only Conrad's extreme rage with Margery that had prevented him realizing that that was the night when Stephanie had said she was going round to visit her friend. Suppose he had remembered and suddenly demanded to know where she had actually been? Stephanie was not a good liar. She would have blurted out something about Stan and then the fat would have been in the fire.

The episode had made her sit down and ask herself squarely what it was she thought she was playing at with Stan. No, it was no good making excuses for herself, or saying that she just found him good company. There was even a question of whether she was being fair to Stan himself. Stephanie's upbringing had given her an excellent understanding of the subtler forms of guilt and self-reproach. Conrad certainly did not deserve to be treated like this. Stephanie recited once again the catalogue of his virtues, and it was no use Margery hinting darkly at goings-on in Abenbury. She knew her husband better than Margery did, and womanizing was not one of his faults. Perhaps it would have been better if it had been.

Stephanie had once answered one of those silly quizzes in a woman's magazine entitled 'The Man in your Life', which had offered alternative answers to a number of questions; you had to tick the answer which you felt to be right. Conrad's score had been alarmingly low. 'Watch out for danger signals here,' the verdict had been, 'you have married a perfectionist and he may find difficulty in living up to his own ideal standards. Worse still, you may find it impossible.'

It was only a game, she had known that it was only a game, but it had disturbed her. She tried not to think too much about it but the sex part of their life together had been, on the whole, disappointing. Probably a good deal of it was her fault; certainly she felt that Conrad blamed her. She had been tense and nervy on their wedding night, her education had by no means prepared her, and the difficulties had continued for quite a long time. This, she knew, had been in part responsible for Conrad's own problems, but only in part. He always approached love-making in a tense, anxious frame of mind. He needed reassuring all the time, and refused to believe the reassurance when it was offered. Sometimes he was unable to achieve anything at all, and because the insecurity which these failures bred in him was great, they were never to be referred to. He would turn away from her afterwards and lie there, tense, screwing up his muscles, not to be touched, and she could sense, although she could not see, that his face in the dark was contorted. Sometimes she found herself almost envying Brenda David-son. Brenda did not have the easiest of times with Cyril, but he did at least get a fair amount of relaxed fun out of life. Stephanie liked Cyril. He could make her laugh, and his amorous propensities were so entirely automatic that they had no more significance than a kind of glandular disorder. He had made a pass at her, of course, in the early days, and she had rejected him more in sorrow than in anger.

'Don't mind me, Stephanie. You don't know how it is. I see an attractive girl and it's a compulsion. Conrad isn't like that.'

No, she had agreed that Conrad was not, and at the time she had been proud of Conrad, but she was beginning to see that his brand of rectitude had its own reasons, and its own inconveniences. And her husband's failure with women seemed to be as much rooted in the peculiar organization of his psychology as Cyril Davidson's compulsive following of them.

She braved another question.

'You never do give lifts, do you? What was it you said about hitch-hikers last summer, yobbos and scroungers, was that it?'

'When I was their age,' replied Conrad heavily, 'either I paid for myself or I stayed at home.'

Stephanie made a little face. 'Very virtuous.'

'It was the way I was brought up. The sort of home I came from did not encourage sponging on other people.'

Stephanie suddenly hardened against her husband. Was this intended as a hit against her father? It would not be the first time Conrad had balanced his own parents' rigid up-rightness against her parents' more Bohemian ways. Her indignation led her to feel, without any pleasure, that she was starting to see through him at last. All this careful keeping himself to himself, the pose of not being beholden to others, sprang from his deficiencies of spirit. For the first time she saw him as a mean, sour little man, incapable of giving spiritually and resentful of receiving.

'They're only trying to get about, Conrad. Look at the fares these days.'

'The fares were not low in my day, Stephanie. Anyway I'm surprised at you. I didn't realize that you wanted me to turn myself into a free transport company for young, unattached females.'

She laughed. 'Oh, don't worry, Conrad, I'm sure they'd be quite safe with you.'

He turned pale. He never lost his temper openly; instead he would become rigid, his skin would seem to pull close across the bones of his skull, his eyes would gleam.

'What, precisely, do you mean by that, Stephanie?'

'What I said. I'm sure they'd be safe with you – you

wouldn't do anything. It's a compliment, isn't it? You're always going on about people like Cyril.'

'It wasn't a compliment, not the way you said it. I may not be an absolute bloody goat like Cyril, but I've still got all the fixings, and everything still works, though you don't sample them much yourself these days.'

For the first time in their occasional quarrels Stephanie did not feel intimidated, at least, not to the point of making her retreat. In fact his words provoked her to another charge.

'Make up your mind, Conrad. Are you trying to tell me now that a girl wouldn't be safe with you?'

The question had a peculiar effect on Conrad. The expression of pain returned, again fleetingly, followed by one of malevolence. He spoke quietly, with venomous self-control.

'I don't want you to run away with the idea, Stephanie, that you have succeeded in making an absolute bloody eunuch out of me. I have the normal instincts and appetites, though I hope I have them under control. You must admit that you have always allowed me a strictly limited expression of these appetites. I don't think you understand how fortunate you are, Stephanie. A good many men in my position would have used your behaviour as an excuse to find satisfaction elsewhere.'

He said more, and finally Stephanie's old timidity and insecurity returned, and she was brow-beaten into silence and left, when he retreated to his study, guiltily accepting that she was in part at least to blame. For all his prickliness, and his sulks, and his pretended indifference to her opinion her husband was very dependent on her. It was her role, which she had for a long time delighted in playing, to arrange everything to suit him and to efface herself. She could not suddenly change this and expect him to be happy about it. The face of agony that he had just shown her was his response to what he felt was a change of mood on her part.

In a way it was an expression of his love. Stephanie knew

that she was not considered clever, but with regard to her husband she had very delicate perceptions. She told herself that she must try to do better. Yesterday, for instance, he had come in full of complaints about some class that he had taught, and she had listened very inattentively and failed to offer the usual consolations. Then, later on, he had told her about being short-listed for that job and she had not made enough of a fuss about it to please him. Not that he had made any complaint, but his mood during the rest of the evening had told her. It was in ways like this, trifling individually but important when added together, that she was failing him. In the past it had been a joy to her to offer this support. Why was it so no longer?

15

'If you don't mind, sir, I'd like you to accompany me to headquarters.'

Conrad stared blankly. This was a most unpleasant surprise. He had come down to Abenbury early on the Tuesday morning to make a punctual start on his school visiting, and his old chum Sergeant Rosen had been at the hotel to greet him on his arrival.

'They told me you'd be here to leave your bags at about nine o'clock,' he explained, smiling.

Conrad felt the stab at the pit of the stomach that he always experienced when he received a shock. He wondered sometimes if it was an early symptom of cancer, or a sign of a growing ulcer. The shock had been extreme, partly because he had managed to convince himself that the police had finished with him, but also because until catching sight of the Sergeant he had been in a particularly buoyant mood. The Monday meeting of his BEd committee had been marked by a signal victory over Cyril Davidson and the triumphant reinstatement of his own proposed course, since which time he had basked in the feeling that the gods had finally come over to his side. This proof that they had not was therefore doubly disturbing.

'What's this all about, Sergeant? I'm rather anxious to get into my schools, you know.'

'Just routine, sir. Just one or two questions that the Superintendent would like to put to you.'

His honest, agricultural face beamed at Conrad. It was impossible not to trust him; what the devil was he up to?

What could a Superintendent want with someone like him? Conrad had a sudden mental flash of the Superintendent's photograph, with the words 'Come hell and high water' underneath it. Superintendents were pretty big guns, weren't they?

The Sergeant adopted a professionally soothing tone. It would not take very long. They would only have to go as far as the murder headquarters at Forton Cross. Conrad's pulses hammered at the mention of the name 'murder head-quarters', but he went tamely along. Sergeant Rosen might be benign and smiling, but he was capable of picking Conrad up and simply putting him in his pocket. It was particularly unfortunate. Conrad had planned to visit Andrew Carney that morning.

Superintendent Pearce looked like a smoother, rather better-finished version of the Sergeant. It was as though the local constabulary had only one basic model, chosen for its ability to blend into the landscape. Conrad had made the Superintendent's acquaintance through the pages of the national press, which had given the impression of some hard-bitten, tough-talking law-officer, who had formed his style on the television prototypes. Seeing him in the flesh was an anticlimax. He looked positively avuncular. He rose from his chair to greet Conrad in the most affable way possible, practically putting his arm round his shoulder, and guiding him to a chair. He apologized for the inconvenience of bringing him in, promised that the interview would not take long, produced his cigarette case and offered Conrad a smoke, and, when Conrad said that he did not use cigarettes, graciously asked his permission before lighting one himself. Conrad's nerves began to settle again. From the moment of seeing Sergeant Rosen they had been twisted as tight as the strings on a tennis racket, but they now began to slacken. He exerted himself to match the Superintendent's graciousness, and assured him that anything that he could do, anything at all, he would be most happy to do. Any public-spirited citizen, he told the Superintendent, would feel the same.

'Sergeant Rosen took a statement from you on Friday, didn't he, Mr Nield?'

'He did indeed.' Conrad beamed at the Sergeant, who was sitting at the side of the room with his pad on his knee.

'The day before that one of our men had spoken to you?'

'Well, it was two days before, actually, Superintendent. I had made a rather silly mistake when I spoke to him, that was what Sergeant Rosen came to see me about.'

'It is very easily done, sir. You gave Sergeant Rosen a pretty full account of your movements last Tuesday evening, didn't you, sir? Is there anything that you want to add to that account now, sir?'

Conrad's nerves tightened again abruptly. The last question had been carefully, almost finickingly articulated, and it had been accompanied by a look that could only be described as 'meaningful'. The Superintendent was not the most subtle of interviewers, clearly he was giving Conrad a chance. The question was, a chance to do what? Conrad did his best to keep his expression steady while he thought furiously.

There was nothing much else for them to find out. He had told them he had been in Abenbury, he had told them practically everything except that he had given the girl a lift. They couldn't have found out anything about that, could they? He licked his lips and cleared his throat.

'I – er – I don't quite see what you mean, Superintendent.'

'You were asked if you had seen anything of a young girl hitch-hiker. You said that you had not. You were asked if you had given a lift to anybody yourself. You said that you had not. Do you want to add anything to those statements, sir?'

Conrad shook his head. He was still doing his best to keep his expression steady, but he had the sensation that his face had drained completely of blood, and he cursed the waywardness of his circulatory system. A fat lot of use

145

keeping your expression still if you gave yourself away by turning dead white.

'I can quite appreciate, sir, that a man in your position finds an inquiry of this sort embarrassing, that there are questions that he might prefer not to answer. But we have to find out the truth about things. We rely upon witnesses coming forward to help us. I must remind you, sir, that it is a very serious matter to give false information to the police.'

Conrad felt again the curious panic tightness around his chest and throat. He wished that the Superintendent would stop calling him 'sir', it was so ludicrously inappropriate, like taking off your hat before kicking a man in the balls. It crossed his mind to ask the Superintendent if he was bullying him, but Conrad decided not to do this. Instead, he asked him what he meant.

'We have a witness, sir, who is prepared to say that he saw a car identical with yours stop on the road out from Abenbury at about ten to eleven on that Tuesday night, and give a lift to a girl hitch-hiker.'

So that was it. One of those damned old buffers, Conrad supposed, walking his dog, or some old woman out calling for her tabby. Conrad remembered where he had stopped. There had been people about, but he did not think that they had been near. In that light they could not possibly be sure of what they had seen. Conrad thought of the neighbourhood he had driven through. 'Select residential.' That, no doubt, was how it was described by the estate agents. People with pots of money and nothing to do with their time. Conrad could imagine them, hard 'county' voices, terribly terribly sure of themselves, retired colonels, that sort of thing. Probably carry a fair weight in the witness box. He drew a deep breath. At least he must stick to his guns.

'Good heavens, Superintendent,' he managed to say, 'there must be thousands of cars like mine on the roads of

Britain. It's a very common model, there's nothing unusual about it. I only use it to get from A to B.'

The Superintendent looked at Conrad like a judge eyeing a pumpkin at an agricultural show, and then made a pretence of consulting some papers. Conrad braced himself. He felt that the Superintendent was about to pull off some subtle stroke.

'The Sergeant tells me,' the Superintendent said, 'that your near-side front wing had suffered some damage. Is that so, sir?'

Conrad nodded.

'That makes it more easily identifiable, doesn't it, sir?'

'Did the witness identify it?' asked Conrad.

The Superintendent smiled. 'You had a passenger in your car recently, sir?'

Conrad again asked him what he meant. His heart was hammering away inside his chest, and he felt the customary tightness in his stomach. These reflex physical symptoms, normal for him in moments of stress, were a nuisance, but he must not allow them to take over. He felt very hot and was sure that there was sweat on his forehead. He feared that if he relaxed control of himself he would suddenly pass out, swoon at this man's feet. He used to have fainting fits when he was a child. He could remember standing in school assembly and unexpectedly being assailed by the idea that he was going to faint. One moment he would be quite all right, and then the idea would come into his head that he was going to faint, and shortly afterwards, however hard he tried to prevent it, he actually would faint. This must not happen now. He remembered a Chinese remedy he had once read about, and he dug the nail of his thumb painfully into the flesh of his little finger, at the side, by the nail. He must keep his head, answer carefully, and then they would let him walk out of this room again.

The Superintendent was speaking and Conrad struggled

to attend. He did not want to antagonize him, but on the other hand he did not want to appear over-anxious, and it was a nice calculation to hit the right blend.

'Somebody had been smoking, sir. There were cigarette ends in the ashtray, and you don't smoke yourself, so –'

Sherlock Holmes was right, thought Conrad. A detective should not explain his methods. He pleased himself with this thought. It re-established him in his own eyes as being cool and self-possessed. It was really rather splendid that he should be capable of such detachment in a crisis like this. He was even able to notice that the Superintendent was proud of his stroke of deduction. As he had spoken he had half turned towards the Sergeant as if seeking applause. The gesture made him human and helped Conrad to feel superior again, even to smile.

'Oh, come, Superintendent, they could have been there for months. I don't know if you saw the car for yourself before your boys got at it, but the Sergeant there will tell you that I'm not the tidiest of men. I don't feel really at home in a car unless it looks as if a colony of tinkers has been camping in it. Thanks for cleaning it, by the way.'

That was better. That was the right, humorous note. It showed that he was able to stand up for himself without being actually offensive.

The Superintendent's geniality began to wane. He now looked like a farmer whose gates have been left open.

'I doubt if they had been there for months, sir. I would say that most of them had only been deposited a few hours before.'

'On Thursday, you mean?' Conrad could not resist getting this dig in, and he went on to make himself clear. 'You examined the car on Friday. A few hours before Friday takes us to Thursday. I didn't give anybody a lift on Thursday.'

'Well,' the Superintendent jumped in immediately, 'when did you give somebody a lift then, sir?'

Conrad regretted his rashness. His desire to score off the Superintendent had hurried him into a mistake. It would have been more sensible if he had said that he had given somebody a lift on Thursday. Wait a minute. That policeman who had spoken to him on Wednesday morning had looked right into the car. Could he have seen anything? He must improvise with discretion.

'Now I come to think of it, it would be the Tuesday morning, on my way down from Bickleton. I remember now, I did give a girl a lift.'

Conrad remembered that in telling a lie one should stick as closely as possible to the truth. He had better say, for instance, that it was a girl. They had these cigarette ends and for all he knew there were tests which could establish the sex of the person who had smoked them. Saliva tests perhaps. Besides, that bloody girl might have used lipstick. She didn't use soap but she might have used lipstick.

The Superintendent pressed for the details of this incident. Where had he picked up this girl? At what time? How was she dressed? Where had he dropped her? Had she given any name? Was there any other clue to her identity? What had she talked about? There seemed to be no end to these questions, and Conrad was forced to a series of dangerous extemporizations, which he carried off with the old, self-deprecatory appeal to the fallibility of his memory and his generally uninquisitive nature.

'Good heavens, Superintendent, I really can't remember things like that. To tell you the truth I hardly noticed the girl. No, she didn't speak much at all. You know how it is nowadays with these young people. They're not exactly bursting with the social graces; you give them a lift and they just sit there like turnips. That smoking business, for instance. She never asked me if I minded if she smoked, never even offered me one – obviously not that I would have taken it, but I would have appreciated the courtesy – as a matter of fact, in the confines of the car, I'm not all that fond of having smoke puffed in my face. But there it is, what can you do? Where did I pick her up? Good heavens, let me see – the Sergeant there will tell you that I've got a terrible memory – it would be – just before Witringham, that was it, and I dropped her at – er – Cordery. How was she dressed? Well, you have me there, Superintendent, I'm just not the noticing type, especially as far as dress is concerned. Dress is a thing that I'm just blind to. She could have been stark naked as far as I was concerned – correction – I suppose that if she had been stark naked then I would have noticed, but you know what I mean. She was – er – I've got an impression of a sort of denim outfit, is that what it's called? That blue stuff that looks like boiler suits, and she had a duffel bag, at least, I think she had. I'm sorry, but that's about the best that I can do for you. You seem very interested in this girl, Superintendent, I don't quite see why. She can't possibly have had anything to do with this business at Abenbury.'

Conrad thought that he had managed to put out a smoke-screen of helpful noises without actually committing himself to damaging detail. Let them see what they could do with a description as vague as that.

The Superintendent was asking another question.

'Why did she get out at Cordery, sir?'

'I haven't the slightest idea, I didn't ask her. To tell you the truth I was glad to get her out of my car, with her damn smoking and general surliness.'

'It seems a funny place, sir, unless she lives there. It isn't a junction. All she could do would be to get another lift in the same direction.'

This was true. Cordery had not been a very clever invention.

Conrad shrugged his shoulders. 'Search me, Superintendent. As I told you, I didn't ask her. It wasn't any business of mine where she was going.'

The Superintendent rested his mild blue eyes on Conrad for what seemed a long time, then he spoke.

'And you still insist that you did not see anybody that night.'

'I saw lots of people, Superintendent.'

'Nobody hitching a lift on the road out from Abenbury?'

Conrad shook his head.

'And you did not give a lift to anybody that night?'

Again Conrad shook his head. It was all he could do. He had taken up his position and he could hardly abandon it now. He even felt a flicker of hope. It looked as if this damned policeman had run out of fresh questions and would have to let him go soon. Why had they brought him in? It could not possibly be, could it, that they actually, seriously, suspected him of this murder?

Conrad thrust the notion from him as appalling and unbelievable. They had caught him out in a trivial error and felt bound to follow it up. No doubt the truth was, if one only knew, that they thought he had been up to something on his own account – something he would not want his wife, or the College, to know about. He could imagine these policemen exchanging jokes about him 'having a bit on the side', something like that. That was what they were trying to do – get him to come clean about it. Conrad wished that he could oblige them, how he wished it. If only he could say that he had been knocking off some woman at the time: 'Well, we're all men of the world, Superintendent. Naturally I wouldn't want my wife to know, and it would be rather embarrassing if it came out at the College.'

If only it was as simple as that. In reality he had done nothing, nothing at all, and so he found himself in this mess. It was an unfair world, Conrad thought. These police were just doing their duty. They were supposed to follow all lines of inquiry – what was the jargon – 'however tenuous', was that it? They had not been quite straight with him, mind.

That remark about the damaged front wing had been a shade naughty. They had not actually said that the witness had seen the damage but they had given a false impression. It was a good job that, intellectually, he could take care of himself. He had often read accounts of what people had said under police examination, and he had thought what fools they were to incriminate themselves like that, but now he could understand it better. It took a toughness of mind and a sharpness of intelligence to stand up to it. He, Conrad, had come within an ace of making an ass of himself. It was an ordeal, no doubt about it; these police were not to be trifled with.

The Superintendent turned from a whispered colloquy with the Sergeant and addressed Conrad.

'We have your complete statement then, sir, the one you gave to the Sergeant? You do not wish to alter it in any way?'

'I don't think so, Superintendent, I think the Sergeant got it down correctly.'

The Superintendent bowed his head and then suddenly straightened up and looked directly at him.

'It's not the Sergeant's mistakes I was thinking of, sir. You are quite sure that you didn't make any of your own?'

Conrad's confidence began to wane again. What was it? What were they on to? He tried to remember exactly what he had said.

'If you've got a memory like mine, Superintendent, there's always the chance of the odd slip. What had you in mind?'

'You said that you went to the cinema, was that correct?'

'Quite correct.'

'To the Ritz, to see *Nicholas and Alexandra*?'

Conrad swallowed and nodded.

The Superintendent proceeded smoothly. 'We were given to believe, sir, that you would not have gone to that cinema to see that film.'

He paused in case Conrad had any comment to make, but

Conrad had none. He was thinking furiously. Cathy Winters, that was it. He had said to Cathy Winters that he was not going to see *Nicholas and Alexandra*, and she had shopped him. Between them she and Sandra Duckham had done a pretty good job on him.

'When we checked at the box-office they were unable to remember anybody answering to your description.'

'How on earth could you expect them to remember, Superintendent, from all their customers?'

'Most of the customers are locals, sir. A stranger tends to be noticed, particularly one on his own – you were on your own, were you, sir?'

Conrad nodded again. He did not want to speak, although the Superintendent gave him plenty of opportunity before asking, 'Do you still say that you went to the Ritz, sir?'

Conrad preserved his silence, and the Superintendent, after a pause, in a gently coaxing voice, continued. 'What *did* you do, sir?'

Now that he had been beaten into this unpleasant corner Conrad saw an opportunity. He had been very stupid. These policemen were bound to be suspicious because of his pre-varications; perhaps he could now suggest a reason for them. 'If you must know, I went to the Lido.'

The Superintendent looked puzzled.

'I went to see a film called, I think, *Sex Confessions of a Nymphomaniac.*'

The Superintendent greeted this magnificently. He neither smiled nor looked shocked. In fact his expression of courteous inquiry did not vary in the least degree, nor did he exchange meaningful glances with Sergeant Rosen. He did not even speak. He just left a sort of hole in the dialogue that Conrad felt impelled to fill.

'I'm not particularly proud of the fact. I was at a loose end, I'd never seen that kind of film before, and I yielded to curiosity. When the Sergeant asked me I – er – rather funked telling him. It didn't seem to me to have anything to do with your inquiry.'

Conrad stopped talking. He would have preferred not to have to make such a confession to these men but, since it had been forced out of him, he thought that he had done it right. The Superintendent's answer surprised him.

'Are you in a position to prove this, sir?'

'Why on earth do you want me to prove it?'

'Well, by your own confession, sir, you've told us one story that was a lie. I'd just like to be sure that this one isn't.'

Conrad was non-plussed. When he had visited the cinema he had taken every care to make himself as inconspicuous as possible – proving the fact of his visit had been very far from his mind – and he could not now see how he could do it. What a wretched thing.

'Could we find somebody who saw you?' suggested the Superintendent.

'I hope nobody did see me.'

'Perhaps you would come along with us to the box-office to be identified,' said the Superintendent.

This was awful. There flashed across Conrad's mind a vivid picture of a nationwide press campaign with photographs of himself and underneath the question: 'Did you see this man visit the porno-show?'

'Is that absolutely necessary?'

'It would be nice to get it cleared up, don't you agree? We'll have to check with the box-office anyway.'

'I may have the ticket in my pocket. My suit's at the hotel. It really does seem to me, Superintendent, that you are making a good deal of fuss over nothing at all.'

'It's not quite nothing at all, sir. You see, there is something else that is puzzling us.'

The Superintendent sat back in his chair. His hands were clasped together in his lap and he smiled at Conrad.

'What is that?'

'When we examined your car, Mr Nield, we found the parking ticket that you had bought in Abenbury.'

Conrad stared at him.

'You had put it in the ashtray.'

'Yes, I always do that. It is convenient if I am asked for it.'

'It was underneath those cigarette ends, the ends that you say were deposited there earlier on the same day.'

16

When Conrad finally crawled back to his hotel after his grilling by the police the first person he saw was Soper, popping his head out from the bar and greeting him like a long-lost brother. Conrad groaned inwardly. Soper was young and bright, and go-ahead, and palpably on the make. He had been successful and intended to be more successful still. Already, at the age of – what would he be? certainly not more than thirty-five – he was the fourth in line for the crown at the Education Offices in Bickleton. This was the trouble with staying at the Red Lion. Its reputation for good food at reasonable prices attracted every wandering educationist who happened to have business in the Abenbury area. It had become habitual for Conrad, on returning for the evening, to flick through the visitors' book to find out whom he had to avoid. Sheer tiredness had betrayed him this time, and he smiled a sickly smile and stuck out his hand.

'Good to see you,' said Soper, 'I'd more or less resigned myself to an evening on my own. I'll join you for dinner.'

Conrad heard himself saying something like 'Of course', in a decent imitation of a welcoming tone, and then he got away to have a shower and change his clothes. He felt abominably low-spirited. He had a headache and a pain in the pit of his stomach, and he was limp with nervous fatigue.

At the conclusion of his interrogation by the Superintendent he had been trailed back to the hotel to see if he could find the cinema ticket in the pocket of his suit. Then, at the insistence of the Sergeant, he had gone to the cinema to be paraded in front of a variety of ticket sellers, usherettes, cleaning ladies and ice-cream vendors to be identified. It had been a hellish experience. The walls were plastered with photographs of tits and bums, and Conrad had stood, like some pimply lad with bad breath and bottle spectacles, while those women stared at him.

'By yourself, was you?' one of the women asked.

'I was on my own, yes. Surely you remember me. I was wearing this coat.'

'We get a lot in on their own, single gentlemen, just like you.'

Conrad turned to the Sergeant. 'What about the ticket? I got you the ticket, doesn't that prove it?'

But investigating the ticket was a much more complicated business, requiring the co-operation of the manager, who was never in the cinema in the afternoon.

'We'll look into it in our own time, sir.' Sergeant Rosen beamed at him. He actually seemed to be enjoying this, Conrad thought.

And then a young man approached them with a notebook in his hand and a question on his lips. Conrad saw with horror that it was the abominable reporter who had persecuted him on Saturday morning and he turned quickly away. The Sergeant came to his rescue, cutting the man short before he had got two words out.

'I've got nothing for you, nothing at all. If you want to ask any questions go and see Superintendent Pearce.' And then he uttered the words which Conrad had never before heard a policeman say: 'Move along now.'

Conrad looked straight ahead. Then he noticed that his abrupt turn had brought him face-to-face with a photograph of three naked ladies, which he appeared to be studying at a range of six inches. He hoped to God the man did not have a camera. He and the Sergeant walked off down the street. After a few paces he looked back. The blasted fellow was entering the cinema.

What had made things worse had been the good humour of

the police. They had treated him like a pair of kindly uncles. When the Superintendent had dropped his bombshell about the parking ticket and those cigarette ends Conrad was sure that he must, if only for a split second, have given himself away. Questioners who remain polite under these circumstances begin to seem dangerous.

It was all turning into a great mess. And yet, as Conrad showered and dried himself, he could not feel that he had been in any important respect wrong. He still felt that, in the circumstances, to have told the police about giving that girl a lift would have been a mistake. He had told a small lie to prevent a great injustice, or at least an embarrassing misunderstanding. And he had been sickeningly unfortunate. If he had not been kind to that damned girl, Sandra Duckham, this would not have happened. It would be a lesson to him. There had been almost a conspiracy against him, the Duckham girl, Cathy Winters, masterminded by Milne. The more he thought about it the more actually physically sick and faint he felt. Now he was in a very tricky position.

Of course he had carried the matter off. The Superintendent had brought out all that about finding the cigarette ends on top of the parking ticket with such an absurdly coy air, like Sherlock Holmes demonstrating the peculiar properties of a little-known trichinopoli cigar ash, that he had played into Conrad's hands. Conrad's answer had been instantaneous, apart from his tiny hesitation: 'Good heavens, Superintendent, what a marvellous piece of deduction. What is it that you expect to prove from that? What a quaint idea you have of the running qualities of my car. It's a good little car, it does all I want it to, but it isn't exactly a Rolls-Royce, you know. I can't carry eggs on the radiator without cracking them. I suppose that it has, just possibly, occurred to you that things might get joggled about in the ashtray as I drive along. Isn't it just a little bit far-fetched to try to prove anything from the fact that when you looked into my ashtray the things there were in a particular position. If you'd driven it fifty yards further, you know, you might have found them differently arranged.'

He had said more. Those policemen had not been allowed to have it all their own way. In fact, looking back over it, as Conrad had done all the way from the murder headquarters, it might have been better if he had said less. The Superintendent had sat there, no whit abashed, nodding from time to time, mildly agreeing that one could not attach too much importance to the fact that he had noted. But he had watched Conrad with cold eyes which belied the smile on his lips and which made him suddenly fear what the Superintendent might be thinking.

It was with these worries on his mind that Conrad returned to the hotel to be taken captive by Soper, and it had required a considerable effort, fortified by the consciousness that Soper's good opinion might be important to him, to look pleasant and keep his manner relaxed. And the effort had become almost impossible when Soper, pinning him in a corner of the bar, had said, 'I say, Conrad, when I wanted to know what time you'd be coming in that woman behind the bar asked me if I was one of these policemen. Whatever did she mean by that?'

Conrad just managed to avoid spilling his gin and tonic down the front of his suit. He attempted a ghastly light-heartedness.

'I'm surprised you haven't heard. I've been the subject of quite a lot of police attention lately. It's this murder that's been in all the papers.'

It was a relief to see how quickly Soper lost interest. He did not know about the murder, he did not read about things like that because they had no possible reference to himself. Politely he invited Conrad to explain.

'A girl, found on the moors, strangled I believe. I was unfortunate enough to be travelling along the road at about the time it happened. It seems that when you do that kind of thing the police are very concerned. They keep coming back to go over my story to see if they've got it right.'

'And have they?'

'More or less. They keep reading me their accounts. I give them alpha for effort and delta minus for style.'

Soper was good enough to smile at this and Conrad's pulse gradually returned to its normal beat.

It would have started racing again if he had been privy to the conversation between Superintendent Pearce and Sergeant Rosen which had followed his departure from the murder headquarters. Rosen had sketched the case he was forming against Nield and offered, as a final touch, the magazine which had been impounded from the suspect's car.

'I don't see that we can make much out of this.' The Superintendent turned it in his hands, holding it distastefully at arm's length. 'It's very mild stuff.'

'He went to that sex film on his own.'

'You can't arrest a man for that.'

'They're pointers, sir. They show the way his mind was running. He was by himself, with sex on the brain, walking about the streets of Abenbury late at night. And he had someone in that car with him, and we have got a sighting of a car similar to his stopping along that road.'

'Not a piece of evidence that I'd like to take into court, Rosen.'

The Sergeant agreed, but surely, he felt with exasperation, the Superintendent could see that they added up impress-ively.

'We can link him pretty directly with the first murder, sir.'

'Did you get that Tapscott to look at Nield's car?'

'Yes, sir.'

'Did he identify it?'

'He said it might be the one.'

Superintendent Pearce threw his hands apart. 'How long

would it take the defence counsel to pull that to bits? I want something, Rosen, that I can prosecute on without making a fool of myself.'

There was a pause while the Superintendent ruminated. As far as it went it was a promising case, and so, for that matter, was the one that Nicholson was building against Bronniford. But neither had that finality that encouraged him to risk issuing a warrant. It was very irritating. The press was breathing down his neck and there was nothing he would have liked better than to announce an arrest soon.

'What I must have, Rosen, is one piece of clear evidence linking Nield with either of these girls. And I'd be happier if I had a more precise time for the first murder. If Nicholson's right and it happened later than about five then this man of yours is out of it.'

There was another silence which Sergeant Rosen was too wise to break.

'Keep on at him. Be discreet about it. Find out who was in that car of his, find out a bit more about what he was doing on the twenty-ninth. He was up to something, that's for sure.' And he smiled, for he had not found Conrad's manner any more agreeable than his Sergeant had.

Fortunately for his peace of mind Conrad knew nothing of this, and he passed a relaxing, even therapeutic evening listening to Soper, whose solemn chatter about the educational politics of Bickleton put this police business into perspective, reminding him that the really important issue was how he should get Penniman's job. One thing he did learn that surprised and irritated him. Stan McHale had not only put in for the vacant post of headmaster of the largest comprehensive school in the county but he was on the short-list. The interviews were tomorrow. That was why Soper was down in the Abenbury area; he was on the appointing board.

Conrad listened astounded. A lot of people, Stephanie

included, must have known all about this application and had entered into a conspiracy to keep him in the dark. It was pretty disloyal. Apart from which the idea of someone as unsatisfactory as McHale even being considered for such an important post was absurd. A vivid picture came before his eyes of Stan fondling Stephanie and sniggering at him behind his back. It was lucky he had found out in time. Soper went on about this headship being a key to the educational developments in the county for the next twenty years, and Conrad managed, he hoped, to cast doubt on the suitability of his colleague for such an appointment. He did it skilfully, just hinting that old Stan was not the best administrator in the world, saying how surprised they had all been that he had got so far and that nobody seriously expected – etc. etc. A clever performance which left Soper thoughtful.

Towards the end of the evening, when Soper had been mellowed by repeated applications of brandy, he let slip a significant item. He had been a member of the panel that had considered Warley Hey's new schemes and he confirmed that Carnaby had been the chairman. This was depressing. It looked as if Jacks had been right. Carnaby would not favour the sort of course Conrad had planned.

'I suppose, then, Carnaby will be the chairman when they do ours?' Conrad had asked, and he had been astounded by the answer.

'Well, as a matter of fact, no.' Soper had become exaggeratedly confidential at this point, lowering his voice and drawing his chair nearer to Conrad's as though fearing the presence of a spy from the offices. 'Strictly between you and me, Carnaby's off to America. No, they've persuaded Templeton, of all people, to come back.'

Conrad suppressed an impulse to jump out of his chair and caper about the hotel lounge. Soper might not, as his tone suggested, favour having Professor Templeton, but Conrad did. Templeton was his own professor, long since retired. He had formed Conrad's mind and his teachings remained preserved in Conrad's present practice. If he could not devise a course which would gain Templeton's approval then he did not deserve Penniman's job.

'Very few people know about that, Conrad,' Soper said, looking as if he was already regretting his indiscretion.

'I won't tell a soul, Kenneth,' Conrad answered.

'Personally,' said Soper, 'I regret it. I would have liked somebody much more forward-looking than a has-been like Templeton.'

At ten o'clock they were interrupted. Conrad was wanted on the phone. The caller was Davidson.

'Hullo, Conrad, I hope I haven't spoiled your meal, or anything else.'

What did he mean, 'or anything else'?

'It's about the submission for the new course. Jacks has got hold of some inside information about what went on at Warley Hey's validation, and he reckons it gives us an insight into the way their minds work.'

Conrad smiled, found a seat, pulled it towards him, and sat down. 'What sort of an insight, Cyril?'

'Well, Carnaby was the chairman, he was right about that, and he knows the sort of thing that Carnaby would expect from us.'

Conrad screwed up his face and silently mouthed obscenities at the receiver, scandalizing two elderly ladies who were on their way to bed. Davidson's voice had been too carefully neutral. This was Jacks moving in for the kill.

'What sort of changes does he want, Cyril?'

He knew damn well what sort of changes, but it would be amusing to hear Cyril spell them out. When he had finished, Conrad said, 'The kind of thing you've been pushing all the time, in other words.'

'More or less. I don't want to say "I told you so", Conrad, but I did.'

Conrad could hardly contain his amusement at this.

Cyril continued. 'What I've rung for is to tell you that there's to be a meeting of the panel on Friday, at three o'clock, to consider making changes. Do you think you can be there?'

Conrad could not imagine a force strong enough to keep him away.

'If you can't, Jacks says, not to worry. I can take over for the one session and see the thing through.'

Conrad assured Cyril that this kindness would not be necessary.

When he put the phone down and returned to Soper there was a smile on his face. It was wonderful, after the miserable business with the police, how things had finally turned to his advantage. There was justice in the world, the gods did have their favourites.

'Nothing very important, Kenneth,' he said in reply to Soper's inquiring look. 'A problem had come up in College and they wanted my advice. I'm going to have another brandy. Join me?'

17

When Conrad awoke on the Wednesday morning his spirits
were still high, and he sprang out of bed with fresh, keen
purpose. The dinner with Soper had acted like a catalyst,
releasing new sources of energy and confidence and
banishing his foolish, negative thoughts about the police,
who had seemed so terrifying twelve hours earlier. In truth
Conrad had been flattered by Soper's attentions. You could
say what you liked but he was a pretty important fish, who
did not waste his time on people of no account. That he had
sat with Conrad, drunk his brandy, engaged in confidential
talk with him, seemed to be an earnest of future greatness. It
was almost, dared he fancy it, as if Soper, knowing of the
appointment to be made at the Alderman Robertson, was
acknowledging in Conrad the heir apparent. Conrad the
controller of the new course, Conrad the principal lecturer,
Conrad the member of the University staff, was worthy of
Soper's most affable attentions.

With these glittering prospects before him Conrad began
his day by performing a series of exercises culled from a
manual of yoga. He was supposed to do them every day, the
promised benefits would be immense, but when things were
going against him he tended to let them drop. This morning
he did them if anything over-enthusiastically. He stood on
his head until he felt giddy and the room swam around him.
He lay on his face and lifted his head and shoulders as far off
the floor as they would go, experiencing agonizing pains in
the small of his back as he did so. He stood with his legs apart
and drew in his stomach until, as the manual said, it
appeared to touch his spine. He wondered what the dull

aching sensation was on the left-hand side of his abdomen. When he had finished he felt a little sick and had to lie down on the bed to recover. Then he went downstairs to take breakfast with Soper.

It was clear to Conrad that what he must do now was to get a grip on himself and start taking control of his own destiny again. Through sheer loss of nerve he had been allowing the game to drift out of his hands. He ticked off the items. He had made a mess of the lecture last Saturday, he had let Jacks and Davidson come dangerously near to stealing his course from him, and had let Milne harass him about Andrew Carney and, Conrad's face darkened, play a really dirty trick on him about that Sandra Duckham business. Now, with the cards that fate had dealt him, he was in a position to counter attack. The meeting on Friday, when he would put Jacks and Davidson to flight, would be crucial, but before that he had routine business to catch up with here.

The first priority was to get in to Miss Cranston's school to have another look at Sandra Duckham. If Miss Cranston chose to complain about him, as she had complained about McHale last year, that would do him no good at all. Then he must look in to see Andrew Carney a couple of times. He had already put in a preliminary, unfavourable report on the lad, so he must scotch any protests from that quarter. In fact a general bustling show of energy would serve his turn best, and Conrad went on to provide it, and as he swept about his business, collecting evidence against his students, shoring up his own position, his spirits continued to rise.

Immediately after breakfast with Soper he took himself off to Miss Cranston's school and reduced both the girls there to a state of nervous prostration by a list of complaints about their work. He left a copy with Miss Cranston, saying that he had been seriously disturbed by what he had seen, and departed with the pleasant feeling that she could hardly accuse him of being overly lenient after that. In the afternoon

166

he did the same thing at another school, so Wednesday went down in his book as a thoroughly successful day.

On Thursday morning, still full of bounce, he presented himself in Mr Buick's study just after nine o'clock, with every intention of finishing young Carney's career on the spot, and when the Headmaster told him that Carney was not even in school he put on a fine show of indignation.

'Not in school? This is really too bad, Mr Buick, this is quite inexcusable. I shall take the firmest action about this, I promise you. Did he have the decency to send you a message?'

Buick waved a calming hand. 'No, no, you misunderstand. Andrew has gone with the trip. No, I have no complaints about Andrew at all, he is an excellent boy, most helpful.'

Looking happy and relaxed, as headmasters are wont to do when most of their school is away for the day, Mr Buick put on the kettle and explained that they had gone on a trip to London. 'I ought to have gone myself really, I suppose, but what I say is that after the way they've treated me I don't owe them anything – I don't owe them anything at all. I've stayed behind to clear up.' He beamed at his visitor. 'There is an immense amount of clearing up to be done. Do you take sugar and milk?'

Conrad replied that he did not take sugar. He was feeling deflated and asked Buick if he was sure about his estimate of Carney's excellence.

'Quite sure. I think he will make a first-rate teacher. You've nothing to worry about there, nothing at all. And Stan thinks so too. He was in yesterday and had a look at him.'

Conrad looked blank.

'Stan McHale, you know. I think he said he was in your department. He told me he knows you.'

Conrad could still not take it in, so Mr Buick explained.

'I know Stan very well. He was down here supervising last

167

year – stayed near the village, brought his rods, we did some fishing together. He's a grand lad is Stan. I was awfully glad to hear about the job.'

'The job?'

'He got it. The headship of the William Rufus. You knew he was in for it, of course? Well, he was appointed. The interviews were yesterday morning. He came in afterwards to see me and to cast his eye over Andrew. He said he'd been asked to, so I naturally thought that you'd asked him yourself. Didn't you?'

Controlling his temper with difficulty Conrad answered that he had made no such request.

'Well, anyway, it's all right. He found Andrew very good, agreed with me entirely, so you don't need to worry about him any more.'

And Mr Buick amiably offered Conrad another cup of tea, which was refused with less amiability, and Conrad took his leave as soon as he could.

Conrad's reactions to Buick's news were complicated. First he remembered that he had sent in an unfavourable report on Carney, and now, contradicting that report, were verdicts returned, not only by Buick, who was negligible, but by one of his own colleagues also. Secondly, somebody – Milne? Jacks? Gorning? – had deliberately affronted him by sending another tutor into the school over his head, and what was worse that tutor was a junior in his own department. Thirdly, that junior had now been appointed to the biggest headship in the county, a job that must be worth getting on for £20,000 a year.

Conrad stopped in a lay-by to concentrate on his grievances. Just look at McHale, look at him dispassionately. He was young, about thirty-three. He had very little experience in the classroom. He was careless and casual. He had no standards which Conrad had ever been able to recognize. Complaints had been made about his professional work – the catalogue of deficiencies could be continued. How did you explain it when such a man got such a job? And there was somebody like himself, still, at the age of forty-six, desperately uncertain about his future.

As he went about his duties for the rest of the day Conrad's indignation worked and swelled within him, eventually focusing on McHale. He it was who had actually gone into the school, in defiance of all etiquette, and pronounced glowingly on young Carney. Conrad wanted to hit back at him, to make him smart. What young Master McHale needed was a lesson in good manners, and that evening, before his meal, Conrad went to the phone to administer it.

18

At about two o'clock that Thursday afternoon there had been a knock on Stephanie's front door. She had answered it to discover a large, red-faced man in a shiny blue suit, holding out a card towards her.

'Mrs Nield? My name is Rosen, Detective Sergeant Rosen. I'm just making a few inquiries and I wonder if you would answer some questions.'

She had shown him into the front room. Her heart had jumped, as honest people's hearts do when they are suddenly confronted by the police. She saw the quick, approving look he gave to the antique furniture she had brought with her from her mother's. He seemed to be a noticing sort of man. He waited politely to be offered a chair.

'It's about this business down at Abenbury, Mrs Nield. I daresay your husband has told you all about it.'

Stephanie nodded. In fact Conrad had told her very little, but still she nodded because she would have had difficulty in speaking. What did this man want with her?

The Sergeant produced a notebook and consulted it in a splendidly leisurely manner. 'I understand that your husband visited the Abenbury district on April the twenty-ninth – that was a Thursday – is that so?'

Stephanie remembered clearly. The date was fixed in her memory by the row she had had with Conrad. She and Margery had gone out in the evening and he had had to get his own meal.

'Yes, he was down there.'

'What time did he arrive back that evening?'

The question was thrown out very casually, too casually. Stephanie was acute enough to understand that the matter was important. She wondered why.

'About half past six, I suppose.'

'You suppose, Mrs Nield? Don't you know?'

'He usually gets in about that time when he comes back from Abenbury.'

The Sergeant looked at Stephanie with the same suddenly-awakened attention that he had given the furniture. Something unexpected had happened that interested him.

'It's not when he usually gets back that we are bothered about, Mrs Nield. What we want to know is, what time did he get back on that particular day? Can you help us?'

'I – I don't think I can. You see, I wasn't here when he got back.'

The Sergeant smiled as if somebody had given him a present. 'You weren't here. Where were you, then?'

'I'd gone out to a meeting, with a friend.'

'And what time did you get back?'

'Just after eleven – about half past eleven – something like that.'

'And your husband was in at that time?'

'Yes, he was in, of course.' Grim of face, she might have added, complaining bitterly about having to get his own food.

'But, from your own knowledge, Mrs Nield, you cannot say that your husband got home any earlier than some time after eleven o'clock.'

'He must have done, there'd be no reason for him to stay down there. Besides –' a memory of his complaining face came to her aid – 'he'd eaten the meal that I'd left him.'

'But you did not actually see him?' He looked at her again with his uncomfortable, mild, intense gaze.

'No.'

'Do you know anybody who did see him?'

171

'No, why should anybody? I mean, there's nobody else in the house.'

And he had smiled once more at this.

The questioning had not ended there. What sort of a mood had her husband been in when she finally came back on the twenty-ninth? She could have replied, 'A foul mood,' but instead she said that he had been quite normal. Had he been agitated? Abnormally excited? Had he behaved in any un-usual way? Had he been depressed? He had gone on and on like this. She had been asked to recall all his behaviour over the last weeks, and her stubborn reiteration that he had been perfectly normal had begun to sound false simply through repetition.

There had been other questions. What did she know about the damage to the wing of the car? Had she noticed anything unusual about the car itself? Had he been cleaning it careful-ly, for instance? Anything unusual about his clothing? The man had gone on and on and on, perfectly polite, kindly even, but hatefully, frighteningly persistent. When he had finally taken his leave she had felt nervously drained. She had watched, from behind the curtain, as he went down the path. He had gone straight to the house next door.

Stephanie went to the shed, where old newspapers were put to await the bin-men, and fished out the copies for last Sunday, the ones that Conrad had been studying so hard. April the twenty-ninth, here it was, that had been the day when that girl had gone missing in Abenbury. Stephanie refreshed her memory of the details and began to feel quite sick. It was clear what had been in that policeman's mind. She sat on the floor of the shed, with the newspaper in her hand, appalled and frightened. It could not be true, could it? Conrad, the man she had known intimately for all these years? She oscillated between an indignant repudiation of the notion and a frightened acknowledgement that the police would hardly be behaving like this unless they had good reason for it. She had read about other women who, finding that the man they had married was a murderer, had been unable to believe it. No, it was a nonsense, it was a mistake of some kind. She thought again of the answers she had given to that policeman and wondered if she should have replied in some other way, more helpful to Conrad. Had she made things worse for him?

After a while she put the paper back on the pile and went into the house again. She needed to talk about it with somebody, somebody sympathetic. She might have gone round to her mother, but any consolation she would have given would have been on the lines of, 'Well, I warned you, but you wouldn't listen to me.' She might have gone round to Margery, who would be back home from school by now, but Margery would have urged her to stand on her own two feet and let Conrad go to hell. She wanted reassurance, she wanted to be told that her fears were unreasonable and be made to feel cosily safe, and it was in this frame of mind that she decided to visit Stan.

Margery could say what she liked but there was no doubt about it, in a crisis like this a man had a kind of authority, a presence, that a woman simply did not have. Stan had been wonderful. He had a young, slim figure, he was dressed casually in slacks and a shirt, with short sleeves, unbuttoned down to his waist, showing a nice chest with light golden hairs curling on it. His arms were sinewy and brown. He had been kindly, protective, massively at ease. He had told her not to worry, assured her that there was nothing else that she could have said to the police, that she had nothing to reproach herself with at all. He got drinks and they sat side by side on the settee while he helped, as he put it, to get her to see things in perspective. There was a wonderful kindness and consideration about him; he did remind her of what Conrad had been like in those early days.

Gradually she had got back to normal. They had a second drink and he even began to rally her on her suspicions. She could not really see old Conrad as a murderer, could she? The idea did indeed seem absurd. She giggled over it.

They made a nice-looking couple, she thought. She was wearing a light, sleeveless summer frock, with a simple neckline, cut rather low. It had been another hot day and she had the minimum underneath. They sat together on the settee, and their arms touched, and she thought it very pleasant.

And then suddenly the phone, which was on the table just behind them, had rung, and with a spasm of irritation Stan had picked it up. She saw his face change to something like consternation, and he put his finger to his lips to warn her to be silent.

'Hello, Conrad,' he said, 'good to hear your voice. What can I do for you?'

Stephanie went cold. She did admire Stan's calm and the absolute naturalness of his voice. All she could hear from the receiver was a quacking, but it sounded like an angry quacking. Stan, plainly restricted by her presence, was reduced to apologetic, indignant interjections.

'Well, I'm very sorry, Conrad.' 'I can only say that it was Jacks who asked me to go into the school.' 'I had absolutely no intention of being discourteous.'

Stephanie made a movement to get up and leave Stan alone, but his free arm was round her shoulder and he pressed her back into her seat. Then a natural curiosity overcame her. In what followed she acted innocently and without premeditation. She twisted round to face Stan and squirmed herself across his knees, steadying herself by placing her hand on his shoulder. This manoeuvre ensured that her ear was by the receiver, but the unforeseen consequence was that her breasts, through her thin frock, lay lightly on his chest, and her hair tickled his face and fell across his mouth, making it difficult for him to control his voice.

Stephanie listened intently to what Conrad said. She could make out the words only with difficulty, but the self-righteous whine, stalely familiar to her, came through very clearly, and any lingering concern which she felt for him ebbed away. Her hand moved more securely over Stan's shoulder and she relaxed against him. At the other end of the line she heard her husband slam the receiver down with theatrical effect, and so she took the phone out of Stan's hand, raised herself, and leaned over him to replace it on the table. It was a natural result of this movement that her breasts, as she leaned over him, caressed his face, so that the words 'Stupid prick', which he had directed at the distant Conrad, had been half-smothered. She looked down on him and then, slowly and firmly and deliberately, kissed him.

He looked up at her with a lazy satisfaction and responded.

19

Friday was another day of shocks for Conrad. The first shock came at breakfast time, which was a pity, because he had more or less thrown off Thursday's gloom and come to the breakfast table feeling quite cheerful. He had worked out what he was going to say to Milne and Jacks, and anybody else who cared to challenge him, and felt that it was pretty good. As to McHale actually getting that headship. At least it got rid of the bloody fellow. He sat down with a light heart and ate his cornflakes and glanced at the headlines in the day's press. Then the waitress brought his eggs and bacon – Conrad always had two eggs – and he turned the page and found himself reading an article about the recent murders. It was an interview with a 'high-ranking officer' and it destroyed his peace of mind in the first paragraph.

The officer began by making the customary excuses for the inefficiency of his police force, which Conrad received with a curling lip, putting the blame squarely on the shoulders of the British public, who had not been giving him the co-operation that he thought he deserved. But the article went on:

'We know that there are people who find it embarrassing to have to give an account of their movements, but they should appreciate that they have a duty to give the police all the help in their power. Everything said to the police is treated in the strictest confidence. It may be that the witnesses who can help us have their own reasons for wanting to keep quiet. They may have been visiting a strip joint, or watching a pornographic film; they may have been carrying on a liaison which they would prefer their

wives or colleagues to know nothing about. One knows
from experience that in an inquiry of this kind many
unsavoury practices are revealed which have nothing to do
with the main case. We appeal to all such men to come
forward frankly and tell us what they know. Otherwise
much valuable police time is wasted following up false
trails and checking misleading stories.'

There was more in the same vein, and Conrad's bacon
congealed on his plate as he read it. Great heavens, it was
monstrous, it pointed directly to him. He read again the
reference to the pornographic film and had a brief vision of
the reporter from the *Bickleton Herald*, notebook in hand,
entering the Lido cinema. And what a wealth of insinuation
there was in the rest of it. Once get him established as the
frequenter of blue movie palaces and the public mind would
leap easily to the belief that he went to strip joints, had a
mistress down here, and engaged in a number of unspecified
unsavoury practices. Conrad felt giddy with fury. He made
convulsive squeezing movements with his hands expressive
of a desire to seize Superintendent Pearce by the throat and
shake him like a dog. It must be Superintendent Pearce who
was at the back of this, irritated by his demeanour at their
interview, getting his own back in this fashion. Conrad found
that he was sweating, and he felt a familiar constriction in his
throat.

But even worse was to come. In an adjacent column a
'noted psychiatrist' had contributed a sketch of the possible
character of this unknown murderer, and, mechanically
swallowing his food, which had lost all taste, Conrad read
this:

'It is likely that in outward appearance this murderer is
completely normal. He will be a quiet, well-behaved man,
rather introverted, regarded by his family and neighbours
as a model citizen. He will have no girlfriends, in fact he is

likely to be sexually inadequate, even, perhaps, impotent, and he may well gain a furtive relief from his repressed desires through pornographic literature and films. The first of these murders was probably the result of a sudden impulse. Rage at his own sexual failure would have contributed, and a real or imagined insult offered by the girl could have tipped him over the edge into violence. Suddenly the girl is dead, he has triumphed, he has asserted himself. His immediate thought is to cover his tracks, but when this is done, when the police are baffled, when the countryside is in fear, he will enjoy privately a wonderful sense of power, and he feels an overmastering wish to repeat the experiment. Now he has killed a second time, and he will kill again. Make no mistake about it: this man is dangerous, he needs help, and until he is apprehended no woman is safe.'

This was too much. It was appalling to consider how well, in outward respects, the character sketch fitted him. 'Quiet, well-behaved, model citizen, completely normal.' Every respectable man walking about the streets of our cities was comprehended in this description. But if you took it with the other article, then it appeared to be a direct attempt to traduce him. The double reference to 'pornographic films' made the link clear. They were not only on the same page; by an accident of printing they were almost on the same line. The words started out of the text and called attention to themselves. Because he had gone to that cinema then he must be the murderer, that was the only construction you could place on it.

At this moment, prompted doubtless by the reference to pornographic literature, Conrad remembered, for the first time, that soft-sex magazine he had bought in Abenbury along with the local paper that had caused so much trouble. He had hidden it in the back of the car, under the seat. He got up and dashed outside, but he knew before he looked that it would not be there. The police were too thorough for that. He returned slowly and slumped in his chair. Pornographic literature and blue films, was that the way their minds were working? Conrad looked at the article again. It was clever, no doubt about it. No names mentioned, no direct accusations made, but the implications, for his friends and colleagues, who, of course, would be keenly interested in the case, were clear enough. How could he meet them after this? He imagined the jokes. Colleagues asking where he had left his dirty raincoat, Davidson requesting a blow by blow account of the film, Skillington peeping into his copy of the *Guardian* to see if he was concealing *Spanking News* or *Buttock Pummellers Weekly* in its pages.

Conrad read the paragraphs twice more before forcing himself to leave the table. After that, with a great effort of will, he compelled himself to carry out his routine of school visits exactly as if nothing had happened. Whatever the people he met might be thinking about him he was not going to show that anything was wrong. He would be business-like, quiet, and efficient; he would speak strictly about the matter in hand and allow no time for casual conversation. So he parked outside the school where he intended spending the morning, walked briskly in through the main entrance, nodded curtly to those members of staff who happened to be about, and strode purposefully to the first classroom he planned to visit. Nobody said anything, they did not seem to be looking at him in a meaningful way or sniggering; perhaps they had not seen the papers yet.

He settled himself at the back of the room and scowled at the student teacher. She was a timid girl. The report on her previous school practice had said that she needed plenty of support and it was clear that this morning she was not going to get it. She had set out to teach the class about the Napoleonic Wars, and either she was grossly ill-prepared for the task or Conrad's scowl had wiped all recollection of them from her mind, for she made a very bad fist of it indeed. She would make a statement hesitantly, shoot a glance at Conrad to see whether he approved or not, correct herself even if she happened to be right, and then qualify the correction. Every time Conrad made a note she shrank within herself. She tried to draw a map on the board and confused the places hopelessly and finished by rubbing it out. The children asked her questions which she was unable to answer, and on at least two occasions they pointed out mistakes to her.

Through it all Conrad sat implacably scribbling into his notebook, grim-faced, remorseless; yet he was hardly noticing what was going on. As his pen jabbed at the paper it jabbed at ghostly representations of Superintendent Pearce. His ears did not hear the quavering voice of the student but the derision of his colleagues. His notes were a species of automatic writing. Phrases like, 'You should anticipate what the children are likely to ask so that you will be able to answer intelligently,' or 'The map should have been carefully prepared beforehand so that it could have been drawn without error,' formed themselves on the page, but in his mind he was picturing the interview, and himself putting forward his ideas about education, and Gorning and Jacks leaning back in their seats with supercilious smiles on their faces as they remembered that he was addicted to dirty films. He rose and stalked out of the room. As he passed the student he tossed onto the desk in front of her the sheaf of notes that he had written. She stopped in mid-sentence and gazed at the terrible documents, convinced that her performance had destroyed her utterly, while Conrad left the room without ever having seen her distinctly at all.

The second shock came at the end of the morning. Conrad came out of the school and was preparing to get into his car when he saw Detective Sergeant Rosen standing on the other side of the road smiling at him. The Sergeant strolled over.

'Good morning, sir, we thought we'd better wait outside. Didn't want to disturb you in the school. I phoned round, that's how I found out where you were.'

Conrad was struck dumb. The sight of the Sergeant had induced a feeling of nausea and fear, and this had inhibited another feeling, which he had been nursing all morning, one of sullen rage against the police. This chaos in his mind was compounded by the realization that the police had just been advertising their interest in him in every school in the district. So Conrad found himself unable to make any reply at all, and the Sergeant had continued smoothly.

'Superintendent Pearce would like a word with you, sir. It won't take very long.'

They allowed Conrad to drive himself. That, at least, was something. If they had been on the point of arresting, he reasoned, they wouldn't have done that. They did not even put a policeman to sit with him. Mind you, that damned police car was just behind, and they had probably calculated that he was not the type to make a sudden dash to the ports. What the devil, Conrad asked himself, was it now? What could it possibly be? He went over all that he had said to them and tried to think of something that they might have found out, but what was there? For a wild, whimsical moment Conrad even thought that the Superintendent wanted to apologize for the newspaper paragraph, but it did not seem likely, and the idea withered away at the sight of his face and the sound of his first words.

'Well, Mr Nield, you seem determined to make things difficult for us.'

Everything was arranged as on Conrad's previous visit, except that it was a young constable instead of Sergeant Rosen who sat at the table by the window and made notes. The Superintendent was behind his desk. His face lacked affability and he did not rise as Conrad entered, nor did he waste time in polite preliminaries. But his first words, after that reproachful remark, only deepened Conrad's sense of mystery.

'You'll be pleased to hear that we have traced that driver, Mr Nield.'

Conrad looked blank and the Superintendent explained.

'The lorry driver. You told Sergeant Rosen that you had had a scrape with a lorry, that that was how your near-side wing got damaged. Well we have traced the driver.'

Conrad suppressed the impulse to congratulate him and contented himself with expressing surprise that they should have bothered with such a trifle.

'We have to check everything, Mr Nield. You didn't quite tell us the full story about that little incident, did you?'

Conrad again expressed incomprehension.

'From what the driver told us you seem to have had a real barney. He thought that you'd made a complaint about him.'

Conrad explained as best he could. It depended on what one meant by a barney. The lorry driver had been in the wrong, absolutely, in Conrad's submission, in the wrong. He had been grossly abusive and bullying, he had behaved quite disgracefully, putting Conrad in actual fear. Conrad had positively had to drive into the ditch and ram his wing against a gatepost to get out of his way.

'But,' he added, 'there didn't seem much point in going to the police about it. I hadn't even had the sense to make a note of the man's number. I just decided to forget about it. When your man spoke to me, frankly, it didn't occur to me to say anything.'

The Superintendent nodded at this and tapped his teeth annoyingly with his fingernail. He looked at Conrad searchingly and Conrad felt uneasy again. What had this to do with what the Superintendent wanted to see him about? Finally the Superintendent broke the silence.

'The driver was able to tell us one thing, Mr Nield. He told us that in the course of the row he came right up to your vehicle and actually looked into your window. Is that right?'

'He stuck his face close to mine. It was pretty unpleasant, that's what I meant when I spoke of his bullying manner.'

'He saw right into the car?'

Conrad nodded warily.

'He told us that you were alone.'

It was Conrad's immediate impulse to reply that of course he was alone, to ask who had said that he was not alone, why he should not have travelled alone, but an instinct for caution stifled the impulse and he said nothing at all. That was the best ticket. Say nothing. Leave all the talking to them.

'You see, Mr Nield, I understood, from what you said the other day, that you had a passenger with you. If you could just cast your mind back, Mr Nield, to our last little talk. I asked you about all those cigarette ends that were littering your car, and you replied that they had been deposited there by a passenger, a girl that you had picked up on the Tuesday morning, on the way down. I have a note of your evidence here –' the Superintendent consulted his notes – 'and, according to what you said then, you picked up this girl just before Witringham and put her down at Cordery. Now, of course, Wearmark, where you had this altercation with the lorry driver, is situated between Witringham and Cordery. If you had had a passenger in the car with you then the lorry driver would have been sure to see her, and he didn't. You follow me, sir?'

Conrad heard this speech unfolding with the same sensations he had had when he had seen that dreadful man's lorry bearing down on him. He had the same helpless sense that an inexorable force was moving in to crush him and that he could do nothing about it. The Superintendent's speech crashed on him and engulfed him, and he heard the man's voice pressing home his advantage.

'I think you owe us an explanation, sir.'

'All right, Superintendent.' Conrad's voice was a conversational white flag waved over the wreckage. 'You don't need to go on. I'll tell you what actually happened.'

20

'So I put her bag out onto the grass and drove off.'

By the time Conrad reached this point in his story he had to admit that it had not been a success. The effect that he had wanted to produce had been that of a well-meaning albeit casual and slightly muddled attempt to do a kindness, and of the comically ungrateful, even curmudgeonly response to it which had resulted in its being abandoned; but he had not carried his audience with him. The Superintendent had listened to Conrad's story without any interruption at all, but this courtesy had not made the task easier. It is helpful if the person you are talking to occasionally makes a noise of some kind to indicate assent, understanding, or even criticism, but that help had not been forthcoming. Conrad's voice had fallen on the still air of the murder headquarters and echoed round his head disconcertingly, reaching his ears sometimes as a bleat, sometimes as a whine.

'I – I just saw the girl there – I felt a bit sorry for the child – I mean, it seemed a kindness to offer her a bit of a lift. There wasn't much traffic about at that time of night, and she was all alone, so I stopped.'

The Superintendent sat very quietly, his eyes fixed steadily on Conrad's face, a stony expression on his own, and this intensified as Conrad continued with an attempt at jocularity.

'I'll be frank with you, I regretted it almost as soon as she had got in. She wasn't exactly the ideal sort of passenger. She was the silent type, you know what I mean, she hardly spoke two words after getting into the car. And as soon as she'd got her bottom on the seat she was fishing in her bag and getting out those bloody cigarettes. She didn't even offer me one, not that I would have taken it anyway because I don't smoke, but you'd think common civility would have made her offer. She absolutely filled the car with smoke, and it played up my eyes and irritated my sinuses. In fact, to tell you the truth, Superintendent, the whole atmosphere got a bit oppressive. It got hot in the car and, between you and me, I didn't get the impression that her personal hygiene was exactly five-star class. In fact, not to put too fine a point on it, she stank to high heaven.'

It was impossible to judge how the Superintendent responded to a remark like this, his face seemed to have set into a particularly hard form of concrete, but as it echoed back from the Superintendent's silence it sounded to Conrad less satisfactory than he had hoped. The girl's sullen demeanour was his only excuse for getting rid of her. Conrad had already decided not to trouble the authorities with the detail that he had placed his hand on her knee and that she had pushed it off again, and he must get the quality of it across, but he was not encouraged to think that he had. It did not seem to Conrad that the Superintendent was a great one for nuances. He looked the sort of man who will take a skilful description of a complicated situation and simplify it to a damagingly plain statement. Still Conrad persevered.

'We bowled merrily along, me chatting, she smoking, and then we hit a sheep. It just jumped down from the side of the road and I biffed into it before I could take avoiding action. So, of course, I stopped and got out to see if there was anything I could do for the poor animal, and this girl got out as well and announced that she was going to have a pee – just like that, in exactly those words – and she wandered off over the rise to have it. So I went back to the car to wait, and it struck me that this was as good an opportunity as I was likely to have to get rid of her, so I put her bag out onto the grass and drove off.'

He stopped, and the Superintendent continued to look at him with a grave distaste. There was silence.

'On reflection,' Conrad continued, when this became unbearable, 'I wished that I hadn't. It was rather rotten to leave her like that, I know, but frankly, Superintendent, I'd had about enough of her company. I knew there'd be another car along pretty soon. She was no worse off than when I had picked her up.'

At this point Conrad's memory prompted him with fragments of his voice from a few minutes earlier reporting that there was not much traffic about at that time of night. But the two statements were not in contradiction. To say that there was not much traffic was not to say that there was none. Another vehicle would come along – in fact one must have done. It could hardly be laid at Conrad's door that the driver had been homicidal. Conrad closed his mouth tight. This silence was beginning to get on his nerves. Well, he would say no more. His story was over, every word of it taken down by that constable by the window, and now it was up to them. The less he said now the better. At least they had the truth and his conscience was clear.

Finally the Superintendent spoke. 'We didn't see a sheep. You say you killed a sheep; we didn't see one.'

'I didn't say I killed a sheep, Superintendent, I said I hit one. Shortly after I stopped the car the sheep got up and walked away.'

The Superintendent brooded on this for a minute or two. 'You gave this girl a lift, you took her up on to the moors, and then you got her out of your car and left her there for no reason at all?'

'I've given you my reasons, Superintendent.'

'They didn't sound adequate reasons to me for leaving a young girl all alone, at that time of night, in a place like that.'

'But she was no worse off than she was earlier. Look, Superintendent, she was hitching lifts, right? Now I came

187

along that road and gave her a lift. If I hadn't done it then she would still have been there getting a lift from some other motorist. When I left her she was on the same road, still hitching lifts, probably from the same motorist who would have picked her up earlier if I hadn't. Where's the difference?'

'If you can't see the difference for yourself, Mr Nield, then I can't tell you. Now, let us go over this tale of yours in detail.'

And patiently, never raising his voice or losing his calm demeanour, the Superintendent went over Conrad's story. It wasn't like the sort of thing you saw on television, where the officer strides up and down, or puts his face close to his victims and bawls. He was courteous, and persistent, and repetitive. The same questions were asked over and over again in slightly different ways, or presented in a different order. Conrad could understand the purpose behind the technique and could admire the skill with which it was deployed. He had underestimated this chap, he was no fool. He was looking for inconsistencies, but there weren't any. That was the grand advantage of telling the truth. If you could remember it clearly, and Conrad could, then you were not to be shaken. It was a pity, Conrad could see it now, that he had not done this earlier. There was only one danger. This style of questioning seemed designed to be irritating, as though the police were hoping that he would lose his temper and commit some indiscretion. Conrad congratulated himself that he was too shrewd to be caught by a trick like that, and his voice matched the Superintendent's for calmness and lack of expression.

'You say she was smoking when she got into the car?'

'No, I said that she started smoking after she had sat down.'

'We found three cigarette ends. She could hardly have smoked three cigarettes between getting into your car and reaching the moors.'

'I fancy they weren't complete cigarettes. Certainly the first she pulled out had been half smoked already.'

'Perhaps that was why she didn't offer you one.'

'Perhaps.'

There were lots of questions about the girl's appearance.

'I'm sorry, Superintendent, but I'm not a fashion expert, and it was pretty dark. One of those long, straggling, dingy dresses, I think, or it might have been a blouse and skirt. I'm pretty hopeless on these things.'

Conrad nearly added, 'Ask my wife,' but stopped himself because he hoped that the Superintendent would do nothing of the sort.

For the sixth or seventh time Superintendent Pearce got Conrad to repeat that he had left the girl all alone on the desolate moorland.

'She found a dip in the ground, you say?'

'She went to the back of a small rise so that she was out of sight.'

'And you went immediately to the car?'

'Not immediately. I told you, the idea of going did not occur to me straight away.'

'You were cautious – about making a noise – you didn't want her to hear you?'

'Not particularly – I mean, I wasn't on tip-toe or anything like that.'

'But you moved as quickly as possible?'

'Pretty quickly, yes.'

'You put the girl's duffel bag out on the road. Did you open her door or your own?'

'Her door. I didn't put the bag on the road, I put it on the grass at the side. I opened her door because it was on the near side, it was next to the grass.'

'Although it made twice as much noise?'

Conrad looked at him questioningly and the Superintendent explained.

'You're standing by the car. Open her door, close it – bang – walk all the way round the car, open your own door, close it – another bang. It all takes time and makes a noise, if the girl is likely to be disturbed.'

Conrad answered calmly and slowly.

'I have already explained that I was not in the road at all. I was sitting in the driver's seat. I returned to my car simply because I felt cold, I had no idea of leaving. Then I looked down and saw the duffel bag and it suddenly occurred to me. I opened the passenger door, from the inside, heaved the bag out, closed the door, and drove off. That was all. It was very quick – a sudden impulse.'

'You heaved the bag out with some force?'

'I don't suppose there was anything breakable in it. She flung it into the car herself with a pretty good thump. I don't think you should make too much of that.'

'You didn't throw the bag out later?'

'That wouldn't have been of any use to her. That would have been a dirty trick. I keep telling you, I threw it out there.'

Conrad's voice was still calm, he was not shouting. He could see what was behind all these questions. If the girl was dead she couldn't be disturbed by noise and she wouldn't need her duffel bag, but Conrad did his best to hide the fact that he understood this. He must appear quite innocent – damn it, he was quite innocent – and speak always as taking it for granted that the girl was alive. It was very odd but telling the truth seemed to have become the same as making up a story. He was having to force himself to pretend to believe what he knew perfectly well was the truth.

The Superintendent spoke again. 'We didn't find a duffel bag at the scene. I ask you again, sir, are you sure that you put it out there?'

'I'm quite sure, Superintendent.'

Conrad tried to hold the officer's gaze and, absurdly,

found it difficult. He was behaving for all the world as though he was guilty. He must hold the Superintendent's eye without any defiance, or sheepishness, frankly, openly, honestly. Why should that be hard to do? Conrad blinked, he felt his face twitching, he wanted to drop his eyes. The pause lasted a very long time. What was going to happen now? Would he be arrested? It was best now if Conrad simply resigned things to fate. Matters were out of his hands, nothing that he could do would help. It was like the moment when a doctor has finished his examination of you, and you button up your shirt and steel yourself to hear your fate as calmly as possible.

The Superintendent spoke. 'There is one other matter, sir. It concerns your movements on April the twenty-ninth. I believe you told Sergeant Rosen that you were down here on that day?'

This was a shock, but Conrad was fortified by the knowledge of his complete innocence on that occasion at least. He nodded.

'You left the school just before half past three and drove back across the moors through Abenbury, arriving home between half past six and seven?'

'That's right, Superintendent.'

'You don't wish to modify that story at all, Mr Nield?'

'No, why should I?'

'You didn't stop anywhere on the way?'

'No –' Conrad cut his speech off abruptly. He had just remembered that he had stopped, in that lay-by, to have a walk and cure his headache.

The Superintendent was staring at him. 'Were you about to say something else, Mr Nield?'

'No, nothing at all. I didn't stop anywhere.'

It would look very bad if, at this stage of things, he were to alter his story.

The Superintendent continued to stare, and finally he went on. 'Sergeant Rosen asked your wife, but she was unable to corroborate your story. She said she was out when you arrived.'

The news that the police had been round questioning Stephanie was a bad shock, but Conrad managed not to show it.

'That's right. She had gone to a feminist meeting, all about wife-beating and such-like, with a friend of hers.'

'We asked the neighbours, but nobody saw you arrive.'

Another shock. They had been pestering the neighbours. Conrad was silent.

'Is there anybody, Mr Nield, who could confirm your time of arrival home?'

'I don't know. I don't think so. Why should there be? I just drove back and went into the house. I didn't see anybody and I didn't go out again. I was working.'

'Nobody telephoned you?'

'Nobody.'

There was a long silence after this. Conrad's head throbbed. It was worse than he had thought. They were beginning to try to tie him up with that earlier business. His resentment settled on Stephanie. If she had been at home, as she ought to have been, she would have supported his story and all this would not have happened. What were they going to do with him?

The Superintendent spoke. 'We'll prepare a statement for you to sign, sir. It'll take an hour or so. Meanwhile, I believe you said, when we spoke to you on Tuesday, that you had in your hotel the suit you were wearing that night.'

Conrad nodded. 'The cinema ticket was in it.'

'I'd like to take that suit, sir. I assume that it hasn't been cleaned in the interval?'

Conrad attempted a light touch. 'Good heavens, Superintendent, I don't have my things cleaned above once in a Preston Guild.'

But there was no smile. 'I'll get someone to take you to the hotel to collect it. By the time you get back the statement should be ready.'

This looked hopeful. 'And then I'll be free to go?'

'Where were you thinking of going, sir?'

'Back home, to Bickleton. There's a meeting I'm supposed to attend.' Conrad looked at his watch. He had forgotten the meeting. Already it was far too late for him to make it. At that very moment, probably, Davidson was taking control of the submission.

'If you think of going anywhere else, I'd be glad if you'd let us know. We may need to keep in touch.'

The Superintendent's tones were heavy and ominous. Conrad promised to let him know and marched out, with a constable who had been summoned, to a police car.

The journey to the hotel gave Conrad time to think. It must look terrible. It was almost as though he had really been arrested. He sneaked a look at himself in the car mirror, confirming his suspicion that he was very pale. As he walked into the hotel he must try to make sure that his legs did not tremble and that his voice did not sound strange. God in heaven, what had he done, after all? He had put his hand on a girl's knee. That was the most serious crime that he could level against himself. He was supposed to be living in the most sexually liberated society the world had ever seen, and he had put his hand on a girl's knee and all this had happened to him – practically frog-marched to the scaffold. And the irony was that nobody even knew that he had put his hand on her knee. That reprehensible act at least would remain a secret.

Conrad thought of Davidson. Davidson put his hands on girls' knees every day of his life. You could see him doing it, sitting next to them in the library or in seminar rooms. It was the most natural thing in the world for Davidson's hands to find themselves on girls' knees, but the police never came to interview him, he was not wanted for murder. There was no justice in it. Here was he, morally as clean as a whistle, faced with all this, and there was Davidson, an acknowledged goat, stealing all the credit for the submission.

At the hotel Conrad put the best face on things that he could. Obstinately shadowed by the constable, he went to reception and collected his case, which he had left there ready-packed. Then he had to carry it into the lounge and open it and get the suit out and give it to the constable, who stood there woodenly, like a cricket umpire, with it draped across his left arm. Conrad closed his case again and went back to reception.

'I shall be returning on Monday,' he said. 'I'd like the same room, please.'

The haughty girl who lived there, and who spent seventeen hours a day, Conrad believed, painting her nails, made a pretence of consulting the register.

'I'm sorry, Mr Nield, but we're full up next week.'

'Full up? You can't be, not at this time of the year.'

She looked blankly ahead of her, avoiding his gaze. 'We're absolutely full, Mr Nield. The Manager asked me to tell you.'

The constable, still with the suit on his arm, came up behind Conrad and asked if anything was the matter.

'No, no, nothing, nothing at all. We'd better get back.' Conrad picked up his case and led the way out to the police car.

At about half past five Conrad was allowed to leave the murder headquarters and begin the drive home. He felt as though it had been touch and go. First of all he had had to answer another series of questions. Then he had had to sign the statement. The Sergeant – it was the Sergeant this time – gave him each page in turn, and he read it and initialled it. He was too low-spirited to put his pencil through the spelling mistakes. They had taken the clothes from him and given him a receipt for them. Shoes, what shoes had he worn that night? Why, Conrad had answered, the shoes he had on now. Could they look at the shoes? Conrad took them off. Had he another pair of shoes with him? Yes, Conrad had another pair in the car. The constable was despatched to fetch them. He was given another receipt for his shoes. Sitting there in his stockinged feet Conrad felt especially vulnerable. Coat, what coat had he worn? The coat was in the car as well and the constable made another visit. A third receipt changed hands. Conrad waited to be asked to surrender his underwear, but they did not go as far as that. Then at last he was free to leave.

21

'Well?' That was all that Stephanie had to say to him when
he finally reached home on that Friday evening. She must
have been waiting for him, waiting and watching, for she
opened the door in his face as he was fumbling with his key,
and the house was heavy with the burden of her displeasure.
She hardly gave him enough room to enter, his suitcase
bumped awkwardly against the door jamb, and she put her
question before he was fairly in the hall.

'Well?'

It was, Conrad thought, a Donald McGill caricature. She
ought to have had her hair done up in curlers and been
brandishing a rolling-pin.

'What do you mean, "Well"?' he asked, all innocence.

'I'd just like a bit of an explanation, Conrad, that's all. I do
think I'm entitled to that.'

'And what is it that I'm supposed to explain?'

'Oh, Conrad, have you any idea what I've been going
through? The police around asking questions, reporters
pestering me, people wondering what you've been doing, and
all the stuff in the newspapers, and you couldn't even pick up
the phone and give me a ring.'

Her tone, Conrad noticed, was hard. There was no recog-
nition that he might have been going through rather a bad
time himself. Stephanie was angry on her own account, so
she stood there, her mouth screwed up in a narrow, peevish
line, scolding him like a naughty schoolboy. He pushed his
way past her and carried his case upstairs, thus giving
himself a moment to think. He was damned if he was going to
take this lying down.

Conrad's conscience had pricked him more than once into wondering how Stephanie had reacted to the police visit and what she would say to the stories that must be circulating about him. Well, now he knew, and he was almost pleased that her attitude made an apology unnecessary and gave him an excuse to retreat into indignation.

Stephanie's feelings were in a thorough muddle. The experience with Stan had been ecstatic, and it ought not to have been, but all her guilt could not erase the memory of its pleasure. At one moment she was finding excuses for herself, and the next she was telling herself angrily that it was not she who needed to apologize. She was disturbed at what she had found out about her own nature. Margery had known. Margery had insisted weeks ago that Stephanie had a lech for Stan, but she had earnestly denied it and had believed her denial. Stan was a very sweet and attractive person but they were simply close friends. Couldn't you have friendly feelings for a man without people saying nasty things about you? Margery's reply had been ribald and finally practical. 'Why don't you make the most of it while you've got it? It's your own body. Do what you bloody well like with it.' Margery had been right. What Stephanie had considered simple, old-fashioned virtue had been nothing more than funk.

When Margery had said what she did, Stephanie had naturally thought about it. Perhaps Stan was keen on her like that, though he had always been a perfect gentleman. She wondered what she would do if he did become – pressing – and she had hoped that he wouldn't. At least, it might be lovely, but it wouldn't be right, and it might not be success-ful. Conrad had given her a deep sense of her inferiority as a sexual partner and it would be terrible if Stan found her unsatisfactory as well. A really nice girl was not supposed to find that sort of thing enjoyable. She would be ashamed of herself – that was how she had reasoned it out.

The reality had been different. When she had gone round

to Stan's she had been feeling abominably low and wretched and Stan had been kind and tender. When Conrad was so nasty on the phone she had just kissed him on impulse, to make up for the nastiness and show that she appreciated him. He had responded enthusiastically, and one thing had led to another, and, well, there they were, and it had been absolutely marvellous. Never had she experienced anything remotely like that with Conrad, and it was quite untrue to say that she was frigid, or unresponsive, or incapable. She had come to see clearly the extent to which Conrad had loaded the blame for his own inadequacies on to her and this had made her feel both sorry for him and angry with him. She was also relieved to find herself normal, and when she was not feeling guilty about what had happened, for old mental habits die hard, she was feeling proud of herself.

On Friday morning she met Brenda for coffee, and Brenda had shown her a copy of the *Bickleton Herald* in which she read about Conrad's visit to the cinema. At mid-day, on her way back from school, Margery had pushed through the letter box a copy of the newspaper that had caused Conrad so much distress the day before. Stephanie had read the same police warning, and, heavily marked by Margery, the same psychiatrist's character study, and her understanding of her husband's deficiencies had deepened. What exactly had he been doing down at Abenbury? He began to look like a stupid, pathetic little man.

The character study fitted Conrad remarkably closely, closer probably than any other person could imagine. 'Sexually inadequate, even, perhaps, impotent.' Well, no, Conrad was not impotent, at least, not all the time. He had his difficulties, but Stephanie supposed that most men did. He certainly did not have any girlfriends, that part was right, and he did not get on very well with women. He was quiet, he was introverted. Stephanie read over the analysis a number of times. It was very general, it would fit lots of men. Odd, that bit about pornographic films. She looked at Brenda's *Herald*. What was the name of the one that Conrad had been to? She had known him all these years and she would never have thought that he had tastes in that direction.

Every so often she pulled herself together. She and Conrad had been married for a long time, and it had been a good marriage, and she had been happy. His virtues could not have just vanished. He had been under a great strain and his peculiar behaviour was a result of this. She ought not to be disloyal to him now. It was unfortunate but inevitable that the more she forced herself to revive her old feelings for Conrad the more her conscience pricked her about Stan. So when she met him at the door it was a mixture of anger, resentment, guilt, frustration, contempt, fear, and even pity, that made her say 'Well?' so aggressively.

Conrad charged down the stairs two at a time, bounced into the sitting-room and looked at his wife directly and fiercely.

'What do you mean – all the stuff in the newspapers? What are you talking about?'

'There's a big story about it in the *Herald*. I hadn't seen it myself. Brenda Davidson showed it to me, she knew all about it before I did.'

It was difficult to tell whether Stephanie was more aggrieved because of what had happened or because she had not been told first. Conrad decided to take a high-handed line.

'Big story about what, for God's sake? I've just been down there doing my job, that's all, watching bloody students teach.'

'Oh, yes. And how many pornographic films did you see this week? That's all been in, you know. And how many girls did you give lifts to? It's about time you woke up to the sorts of things people are beginning to say about you.'

Conrad took up his prepared position.

'What do you mean, pornographic films? I went to the pictures one night because I was bored bloody stiff. What about it? It's difficult to find a film nowadays that isn't pornographic. The only alternative was *Nicholas and Alexandra*; you wouldn't expect me to see *Nicholas and Alexandra*, would you? And then, when I came out and was driving back to my hotel, I passed this girl and gave her a lift. It was late at night, there wasn't much traffic about, it seemed to me a slight kindness to offer. Evidently you think differently.'

By this time Conrad had got to the sideboard, where he could pour himself a drink. He was about to ask Stephanie whether she would have one herself when he was stopped by the look of alarm and astonishment on her face.

'What on earth are you talking about?' she said, anguished. 'The paper didn't say anything like that. The paper said that it was on Tuesday morning.'

Conrad gave up. He could not understand this. Before he said anything else, he decided, he had better have a look at the paper.

It was the *Bickleton Herald*, a rag, in Conrad's opinion, normally given over to reports of meetings of the Women's Institute and advertisements for wool. The murders, with himself as prominent local interest, had been an agreeable change. Conrad spread it out and found that the predictable worst had happened. That reporter he had encountered outside the cinema had been at work, nosing things out, piecing things together. The police appeared to have dropped a few hints. It was broadly the same sort of thing that was appearing in the national press, but alongside speculation about the murderer and accounts of the police activities there was much more direct reference to his own involvement.

To Conrad the juxtaposition was a deliberate attempt to incriminate him, though the report was written in the careful style of a man who has prepared his copy with a couple of legal experts breathing over his shoulder. Conrad was referred to as a 'local resident', which he could hardly object to, and as a public-spirited citizen he should have been pleased to learn that he had given the police 'valuable information' and that he was a 'key witness'. 'Mr Nield, it appears,' the writer continued, 'was driving along the road towards Forton Cross near the time at which the murder is thought to have been committed. Earlier in the evening he had attended a performance of the film *Sex Confessions of a Nymphomaniac*, showing at the Lido cinema in Abenbury. It is understood that, driving down from Bickleton to Abenbury on the morning before the murder took place, Mr Nield gave a lift to a girl hitch-hiker, and the police are anxious to trace this girl.'

Conrad helped himself mechanically to another drink and subsided into an armchair. It was just what he had expected, except that now it had happened it was worse. It was outrageous – all that gloating over the girl's injuries and the state of her body, 'half naked', 'evidence of a considerable struggle', 'bruising on the upper thighs'. To find your own name linked even in the most indirect way with this sort of stuff was defiling, but to have it linked like this was cata-strophic. Conrad read the passage for the third time. He began to see what had happened. This report had been written after that interview on Tuesday, when that reporter had followed him and Sergeant Rosen to the cinema. The revelation that he had picked the girl up that night had not yet come to the ears of the papers. When it did – my God, what would they say? Conrad noticed Stephanie looking at him and felt that he ought to speak.

'It's outrageous, it's terrible. It almost directly implies that I was involved in this filthy business.'

'What did you mean, Conrad,' Stephanie's voice trembled slightly, 'when you said what you did about picking up the girl that evening?'

'I did pick her up that evening,' said Conrad, blunt,

straight from the shoulder. 'It's typical of this bloody rag that it should cock up the whole story. I picked her up on the way home, after I'd been to the pictures.'

'You mean that you actually gave her a lift on the very night that she was murdered?'

'I picked her up, yes, I told you.'

Stephanie was looking at Conrad with horror, and he stared directly back at her. After a moment or two she could not meet his gaze any longer and looked away.

'After I dropped her,' continued Conrad, 'some other motorist must have come along, and presumably it was he who did it. Now you know why the police have been so interested in me. Four hours was it, the paper said, they were questioning me? I didn't think it was anything like that long myself.'

He looked at his wife steadily. She was staring out of the window. He tried to fathom what was going on in her mind. Could she really, seriously, be thinking that he was capable of doing a thing like that? Again he felt a lack of sympathy in her, a sensation that she was drawing in her skirts and moving out of his range. Conrad found himself hardening towards her. If that was how she wanted to be then damn well let her. It was not for him to come whining to her for consideration.

'I suppose,' he said, breaking a lengthy pause, 'that there is a bite of something to eat. Just so that I can keep body and soul together, if you wouldn't mind, that is.'

She moved mechanically to serve him his meal.

'It's been a somewhat tiring day,' he continued, 'I've just spent the afternoon with the police again.'

'The police seem very interested in you.' Stephanie said this in a dead voice, as though she was striving politely to make conversation with a stranger.

'I suppose it's natural. Professionally they were bound to ask me a few questions.'

Why didn't she come right out with it and say, 'Did you do it?'

'How did they get to know that you'd given her a lift at all?' Stephanie asked. It was an opening for him.

'I told them.' Just like that, flat and nonchalant.

'You told them yourself? Wasn't that a bit silly?'

'Not really. After all, I haven't done anything. There are times, Stephanie, when it's a bit silly not to tell the police things. If you don't tell them, and then they find out, that makes it a good deal worse. It wasn't exactly an easy decision to make, to speak up like that. Just at this time, with the job coming up and everything, frankly I could do without a thing like this. I don't suppose it'll make matters easier for me at the interview. It would have been a damn sight more convenient to have said nothing at all, but it went against the grain a bit to do that. Anyway, I told them, like a good little boy, so there it is.'

'And have they finished with you now?'

Conrad stood there wearing a brave smile and shrugged his shoulders. He spoke quietly, without melodrama. 'I'd rather like to know that myself, but I'm afraid the police haven't let me into their secrets. The question, of course, is whether they believe me when I say I didn't do it.'

He wanted her to come up to him and comfort him. The self-pity that he had been feeling all week welled up in him and implored consideration, but she went on mechanically preparing the meal, her mouth set, her eyes anywhere except on him. Finally she brought in the food and put it on the table.

'Aren't you having any yourself?'

'No, I had something earlier. I wasn't sure when you'd be home.'

The food had been in the oven for a long time and was dry and shrivelled. Conrad got himself another drink.

He champed at the meal, swilling down mouthfuls of food

with swigs of lager. It was not very appetizing. Upstairs he could hear Stephanie moving about, and then her voice came down to him.

'Conrad, did you leave your suit behind you, the dark blue one? I can't find it.'

Conrad made an inarticulate noise, his mouth full of meat and potatoes. He rose wearily to his feet and went to the foot of the stairs and paused there, looking upwards. Stephanie was standing at the top. Slowly, with exaggerated grimaces and movements of the head, Conrad masticated his mouthful, and swallowed it. Then he spoke.

'I left it with the police.'

'What?'

'I left it with the police, they asked me for it.'

'Why ever did they do that?'

Conrad put on his long-suffering voice, icily polite, each word articulated precisely: 'They wanted to have a look at it. It was the suit I was wearing that evening, the evening I went into Abenbury.'

Stephanie was halfway down the stairs. Her hand trembled on the bannister. 'What do you mean, Conrad? Why did they want it? What do they want to do with it?'

'They want to examine it, Stephanie. They want to see if there are any stains or marks on it, blood, semen, stuff like that. You see, Stephanie, if I did strangle the girl and assault her sexually and fight with her and all that, there ought to be some marks on my clothes, and they want to see if there are any.'

Stephanie stood on the stairs looking down at Conrad, looking directly at him at last. The trembling had communicated itself from her hand to the rest of her body, and her face worked slightly. She did not speak. After a moment she turned and ran back into the bedroom.

Conrad returned to his seat. Serve her right. She had asked for it. How dare she actually believe that he, Conrad, could possibly be guilty of a thing like that? He prodded at his food again, but it was uneatable by this time and he scraped his plate clean into the fire. He went into the kitchen and peered into the oven where he saw an unappetizing rice-pudding and decided that he would not bother with it. He got himself another drink.

A few minutes later Stephanie came downstairs again. 'I'm going out,' she said.

Conrad waved his glass in her direction, indicating that that was all right by him.

'I'm going round to Margery's, I don't know when I'll be back.'

'Give her my regards,' said Conrad. 'Oh, by the way, before you go, were there any messages or anything for me during the week?'

Stephanie was halfway out of the door, and seemed to be about to say 'No', and close it behind her, when she remembered something and, almost with pleasure, paused in her flight.

'Yes, I nearly forgot. Milton Jacks rang this morning, about mid-day. He wanted to know why you hadn't sent the examination lists in to the University.'

If Stephanie had hoped to smash Conrad's pose of frigid unconcern she succeeded. This was another of those jolts that the Alderman Robertson specialized in. Surely this should have been Penniman's job. Penniman had handed over to Conrad, but Conrad had clearly understood that it was for next year. The lazy sod. As soon as he got a job elsewhere all his commitments were dropped like hot coals.

'I'll have to do it first thing in the morning – when were they due in?'

'You needn't bother. Jacks said that he was going to ask Philip Milne to do it. I said I'd give you the message and I have; there wasn't anything else.' Then she was gone.

For a few minutes Conrad merely cursed. It would be very

damaging if that little chore went to Milne. Everything was going against him, he might as well simply not turn up for the interview. But after a few minutes it struck him that it was futile to sit there moaning about things. God helps those who help themselves. He began to think hard. Jacks had phoned Stephanie about mid-day. Now that afternoon Philip Milne had been at the BEd meeting, the one he had so unfortunately missed himself, which meant that probably he had not even started the job yet. Five minutes later Conrad was on his way to the College, and within a quarter of an hour he had got the keys from the night porter and was in the Records Office. Preparing the examination lists for the University involved taking the student record cards for the final year, all three hundred and ten of them, and abstracting from them details of all the courses that each student was entered for. Conrad braced himself for a tedious night and bent down to get the files from the bottom drawer of the filing cabinet. A moment later he straightened up. The drawer was empty.

Conrad refused to allow himself to be dismayed. Milne must have come for the files as soon as the BEd meeting was over, the slimy little creep. The question was, what had he done with them? There was a strict rule that the files were not to be taken off the College premises for any purpose whatsoever. Conrad looked at the bunch of keys the porter had given him. One of these fitted Milne's study; he wondered which. Two minutes later he was trying them in the lock.

The sight which confronted him when he finally got the door open did much to make up for what he had suffered earlier in the day. Good old Philip, praise to his industry and his devotion to duty and anxiety to please. He really must have worked like the devil. Probably he had started at about five o'clock and by the time he had given up, half blind and giddy from the effort, he had worked methodically through the files as far as the letter S. On the left-hand side of his desk, all neatly written up in Milne's precise script – he could not use a typewriter – were the four lists complete up to this point; on the right-hand side was the small remaining pile of record cards. Conrad helped himself to some of Milne's file paper, licked his lips, and picked up the top envelope. It would not take long.

In fact it took forty minutes. Then Conrad carried Milne's lists, and the ones he had just made, to his own study and typed them all out neatly. After that he returned Milne's lists to his desk, arranging them exactly as he had found them, restored the files to their original position, and locked the door. On his way home he put the lists in the post, addressed to the University Registrar. He felt quite light-hearted for the first time since opening his newspaper at breakfast that morning. God, as he had told himself earlier, helps those who help themselves.

22

'Dear Mr Jacks,' wrote Conrad, 'I am at a loss to understand the note you sent me. Naturally I have completed the examination lists and sent them to the University.'

It was Sunday, and Conrad had settled down to the job of catching up with his correspondence. He had gone into College the day before to deal with it, but finding the atmosphere there oppressive he had brought it home instead. His colleagues had appeared not so much hostile as embarrassed and unwilling to speak to him. No longer was anybody making jokes about his involvement in the murders near Abenbury. On at least two occasions he had approached small groups engaged in animated talk, but each time as soon as his presence was noted the talk had stopped abruptly, they had made awkward and forced conversation with him and as soon as was decently possible the members had drifted away.

Conrad noted this grimly but, he told himself, he must behave as though everything was normal. Once again, as in his interview with the Superintendent, he was struck by the difficulty of acting a role that one knew was true. He was innocent, but the more he strove to appear so the more he appeared to be guilty. He had to calculate what he should say and what tone of voice he should use. He put on a smile when it seemed appropriate, forced a note of cheery unconcern into his voice, turned away with a rehearsed casualness, and after a time stopped even trying to assess how far he was succeeding. Damn them all. They would know the truth some time – if only the police got on with their job of finding that murderer – and meanwhile he could do without them.

The contents of his pigeonhole were spread out on the desk

in front of him. A note from Percival, who looked after the school practice, telling him that Miss Cranston had written making a formal complaint about the inadequate supervision of her students. Conrad put this on one side; it would need thinking about. A letter from Gorning saying that as Conrad had not been able to attend 'the crucial meeting' of the BEd planning committee, Mr Davidson had been asked to take over the chairmanship. Conrad threw this into the waste-paper basket; one didn't waste one's time writing to Gorning, but he must remember to phone Professor Templeton. Gorning's letter would have its answer, he could promise that. And finally there was this message from Jacks expressing surprise and sorrow, the bloody hypocrite, that the University lists had not been sent in. 'I understood from Mr Penniman that you had undertaken this important responsibility. In the circumstances I had no option but to ask Mr Milne to take it over.'

Conrad licked his lips and grinned at the opening sentence of his answer; it is good to smite the enemy hip and thigh. He finished dealing with the hip and then turned his attention to the thigh, which was the real purpose of his writing:

'There is another matter which I wish to raise. I was astonished to learn, when I went into one of my schools last week, that without consulting me, or even informing me, you had instructed another member of staff to examine one of my students. This was a deliberate act of gross unprofessional discourtesy.'

Conrad had come to the end of his sheet and had to pause here to change the paper in his typewriter. It was a fiddly job shuffling the carbons together – he was taking two copies so that he could send one to Gorning – and as he lined them up he thought out his next sentence:

'What is astonishing about the business is your apparent assumption that because I commit the sin of criticizing a student I must be on the point of failing him. I saw Carney teach, he made a number of mistakes, and I pointed them out to him. I understood, in my ignorance, that this was my duty, but it seems that you think I was wrong. I am happy that by the time Mr McHale saw Carney he had so far profited from my advice as to have made a substantial improvement. I have no doubt that, had I been left on my own, by the end of the practice I could have transformed him into a tolerably competent teacher, but now, of course, your interference has undermined my authority and made my work considerably more difficult.'

Conrad stopped at this point and read what he had written with satisfaction. There was a dignity and a restraint about it which were very pleasing. Perhaps a copy should also go to the Chairman of the Board of Governors. He considered his next sentence.

Around him the house was silent. Stephanie had gone out somewhere – she spent most of her time out these days – and when she was at home she spoke as little as possible and almost threw his food at him. She was also having some sort of a spring-clean. All her clothes were in heaps on the floor of her bedroom and she was using her sewing machine furiously. She did this when she was out of sorts. It was her way of sulking to go round the house with a duster and make everywhere as uncomfortable as she could. Well, she would snap out of it. Stephanie was the least of his worries. If he got that job, with the extra salary and the promise of a future University lectureship, she would come round.

At the precise moment when Conrad was penning his letter of complaint to Jacks the police were doing what he had so fervently wished them to do, getting on with the job of tracking down the murderer. A crisis had occurred, and a meeting was in progress in Superintendent Pearce's room.

Sergeant Rosen had great hopes of this meeting. He had been very disappointed by the Superintendent's reaction after the last interview with Nield, confidently expecting that the order would go out for his immediate arrest, but the Superintendent had procrastinated, still secretly convinced of the guilt of Bronniford.

'There's nothing there yet that we could confidently take into court,' he had said, snuffing out Rosen's hopes, 'it would be thrown out at committal. Besides,' he had added, 'Nicholson's pretty sure that he's on to something with Bronniford. Something very peculiar has been going on there. As far as we can make out Bronniford has been falsifying his travelling times in his log. It's beginning to look very promising indeed.'

And that was the thanks Sergeant Rosen had got for what he considered was a rather smart bit of investigation. So he had fretted, and Nicholson had looked triumphant, and then finally Nicholson's patience, never very durable, had worn out, and instead of, as he put it, pussy-footing about trying not to put the bugger on his guard, he had risen to his feet, on the Saturday morning, and announced that he was going to confront the bastard. 'I'll shake seventeen varieties of shit out of him,' he had continued, confident of his powers in that direction. 'By the time I've finished with him I'll have the poor sod on his knees begging me to take him in.' And he had gone off like a knight in a medieval romance intent on tackling the dragon.

Late in the afternoon he had returned crestfallen.

'No luck?' asked Rosen, observing his demeanour. 'Didn't he crack?'

'Oh, yes, he cracked all right.' Nicholson's tone was flat, but he still seemed hurt by the suggestion that anybody tackled by him might not have cracked. 'I busted the sod into little bits.'

'Well, what's the matter, then? You mean you've got him?'

'He wasn't anywhere near the bloody place. Do you know what he's been doing?' Nicholson's voice rose in an aggrieved roar. 'He and his pals have had a regular racket on. They've been systematically thieving Cross's loads.'

The Inspector's indignation was comic. It was not the thieving that had affronted him. That was part of the natural order of things. What had hurt Inspector Nicholson was that an enterprise of this kind had been carried on under his nose for months and he had not had an inkling of it. Inspector Nicholson prided himself on his network of information, and this sort of thing was an affront to his professional competence.

'Even Cross didn't know about it. You should have seen his face when I told him.'

'I didn't think Bronniford had the brains for that sort of thing,' said Rosen, intending to be soothing.

'He hasn't. Bronniford was nothing. Bronniford was just the driver. It was McBain, remember McBain? He shared a cell with Bronniford at Strangeways, and as soon as he heard that Bronniford was driving for Cross's he got this idea.'

And Inspector Nicholson told Rosen all about the scheme, which was very clever and involved making a complicated detour on each trip and off-loading part of the cargo at an old quarry.

'They fixed it so that they never took too much at one time. If Cross noticed any losses he thought they were being pilfered in the depot or at the other end. Clever, and, of course, only a few needed to be in on it.' Nicholson had a professional admiration for a smart piece of thieving. 'They could have kept it on for years, and then something like this happens and they get dropped in it. I tell you what, I wouldn't like to be in Bronniford's shoes when McBain catches up with him. He was shit-scared; that's why it took me so long to get it out of him.'

But Sergeant Rosen had little sympathy to waste on Bronniford. This, surely, at last, left it clear for him to go after that Nield fellow, and this was the question which was being discussed at the meeting in Superintendent Pearce's room. Perhaps Conrad would not have been pleased that the police were taking his advice after all. About the time when he was sealing the letter to Jacks in its envelope and writing the address, Superintendent Pearce was instructing Sergeant Rosen to get a search warrant to go over his house.

'There's that haversack thing that the first girl – what was her name? – Lucy Watson was carrying, and that duffel bag that he said the second girl had with her. If you could find either of those, or any article of clothing to connect him with either of those girls, then we've really got a case. I want one tangible piece of evidence that we can take into court, Rosen, just one piece.'

This was how it came about that on the Monday morning, just before nine o'clock, and an hour and a quarter after Conrad, delighted to get away, had left for Abenbury, Sergeant Rosen, accompanied by six policemen and two policewomen, appeared at Stephanie's front door.

For Stephanie it was the last straw. She had thought, seeing only a dim silhouette through the frosted glass, that Sergeant Rosen was the postman, and the unexpected sight when she opened it of nine assorted police was shattering. Then Sergeant Rosen had produced his warrant and waved it in front of her, and without asking her leave, or even allowing her to look at it properly, these horrid dark blue people were swarming all over her house. They were polite and apologetic, but they were also very thorough, and they roamed everywhere, poking behind cisterns, emptying cupboards, crawling into the cockloft, peering down the manhole outside the back door.

They were most interested in the pile of clothes on the floor of Stephanie's bedroom. Was she going away, then? Was her husband going with her? Had she been looking for something? Had her husband asked her to look for something?

Had she cleared anything out, thrown anything away, burnt anything? Men were dispatched to examine all the grates in the house and look at the incinerator in the garden. It was a point that seemed to fascinate them, and they kept coming back to it. And what was absolutely nightmarish about the whole thing was that they would not tell her why they were there or what they were looking for. And all the time a crowd was growing on the pavement outside the house, pressing against the fence, peering through the hedge. Curtains in neighbouring houses twitched, cynical-looking men appeared with cameras and notebooks and argued with the constable at the gate.

Stephanie sat in the middle of all this on the sofa in the front room, pale, her hands trembling. One of the policewomen sat with her the whole time, watching her. When Stephanie got up and went into the room at the back to see what was happening there, this policewoman followed. Good God, there were policemen in the garden sifting the compost heap and raking through the dustbins. Two of them began to dig up a flower bed which Conrad had recently planted. It was simply awful. Every so often the other policewoman came up to her and showed her an intimate feminine garment and asked if it was hers and seemed disappointed when she said that it was. Didn't they expect her to wear things like that? Did they think she was too old for it? Irrelevant thoughts struck her as immensely important. She remembered that she had not made the beds this morning, she wondered if the cupboards were clean, she noticed that the man who had been looking behind the old wardrobe in the box-room had come out covered with cobwebs and she wanted to tell him that she had been going to clean there in a week or so. She regretted that she was dressed in her oldest, shabbiest clothes because she had been intending to have a great clear-out.

She did not speak unless she had to. Sergeant Rosen put

214

this down to timidity, but it was more a matter of acquired caution and disgusted rage. In fact the Sergeant was under a misapprehension. He had quite taken to Stephanie on his earlier visit. She had seemed to him to be a real lady and had brought out all his protective instincts. She was obviously a cut above her husband, she must have a very genteel background. All these fine antiques and things, he correctly guessed, were hers. Such a lady, he thought, would naturally look to the police as her natural protectors and an invasion like this was worse for her than for an ordinary person.

So, chivalrously, did Sergeant Rosen's mind work, but it worked wrongly. Stephanie's father had steered too near the shady side of the law for his relations with the police to be quite easy, and she had learned from him, in the imitative way that a young child does learn, to be cautious of authority figures. There had been occasions, when her father had been at the bottom of the financial see-saw, when it had been left to her to open the door to landlords, or debt-collectors, or even the police themselves, and to pipe, in childish innocence, that Daddy was not at home. These burly men had often been enchanted by her manner and had given her sweeties and gone away. The insecurity had left its mark. It was this kind of life that Conrad was supposed to have taken her away from for good and all, and she sat there hating the Sergeant for what he was doing to her and hating Conrad for causing it.

As she sat, stonily silent, she reviewed the case against Conrad and finally, after circling about the subject for days, approaching it and then shying away from it, she condemned him. The weight of the evidence was overwhelming. The newspapers were hinting it, even Conrad's friends in College seemed to think it possible. That psychiatrist in the newspaper had pointed directly at a man like Conrad, and the police seemed convinced that he was their man. The magistrate who had signed the warrant must have believed that Conrad was guilty. She could not hold out against this mass of opinion.

She knew Conrad to be capable of irrational rages when he was, as he thought, humiliated. She knew that he could carry a grievance for months. She knew that he had a cold, smouldering anger that could lie perfectly hidden from all eyes except hers. What was it that psychiatrist had said? 'The first of these murders was the result of sudden impulse. Rage at his own sexual failure would have contributed, and a real or imagined insult offered by the girl could have tipped him over into violence.' Stephanie had read the piece so often that she remembered it word for word, and it seemed terribly possible to her.

It was curious. Now that she had argued herself into accepting Conrad's guilt all manner of unconnected things contributed to point in the same direction. She remembered the talk she had attended with Margery about battered wives. That had been, had it not, the evening of the first of these horrible murders? One of the specialists there had explained that wife-batterers were sometimes the most unlikely people. Respectable professional men, outwardly models of behaviour, were among the worst offenders: 'The more these men try to conform to an ideal pattern, the more violent is the reaction.' It all made sense.

Upstairs she heard heavy furniture being moved about, followed by what sounded like a burst of swearing, instantly checked by the Sergeant. She must get away as soon as she could. What a blessing it was that the house and furniture had been kept in her own name. With those and the money her father had left her she should not be too badly off. She must certainly get away from it all. She did not even want to see Conrad again and the thought of his touching her was nauseating. No, she was justified now, amply justified, in leaving him. Nobody could blame her; she could not even blame herself. The tears rolled down her cheeks and she felt a sense of release.

It was nearly four o'clock before the police withdrew. Sergeant Rosen was polite to the last, hoped that they had not created too much disturbance, promised to get rid of the crowd of people outside, but his bland manner hid a bitter disappointment. The house, he was forced to confess, was as clean as a whistle, and he could hear in advance Inspector Nicholson's 'I told you so.' 'You don't suppose he's got that haversack at home waiting for you to find, do you?' Nicholson had asked. The Sergeant was not so sure, you never knew your luck. Christie kept the pubic hairs of his victims in a little box, didn't he? At the very least he might have turned up a pile of pornographic material to go with that magazine they had found in his car, but there had been nothing. It was almost suspicious, if you thought about it. Could any house be as innocent as that? 'It looked to me, sir, as if they were getting ready to do a bunk.' This was how he explained it to the Superintendent. 'His wife had already cleared half the cupboards out, piles of her clothes all over the place. She could have been about to pack.'

He outlined the details of the search.

'I think they'd been burning things. There were ashes in the grates, and in the incinerator in the garden. They'd been having a general clear-out. Looked to me as if we were a day too late.'

This was a reproach offered to the Superintendent for being dilatory. The Superintendent sat looking judicious, stroking his chin and wondering what the hell to do. Had they got enough of a case to proceed against this Nield fellow?

'We've got his statement, sir, that he had the girl in his car.'

The Superintendent scratched his left ear and stared up at the ceiling. Statements were tricky things.

217

'I wonder how much of it will be left after he's got a good defence counsel to look after him?'

That was the question. The case against Nield was wholly circumstantial and however persuasive it looked to these policemen here it might fall to pieces in court. Superintendent Pearce had no intention of spoiling his reputation by bringing a charge that could not be maintained. On the other hand he was by now under considerable pressure and if he did not arrest somebody soon he would not have a reputation to save. It was a devilish difficult decision. One small item stuck in his mind. He had questioned Nield about his movements on the day of the first murder, asking specifically if he had gone straight home after finishing in his schools, and Nield had hesitated before answering 'Yes'. He had been on the point of giving himself away and he had just stopped himself. Nield had been pretty cool so far, but he was hiding something. If he had the shock of being arrested, what would that do to him? Superintendent Pearce thought that he knew the type. He would go to pieces. It would be a different sort of game then.

The Superintendent made up his mind and opened his mouth to speak. At that moment the telephone rang. At a sign from his superior, Inspector Nicholson answered it. He listened and a look of astonishment appeared on his face. 'Bloody hell,' he said. He handed the phone to Sergeant Rosen. 'It's for you.' There was a broad grin on his face.

23

'You're looking very spruce, Conrad.'

This was bad luck. Conrad had taken a short cut through the Science Block, and Charles Halliday had popped out of one of the laboratories and caught him.

'Thank you, Charles. Naturally I'm in my Sunday best.'

Halliday looked puzzled.

'The interviews, Charles, the interviews for the new job. They're today, at eleven o'clock.'

'I'd forgotten.' Of course, he could afford to. His job was safe enough. 'I didn't realize they were so soon. No wonder Cyril was looking sick yesterday. You heard I suppose, that this new scheme of his was thrown out by the assessors?'

Conrad had heard, and made an effort not to show how pleased he was, contenting himself with saying that he had expected it. 'The scheme was radically unsound education-ally. I was against it all along, but they wouldn't listen to me. I would have had a very poor opinion of the University if they had accepted it.'

'Really?' Charles sounded uncertain. 'Well, I didn't see the scheme myself, so I can't comment, but it is unusual for them simply to throw out something which the College has put forward. From what I heard they didn't even suggest ways it might be modified. Cyril was furious. I was in the common-room when he came in afterwards, and he was certain that it had been sabotaged. The University was acting under instructions.'

Conrad laughed. 'Extraordinary thing to say. Sabotaged by whom? I think old Cyril is developing a persecution complex. He tends to believe that any sign of opposition is a concerted plot against him.'

'I suppose,' said Halliday, charitably, 'that he was upset because of the interviews today. I see it now. It's bad luck for him getting a knock like this the day before.'

Conrad preserved a discreet silence. The only bit of luck had been hearing from Soper that it was Templeton who was going to take the chair at the assessors' meeting. Professor Templeton had always been very kind to Conrad. It was he who had offered him the chance to do research, the chance which he had had to turn down. It had been very natural for Conrad to pick up the phone and get in touch with his old teacher to ask his advice about this book that he was writing. It had not been difficult, in the middle of the conversation, to mention the forthcoming assessment. The Professor, kindly as ever, making a natural mistake, had expressed the hope that he might meet his old pupil when he came to visit the College.

'I'm afraid not, Professor. I won't be there. They've packed me off to get me out of the way. The fact is that I'm not particularly enthusiastic about the course that's been put forward.'

When Conrad said this he was mindful of something else that Soper had said: 'If the assessors get the idea that the College is not united in support of the proposals then they won't touch them at any price.' And he had gone on, with much laughter, to give examples of submissions when half the staff of a college had been given the day off just to get them out of the way. 'That's what you'd better do, Conrad, pack your dissenters off.'

Professor Templeton had been very interested in what Conrad had told him, particularly when Conrad had gone into details of the submission he had prepared himself, which, the Professor agreed, sounded very much the sort of thing that was wanted.

220

No, Conrad felt that Charles Halliday was wide of the mark when he spoke about luck entering into it.

'You've had a bit of bad luck yourself, Conrad.'

Conrad braced himself for what was coming and put on an expression of polite incomprehension.

'I saw it in the papers – the police visiting your house and all that. Very unpleasant, especially coming just now.'

Halliday meant to be kind, but Conrad saw only a sneer and a hint of what people were saying behind his back.

'I'm sorry, Charles, but I don't see it. You seem to me to have got hold of the wrong end of the stick. I was unfortunate enough to be near at hand when a particularly nasty murder took place. In the circumstances the police have got to investigate me, and that is what they have been doing. With great courtesy, may I add. If you'd been in my position, Charles, they'd have done it to you. And if you're suggesting that it may affect the interview this morning all I can say is, why the hell should it? Sorry about the language. There is absolutely no comparison with Cyril. He made a botch of a negotiation on educational matters that vitally concerns our whole future.'

He delivered this speech solemnly, looking Charles straight in the eye, and it was Charles who had to look away, embarrassed.

It was the manner, the tone that Conrad had been rehearsing since Tuesday morning when he had opened his paper, casually glanced at a picture of two policemen digging in a garden which looked familiar, peered closer, and seen that it was his own. From that moment onwards he had been reconstructing his defences and this was the result.

Charles Halliday shifted from foot to foot, and found himself saying 'Of course' and 'Naturally I didn't mean anything of that sort', and thinking that, surely, Conrad could not have done anything so very bad. Halliday normally held himself aloof from the gossip of the common-room but he had heard what was being said about Conrad and had come to wonder if there was possibly some truth in it. Perhaps he had got himself involved in some kind of sex frolic that had gone too far. This was a popular theory, but, looking at Conrad, hearing him speak so openly and rationally, Charles could not believe it. He did notice, however, that for all his apparent calm, Conrad's hands were quivering.

Conrad observed the result of his words and felt well pleased. Taking the side of the police was good tactics, showed fair-mindedness and a consciousness of his innocence. The 'with great courtesy' was a late addition to the façade, tied on after he had returned on Thursday evening and had a short conversation with Stephanie, who had broken her vow of silence to mention that the police had been round.

'It means nothing at all, Stephanie. A man like Sergeant Rosen has to follow certain procedures; if he doesn't then he gets kicked up the bum. Now he can go away and look for the real culprit.'

And he had stared her out of countenance, and she had gone away and got on with the spring cleaning, or whatever it was that involved heaping the contents of cupboards on the bedroom floor. With a bit of luck, if he stared at Charles Halliday long enough he would go away too, but he didn't. He held on, hesitating and fidgeting, until he finally came out with what was on his mind.

'What I actually wanted to talk to you about, Conrad, was something else.'

'You'd better make it fairly snappy, Charles, the interview's in about half an hour.'

'Well, I do feel that this is important, Conrad. It is about Matthews; I told you he has been having trouble with his courses.'

It took a moment for Conrad to refocus his mind and to remember that this Matthews was the awful lout who had accosted him on the stairs about an extension to C/P/12.

'To be precise, Charles, you said that you could not tell me about it.'

'No, well, it will all come out now anyway, I suppose. It was his wife, she was pregnant. Had you heard that?'

'I didn't even know that he was married, Charles.' Now that he did Conrad found the idea grotesque. That flabby, greenish creature married to somebody, clasping her in his arms, exuding his sweat over her.

'Well he is, and his wife was pregnant.'

'A fairly common case, Charles. A matter for rejoicing I've always understood. Never had an opportunity myself, but –'

'It wasn't a matter for rejoicing as far as she was concerned, Conrad. In fact, that was the trouble; she didn't want the baby and he did.'

Conrad laughed, knowing that laughter would irritate Halliday. 'You know, Charles, if these people had an ounce of common sense they'd sort out a thing like that beforehand. With all the sex education they get presumably they know what to do.'

'You're not very sympathetic, Conrad.'

'I'm not intending to be, Charles. If these students want to be considered adults then let them behave like adults and take the consequences for their own actions. If you try to be kind to them they do their best to get you into trouble, and if you try to do your duty and tell them what's wrong with them they go whining off to some other member of staff. I suppose you heard about young Carney and Milne's little attempt to put me in the wrong?'

But Charles had not heard, and when Conrad told him he showed signs of impatience and lack of understanding.

'I don't quite see the connection, Conrad.'

'All I'm saying is, Charles, that in future I intend to do things precisely by the book. If this Matthews of yours wants an extension of time then he can whistle for it.'

'You don't understand, Conrad, I'm not asking for an extension.'

'What are you asking for then?'

'I'm not asking for anything, I'm trying to tell you. Matthews tried to commit suicide yesterday.'

Conrad was jolted into silence, and Charles proceeded.

'His wife had an abortion without telling him, and he swallowed half a bottle of barbiturates.'

'Good heavens, Charles, how dreadful.'

Conrad said the expected thing rather than what he actually felt. It was a stupid act, certainly; unnecessary, yes; but he could not, to be honest with himself, actually feel it as dreadful. It was the sort of behaviour that you would expect of a generation that loved without principles and without a sense of responsibility. Is it dreadful to reap what you have sown?

'Isn't it,' said Charles. 'That poor boy.'

'You mean she just had the abortion without saying a word to him?'

'She had talked about an abortion, I understand, and he had said that he didn't want her to have one, so she went to a women's organization – Stephanie's friend Margery is a counsellor for them – and they put it through for her.'

Not a very happy phrase, Conrad thought.

'She said that it was her own body and she had a right to do what she wanted with it.'

Conrad nodded. There was a grim logic about it. Look after your rights, abandon your duties, and enjoy the consequences. There was no point in saying anything like this to Charles, though, so, instead, he asked a question.

'I'm very grateful to you for telling me all this, Charles, but why were you looking for me so urgently? What was the hurry?'

'I thought you ought to know. Some people are saying that it was not only the abortion business that made young

Matthews do what he did. They are saying that he was harassed about his work and that this contributed.'

Conrad moved away from Charles Halliday, took five paces down the corridor, turned, and lunged five paces back again, swearing vehemently as he did so. Charles seemed about to protest but Conrad stopped him.

'Exactly what I might have expected. One tries to have standards and all the thanks one gets for it is to be blamed if something like this happens. Who is it who is saying this? Jacks, I suppose?'

'I haven't heard Jacks say anything, Conrad. I believe the student president is going to bring it up at the students' union meeting.'

'Obviously, if one knows the background of something like this one makes allowances. I was not told the background.'

'It was a confidential matter. I expected you to accept my assurance that it was important.'

Conrad stared at Halliday with a baffled fury. 'How many people know about this, Charles? Has it got through to any of the governors yet? I mean, I've got to meet them at this interview in about ten minutes, so I'd like to know what to expect.'

Charles Halliday's face took on an almost hunted expression. 'Well, naturally, Conrad, I've had to put in a report, and they are bound to have got it by this time.'

'I see,' said Conrad.

'I had no choice, Conrad, did I? After all, the students are bringing it up anyway.'

But Conrad could not trust himself to speak further, and he turned away and hurried off down the corridor. Halliday had the cheek to call after him something that sounded like 'Good luck'.

24

Conrad arrived at the room where the candidates were waiting for the interview out of breath and in a sweat. He was the last to enter. They were all in a circle round the perimeter of the room looking, in their unfamiliarly immaculate costume, like strangers who had just met at a party and had not yet been introduced. Conrad tried to remember when he had last seen Cyril Davidson in a suit. Once again he had the impression that his appearance had checked the flow of talk and that they were embarrassed by his presence, but he steeled himself to greet them as unconcernedly as possible and in a moment things were outwardly normal. Tony Skillington was standing by the window morosely watching the arrival of the last members of the appointing committee, and he was the first to speak.

'Hullo, Conrad, we'd begun to think you weren't coming.'

What did he mean by that? Was he suggesting that it was not worth Conrad's while to turn up?

'I was delayed, Tony. Charles got hold of me.'

Skillington turned drearily back to the window. Outside pensioners were exchanging shrill greetings, a septuagenarian governor was being helped up the steps of the College, and a lady in a flowered hat was banging her hearing aid against the handle of her stick.

Young Aspinall joined him. 'They're not hurrying, are they?'

'Why should they? They've got their hands on our balls. It's more fun to make us sweat for a bit.'

Skillington left the window and sat down. It was evident

from his face that the strain of the interview was already beginning to tell.

'How long do these things usually take?' asked Aspinall.

'Hours, and hours, and hours,' replied Skillington.

'You sound,' said Philip Milne, 'as though you've never been to an interview before.'

'I haven't,' said Aspinall, creating a sensation. Even Porter looked up.

'What about when you were appointed here?' asked Skillington.

'I didn't have to come for interview, I was just sent a letter through the post.'

Conrad, Skillington and Milne all exchanged glances. The same thoughts were in each mind. They had all had a struggle even to get on to the staff of the Alderman Robertson, and this young cub had just walked in. Now, for all they knew, he might even snatch this supreme prize from under their noses. Skillington changed the subject, not trusting himself to say anything more.

'What did Charles want to see you about, Conrad?'

Conrad stiffened, but controlled himself. He must know perfectly well what Charles had wanted. This was designed to embarrass him.

'The business with Matthews, of course. It was the first I'd heard about it. A bit of a shock.'

'How is Matthews?'

Conrad realized that he had not thought to ask Halliday. 'As well as can be expected.'

'He's off the danger list,' said Milne. 'I rang the hospital last night.'

Conrad said that that was a relief and the subject was allowed to drop.

Conrad looked round him. Porter was in the corner, detached from the others, showing no interest in the conversation, gazing down at the floor. Every so often he uncrossed his legs and crossed them again, but apart from this he sat quite passively. Cyril Davidson was on Conrad's right, and was unusually silent. When Conrad had come in he had looked at him very hard and he had given the impression that he was simmering with anger, but he had looked away again and had given no greeting. Conrad guessed that he was as sick as mud about the failure of his BEd submission.

Skillington glanced at his watch. 'High time they began to have us in.' He looked at Aspinall. 'You'll be first, of course.'

Conrad had already done his calculations. Aspinall, Davidson, Milne, and then it would be his turn. He experienced a little tug at his nerves and shifted restlessly in his seat. Then he addressed Cyril Davidson.

'I hear your scheme was chucked out yesterday.'

Cyril sat there, one eye scorching Conrad; after many seconds he uttered the one word: 'Yes.'

'I don't want to say, "I told you so," Cyril, but I did.'

Davidson brought a withering sigh from the recesses of his lungs.

'There was something very odd about the whole business yesterday, wasn't there, Philip? When they came down here those assessors had not the slightest intention of accepting the proposal.'

'They'd probably read it, Cyril.'

'Very funny, Conrad. What I want to know is, what had people been saying to them behind our backs?'

Conrad laughed with the assurance of a man who, if his conscience is not absolutely clear, at least knows that he cannot possibly be found out.

'What could anybody have been saying, Cyril?'

Cyril now turned to face Conrad and was about to launch into his reply when the door opened and Miss Birdsall, the Principal's Secretary, came in to announce that the board would like to see Mr Aspinall. Davidson waited for him to go out before continuing.

228

'I'll tell you what they could have been saying, Conrad. At one stage in the discussion that bloody old fool who used to be in the English Department there – what's his name? Templeton – he said that he understood that there was a very considerable division of opinion about the merits of the scheme on the part of the staff here. Now where could he have heard that?'

'He only had to look at it, Cyril, to guess that a good many of us would not be very keen on it.'

'It was more than a guess, Conrad, he stated it as a matter of fact. Wasn't Templeton your Professor?'

'He was Professor to a good many people, Cyril, and a very fine one. I have a great respect for Templeton. I wish I'd been here to meet him, but I wasn't. You had edged me out, remember? I was down in Abenbury doing my job. Incidentally, why was Templeton in the chair? I understood that it was going to be Carnaby.'

That fixed him. He subsided, still suspicious and muttering, but completely baffled. Conrad pressed his advantage.

'The fact is, Cyril, as I have been telling you all along, your scheme was a bad one. I think I may say that I understand the University mind as well as anybody here and I knew perfectly well that they would not accept it. On the whole I'm very pleased.'

Cyril smiled evilly. 'You haven't all that much to be pleased about. It leaves us all in the shit. Without a course we won't get any students, and if we don't get any students we're all of us dead.'

'But we have got a course, Cyril,' Conrad began to become passionate, 'the one that I worked out, the one that you and Jacks ditched. It could be submitted in a week and I have reason to believe that it would be accepted without much trouble.'

'What reason?'

Davidson looked up, suddenly suspicious, but Conrad merely smiled at him.

'I'll tell you this, Conrad,' Davidson became venomous again, 'Jacks is not going to put your scheme forward, whatever happens. He told me so.'

Conrad was careful not to let this make him angry. For one thing it was probably not true, and even if it was there was no point in getting worked up about it now, but it disturbed him. His whole calculation was based on the idea that since time was so desperately short Jacks would have to accept the course that was actually available. He said as much, but Davidson laughed.

'Forget it. The earliest the assessors could be reconvened is next December. Jacks reckons that that gives us time to plan another scheme.'

Conrad bit his lip. Davidson looked away, and the conversation ground to another halt.

The silence lasted until Aspinall returned, looking, Conrad was sorry to see, pleased with himself.

'Eighteen minutes,' said Philip Milne.

'Eh?'

'Eighteen minutes – you were in for eighteen minutes, I was timing you.'

'Is that good?' asked Aspinall.

'Very good,' said Milne. Skillington and Conrad looked at one another and then quickly looked away again. Eighteen minutes was not very good. They both smiled.

'I suppose there's not much point in my waiting any longer,' said Aspinall.

'Possibly not,' said Conrad. 'The usual drill is that after we've all been seen the successful candidate is asked to go in again and is offered the job. You've got to make your own mind up about that.' That would put the cheeky little bugger in his place.

Aspinall sat down, and a few minutes later Miss Birdsall

came in and asked Cyril to follow her to the Board Room. Milne started to whistle tunelessly, until Skillington asked him to stop. Porter took his hands out of his pockets and placed them on the arms of his chair.

'What did they ask you?' Milne said suddenly, but Aspinall, though new to the game, was not so easily caught.

'The usual things, I suppose. I had to outline my career.'

That, thought Conrad, was why he had been in so short a time. If he padded it out it should take him twenty seconds to do that.

'Anything else?'

'Nothing much.'

Milne leaned back, baffled. Then he took some notes out of his pocket and began studying them, and finally glanced at a letter he had brought out with them.

'Oh, by the way, Conrad, I've been meaning to say this. I do think you might have told me that you had sent those lists in to the University.'

Conrad smiled innocently again. 'Blame Milton Jacks, not me, Philip. I just did the job I was supposed to do. Jacks got it into his fat head that I hadn't and asked you to do it, but I can hardly be held responsible for that, can I? I did drop him a note to say that everything was all right.'

'I know, that was when he told me.' Milne continued to look at Conrad speculatively, and then he went on. 'There was one rather funny thing. On the list that I'd made I got the two Desmond Bennets mixed up.'

These two had been a nuisance throughout their course, so inconsiderate as to have the same Christian names and the same surnames, except that one spelt it Bennet, and the other Bennett.

'Very easily done, Philip.'

'Yes, I know, but the odd thing is that you had made exactly the same mistake.'

'What I say, Philip; it's very easily done.'

'Exactly the same mistake, Conrad. I got their main subjects right, the accessory subjects wrong, and the professional subjects right, and so had you.'

Conrad stared at him. 'Well?'

'It just seemed odd, both of us making that identical error. You didn't by any chance see my list, did you?'

'I didn't even know you were making a list until Jacks left me a message about it. Anyway, as you said yourself, my lists were sent in first. Did you see mine?'

'Of course I didn't.'

'Well, then.'

The pause that followed this lasted until Cyril returned looking defiantly pleased with himself, and Milne received his summons to go in.

'What did they ask you, Cyril?' Skillington said.

'I don't know,' Davidson replied, 'I didn't listen. I didn't care a bugger what they wanted to ask; I knew what I wanted to tell them.'

Again Conrad and Skillington exchanged a lightning glance. This was old Cyril shooting a characteristic line, and he proceeded to tell them in some detail how impressive he had been.

'I wasn't going to let a parcel of greengrocers and garage proprietors start telling me about education. I said to them, "I'm the expert here, that's why you took me on in the first place. What are you paying me for if you think I don't know my own job?" Then I told them what my ideas were. I think I made my point.'

He was quite sickening. He told them what the Chairman had said, and what old Goodey had said, and how Mrs Belleshall had made an ass of herself as usual, and how Jacks had stepped in with a helpful question just at the right moment.

'How long did Philip say I'd been in? Forty minutes, was it? I didn't think it was as long as that.'

232

'Time passes quickly when you're enjoying yourself,' Skillington said.

'It was thirty-four minutes, Cyril,' Conrad said.

'Anybody timing Philip?' asked Aspinall. The others all looked at him, except Porter, who was staring at his shoes.

When Conrad finally entered the Board Room and was requested to take a chair, his nervousness fell away from him. As Milne had so wisely said earlier, it was the waiting that was the worst. Cyril had given him a valuable reminder. His posturings had been absurd, but the right attitude had been behind them. Nobody was going to get a job like this by acting the shrinking violet. So Conrad spoke up boldly, outlined his qualifications for the post, mentioned his experience, spoke of his special relationship with the University.

'One of my duties in College is to prepare the lists which are sent to the University each year of our examination candidates, and I think I may say that I work in fairly close liaison with the University people. I don't need to remind you that the person appointed will become, eventually, a member of the University team.'

He spoke of the need to bring their academic courses closer to those of the University, in view of the projected merger, and was able to regret the failure of their recent submission.

'Perhaps, if we had taken the University more into our confidence in the early stages of discussion it would have saved us this disappointment.' One of the governors, blessings on his head, asked, 'What disappointment?' giving Conrad a golden opportunity to explain about the BEd submission and Davidson's failure.

'Fortunately,' he was then able to add, 'we already have another scheme, fully prepared, which we could offer immediately.'

'I am bound to say,' Jacks chipped in, 'that we are not contemplating an early re-submission.'

Conrad was unabashed. He had expected hostility from that quarter.

'I had heard this,' he said, 'but I hardly believed it. It seems to me so essential to get a course approved as soon as possible, and I would think it very unwise of us, at this juncture, to be at odds with our own University.'

This was a good line. Several of the governors were also members of the University Court, and a number of them nodded assent. Jacks twisted his lips together in annoyance, and Conrad sailed on with growing confidence.

It was Gorning who asked, in what sounded like a pre-pared question, Conrad's views on the proper relationships to be struck with students. 'This new post will involve working with the students, Mr Nield, as I am sure you will agree.'

Conrad agreed, of course. He wondered if the others had been asked this or if it had been reserved for him alone. He paused before answering, looking round the faces watching him. No doubt they had all heard about Matthews. Jacks would have seen to that. Probably his general reputation as a strict, even stern, disciplinarian, was known to them. Well, he must plunge in.

'I think, Mr Chairman, one is conscious that one's respon-sibility here is dual, both to the student as a person and to the profession for which he is being trained. In other words one has to execute a delicate balancing act between friendly co-operation on the one hand and firm control on the other. I do not –' and Conrad boldly faced Jacks again – 'subscribe to the modern theory which suggests that the teacher should abdicate his moral role. We have to awaken in our students a sense that they are citizens of a free society, with all the duties and responsibilities that that entails, and it is through the example that we set that we do this. Clearly this requires that we oblige students to honour their commitments and exact penalties if they do not.'

Yes, he had read the feeling of the meeting aright, there was a general nodding and murmuring agreement. The rest of the interview was a cake-walk. He sat back, relaxed, and talked naturally and with authority. When it was over he felt that he had made exactly the right impression, and he had difficulty, when he returned to the waiting room, in concealing his satisfaction.

'Just over forty minutes,' Milne told him.

'It felt longer. A bit of an ordeal really, I can't say I'm sorry it's over.'

While they waited for Porter and Skillington to be interviewed Conrad felt the customary reaction after a nervous strain. He was suddenly limp, his senses were dull, he did not wish to speak or be spoken to. He did however notice that neither Porter nor Skillington was accorded anything like the amount of time that he had had. Then they all sat waiting while the governors discussed their choice. Nobody spoke much. Skillington attempted a couple of nervous jokes, but they fell quite flat. Davidson dragged on his fifth cigarette of the morning, Aspinall drummed his fingers on the arm of his chair, Porter sat impassively in his corner. Then the door opened and Miss Birdsall came in.

'Mr Nield,' she said, 'will you come this way?'

It was a stunning moment, and Conrad sat for a couple of seconds, unable to respond. He had done it. In the teeth of all the hostility, in spite of all his misfortunes, he had done it. As he rose to his feet he felt his knees trembling. He was safe. More, he was going to be a member of the University staff. The others crowded round him as he tried to twist his features into a modest, self-deprecatory smile.

'Well done, Conrad.' It was Cyril Davidson shaking his hand, his face looking grey and old and lined all of a sudden. Skillington was not able to speak at all; he tapped Conrad on the shoulder and made a fluttering movement with his hand expressive of congratulation, and while he did it he had to look away from Conrad. Milne made his words sound almost sincere.

'If I couldn't get it myself, Conrad, there's no one I'd rather see appointed.'

Then Conrad had to hurry after Miss Birdsall, murmuring his thanks as he went. She was waiting for him in the corridor and led the way as soon as he appeared. Conrad felt light-headed, the relief was almost painful, and he smiled amiably at a passing office girl, fancying foolishly that she looked at him with a new kind of respect. He was secure. He was not going to be made redundant. All that he had done was now about to bear fruit.

At the end of the corridor Miss Birdsall, instead of turning left to go to the Board Room, turned right. Conrad followed, puzzled. He was about to say something when she led the way into the entrance foyer and a very large police constable levered himself out of a low chair and loomed over Conrad.

'Mr Nield?'

Conrad nodded.

'I would like you to accompany me to police head-quarters.'

25

Conrad's immediate sensation was that the world had turned white. His knees shook, and he put a hand on the wall to steady himself. He cast a look of despairing reproach in the direction of Miss Birdsall, but that lady had already turned away from him with an expression that absolved her from all responsibility. He could not trust himself to speak, but made a gesture of assent with his left hand, pushed himself off from the wall with his right, and followed his captor out of the building. The front terrace was deserted, but he imagined faces peering from the windows of all the rooms, and he trudged behind the policeman wondering why they had had to send such a conspicuous member of the force to fetch him in.

The abrupt transition from the highest hopes to bleakest despair had had a numbing effect, and he slumped in the back of the police car while thoughts passed incoherently and in an oddly detached way through his mind. What had they found out? Could they possibly have discovered anything at his home? Had the forensic examination of his clothes given them anything which they fancied they could use as evidence against him? These ideas were prominent, but mingled with them were other thoughts. What was happening at the interview? What was Stephanie going to say? What would the newspaper headlines look like now? It began to seem as if the nightmare he had dreaded was about to come true. The police, under pressure to pin the blame on somebody, had chosen him. At this point the odd detachment which the shock had caused began to operate usefully. The notion of himself actually standing trial on a charge of murder was just too incongruous. For the hundredth time Conrad went over, in his mind, the case which might be made against him. He had picked up that girl and taken her onto the moors. Later she had been found strangled. Would any jury say that that amounted to proof? Oh, God, it was intolerable. He had done nothing, absolutely nothing, and this had happened to him. As he went over the chain of events that had brought him to this he felt a mounting sense of panic, he wanted to cry out and beat on the windows of the car in protest, but of course he did not. He sat there, shivering, nervously clenching and unclenching his fingers.

The car was approaching the police headquarters and Conrad, staring listlessly out of the window, saw something which did not immediately register in his mind. A girl was walking down the road towards them and Conrad's eyes rested accidentally on her. Then he sat up and stared. A moment later, as the car swept past her, he was twisting round in his seat to watch where she went, shouting like a madman to the driver to stop and turn round, and hammering on the rear window of the car to attract the girl's attention. He could not be mistaken. She had been cleaned up, she was dressed differently, she looked almost attractive, but it was his passenger, the girl he had left on the moors.

'Stop that girl,' he found himself calling out, 'it's her, she's alive, we must show her to the Superintendent.' He discovered that he was pounding the driver on the shoulder with his left hand, and that the driver did not like it. As soon as the car drew in to the kerb Conrad scrabbled at the door handle, jumped out onto the pavement, and ran up the steps of the police headquarters with the constable in pursuit. Unfortunately, once he was in the building Conrad realized that he had not the least idea where he was to go and he had to wait for the policeman to catch up with him.

'Whatever is the matter, sir, carrying on like that? We might have had a serious accident.'

'That girl, the girl who passed us on the road. She's an important witness, she's got to be found, it's urgent.'

'Just come along with me, sir, and tell Sergeant Rosen. He wants a word with you.'

It was funny but Conrad suddenly found that, on his part, he wanted a word with Sergeant Rosen, and he burst into his office as soon as it was pointed out to him. The Sergeant looked up, startled, and checked Conrad's clamour with a gesture of his hand.

'All right, constable, leave this to me. You'd better sit down, sir.'

Sergeant Rosen was feeling old and tired and dispirited, which was odd in view of the fact that he believed that his case had now been solved. He looked at Conrad with mild distaste, no longer feeling any pressing interest in him.

'We know all about that girl, sir, we found her some days ago, she's been helping us with our inquiries.'

'Then you know I didn't do it?'

'We never thought you had, sir.' The Sergeant's eyes shone with a rural honesty and simplicity as he uttered this frightful whopper. 'There was never any direct evidence to link you with the crimes.'

The Sergeant was not going to show this man, of all people, the extent of his disappointment.

'Anyway,' he continued, 'something has happened which exonerates you completely.'

Conrad dropped into a chair in front of the Sergeant's desk as though his strings had been cut. This was all getting too much for him. Five minutes ago shades of the prison house had been closing about him.

'What did you bring me down for, then?' he asked weakly.

'We wanted to give you your clothes back.'

Sergeant Rosen did not like Conrad and would willingly have irritated him, but if he had thought for a week he could not have calculated a speech more likely to rouse him to fury.

Conrad thought of the interview, drawing to its close at that very moment no doubt; he remembered his recent terror in the police car; and when he considered that these things had been caused by a parcel of clothes that he could have picked up at any time he felt that he was going to have a stroke. There was malice in this, it had been done deliberately. That bland, gaping, agricultural fool at the other side of the desk was grinning at him in mockery.

'My God, Sergeant, do you realize what you've done? Do you know that I've just suffered agonies? I've had to leave one of the most important meetings of my life, just because you wanted to give me my suit back. I'll tell you something, Sergeant, I take this very ill indeed. I think you did this deliberately. I think this is petty malice, and spite, and police persecution. I shall take this up with your superior officers. If necessary I shall complain to the very highest quarters.'

Sergeant Rosen was surprised, though not, it seemed, unduly worried.

'We are officially required to return your clothes to you, sir. I'm sorry if it was inconvenient. You should have explained to the constable; we could easily have arranged to see you later.'

Conrad might have said that it would have seemed to him futile, when a policeman has called to arrest you on a charge of murder, to ask him to wait for ten minutes so that you can finish being interviewed for a job, but he didn't. Instead he asked, 'Why didn't you just drop the clothes off at my home?'

'We did call, sir. Your wife did not say anything about it being inconvenient.'

So it was Stephanie's fault.

'I hope you haven't been worrying my wife with all this. She has had quite enough anxiety as it is, what with the house being searched and all the publicity.'

'I think you'll find that we were able to set her mind at rest about everything, sir.'

As the Sergeant said this he was thinking of the report he had received from the constable who had been sent round. According to him Mrs Nield had had something else on her mind at that moment. The hall had been full of luggage, and a youngish man, whom she addressed as Stan, had been helping her to load it into a battered old car. They had both been considerably put out he said, by his appearance, and they had edged him out of the house pretty quick. No, he had said, in answer to a question from the Sergeant, he had asked Mrs Nield if her husband was going away anywhere, reminding her that if so the police would like to be informed, and she had said, rather sharply, that he was not going anywhere. From his Panda car the policeman had watched the two of them drive away. None of this was any business of the Sergeant's, and he saw no reason to confide it to Conrad, but he felt justified in saying that Mrs Nield was not unduly worried about her husband.

'We didn't take the clothes themselves round because, in fact, there are one or two more questions that I'd like to put to you.'

Sergeant Rosen looked at Conrad wearily. He was thoroughly tired of this peevish, self-centred person, and he would have preferred to have had nothing more to do with him, but duty required that he should clear up a couple of points. The Sergeant had recently been oppressed by a feeling of futility, and he had not shaken this off yet. It had been an unsatisfactory investigation. After all his work the solution had come about by pure chance, and, what was infuriating, the man they had now got was someone who had been questioned earlier and allowed to go on his way. It had been a stupid, random, botched affair that reflected credit on nobody. A couple of constables last night had been making a routine check on passing vehicles, seeing if they had illuminated rear numberplates. This van had come along which had proved to have no numberplate at all. There was a number, it had been roughly chalked in the rust at the bottom of the rear door, but no plate. The policemen had tut-tutted and walked round and taken in the generally deplorable condition of the vehicle, then they had invited the driver to open the door so that they could look at the condition of the wiring inside. What they had found there, under a plastic sheet, had taken their minds right off trivialities like faulty lighting. When they began to check up it all became doubly annoying.

'We had this man,' Nicholson had pointed out, 'he was the one who was reported by that woman. We actually had him in the station at Forton Cross.'

Sergeant Rosen had stared at the card-index entry in despair.

'Said he was changing his wheel in that lay-by.'

'We went back and found the handle of the jack that he said he'd left there.'

'I checked on him again later, after the second murder.'

No, it was not a business in which anybody could take any pride.

He addressed himself to Conrad. 'The first point is quite a small one, I daresay you won't be able to help us at all. Do you remember, on the afternoon of April the twenty-ninth, you left your school just before half past three, you told us. Did you happen, as you passed, to notice a lay-by a couple of miles outside Forton Cross, as the road goes up to the moors?'

Conrad had made up his mind that from now on in his dealings with the police he would tell the strict, literal truth, so he nodded. 'I know the lay-by. It's at the foot of the hill, the beginning of a nature trail.'

'You didn't notice, did you, when you passed it on the twenty-ninth, if there was a vehicle there or not?'

'Yes, I noticed,' said Conrad, 'there wasn't.'

Sergeant Rosen was surprised. 'You seem very definite.'

'I stopped there.'

It gratified Conrad to see that this information seemed to

242

give the Sergeant distress. His jaw dropped and he repeated Conrad's words in disbelief.

'Yes, I stopped there. I had a bit of a headache so I thought I'd stop and walk up and down a bit to clear it.'

'Go on.'

'Well, I looked at the map of the nature trail, then I decided to walk to the top of the hill to catch the fresh air.'

'You were within sight of the lay-by the whole time?'

'Of course. The path goes round the edge, you can look down at the road.'

'And how long, would you say, were you there?'

The Sergeant ground these questions out from between his teeth. Conrad could not understand his emotion.

'Let me see. A quarter of an hour up, quarter of an hour back. I stood at the top for a few minutes, sat down on the seat for a bit coming down. Might have been three quarters of an hour to an hour. I wasn't hurrying.'

'And during all this time did any other vehicle come into that lay-by?'

'No,' said Conrad, 'not one.'

He felt that never, in his whole life, had he been looked at with such concentrated hatred as he experienced now from the Sergeant. Davidson had been hostile before the interview, Milne had looked at him bleakly, but neither had been anywhere near the class of the Sergeant.

'Why the hell,' he shouted, 'didn't you tell us this before, Mr Nield?'

'It slipped my memory.' Conrad's voice was soothing. 'It didn't seem to me important.'

'I asked about it specifically at our very first interview, and the Superintendent himself put the direct question to you: when you left school on the twenty-ninth did you go straight home, and you said "Yes".'

'I forgot. What the hell does it matter? It went clean out of my mind. Then, after the Superintendent asked me, I remembered, but I thought you might think it funny if I changed my story, so I didn't mention it.'

'We wouldn't have thought it funny at all. We'd got quite used to changes in your stories.'

Sergeant Rosen breathed hard and seized his vanishing temper by its coat-tails. Christ! The case could have been solved then and there if this silly sod had only been a bit straighter with them. The evidence had been in his card-indexes, and the one piece needed to complete it – he pulled himself together.

'We did put out a public notice, Mr Nield, asking any driver who had been along that road at that time to come forward. You ignored that too, didn't you?'

Conrad did not say anything. He was perplexed. This man obviously took his omission very ill. It was safer not to speak.

'Perhaps we'd better go on to the next question, Mr Nield. That girl you picked up told us quite an interesting story. She got a lift, she said, from the next lorry that came along, about twenty minutes after you left her, she said.'

Conrad nodded.

'She said that you had scattered her things all over the place. The driver helped her to pick them up, most of them. As a matter of fact we should be grateful to you for one thing, Mr Nield. We couldn't understand it but those knickers that we found, the ones that led our boys to discover the body so quickly, the girl's mother didn't recognize them. They didn't seem to belong to the victim. Well, they were your passenger's, they had nothing to do with the dead girl at all. If you hadn't thrown them about then our police car wouldn't have stopped and the body might have been hidden there for months.'

Conrad sat quietly, he was very pale. It would all be recorded in the files – throwing the clothes about, putting his hand on her knee –

'When they had got all her things together,' continued the

Sergeant, 'they drove off. Now the girl said that no other car passed in either direction from the time that you drove off to that moment. Do you follow me?'

'I could follow you a bit quicker than this, Sergeant. Would you mind very much getting on?'

'Half a mile down the road, of course, they passed that lay-by, the one we were talking about a moment ago, and both the girl and driver say that there was a vehicle parked there, but they couldn't give me much of a description of it. Now, you must have passed that lay-by. Did you see anything of one?'

Adhering to his resolve to be strictly truthful Conrad answered that he had seen a vehicle.

'Can you describe it, sir?'

'It was a van, a dark-blue van, rather old, very dirty and rusty. I think it was a Commer, but I'm not sure. I'm not very good at identifying vans.'

The Sergeant again looked surprised.

'That's a very accurate description, considering that you only saw it for a second in the dark.' And considering, the tone of voice added, that Conrad had not been notable, hitherto, for the accuracy of his observation or the retentiveness of his memory.

'I actually stopped in the lay-by, Sergeant. I left that girl in rather a hurry and didn't shut the door properly so it rattled as I drove along. I stopped to pull it to and to pick up the fag-ends she had littered the floor with.'

'Do you think you could identify the van if you saw it again? I suppose you didn't, by any chance, observe the number?'

Conrad giggled. It was too good an opportunity to miss. This bugger had ruined his chances of that job, he had made his life a misery, he had abused him for being uncooperative. Well, he would jolt his calm if it was the last thing he did.

'I can't tell you the number, Sergeant, but perhaps I can

do better. I can tell you where you can find the numberplate.'

It was lovely. The Sergeant was rigid, his face a mask of astonishment.

'What do you mean?'

'The van hadn't got a numberplate, not at the back anyway, it had dropped off, and I can tell you where you can pick it up. I can't very well do any better for you than that, can I? You were hinting that I've not been very helpful so I'm trying to make up for it. The fact is, Sergeant, that it wasn't the first time that day that I'd seen that van.' And Conrad explained how it had been behind him when he had had his altercation with the 'Happy Home', and how he had noticed the numberplate dangling loose.

'And then, when I was in the car park in Abenbury I saw it again.'

'Yes?'

'It was in a quite disgraceful condition, Sergeant, hanging on by no more than the thickness of a thread of rust.'

'Indeed.'

'I bent down to examine it. I just put my finger out and waggled it from side to side.'

The Sergeant swallowed hard and stared at Conrad fascinated, but he seemed to have passed beyond speech.

'And it just dropped off. I barely touched it and it dropped off. So,' Conrad continued, 'I picked it up and put it over the fence that runs alongside the wall of the laundry. I imagine it's still there.'

'Whatever did you do that for?'

Conrad smiled charmingly. 'An instinct for tidiness, Sergeant. I didn't want to litter the place up with his damned numberplates.'

26

When Conrad left the police headquarters it was nearly four o'clock, and as he walked down the road towards the bus station he reflected ruefully on what had just occurred. The police had not, he thought, been fair with him. Instead of being grateful for his help they had blamed him bitterly for not giving it earlier. The numberplate had been retrieved, confirming his story, Superintendent Pearce had been summoned and been given a highly-coloured account by the Sergeant, and all hell had broken loose. Conrad had made matters worse by telling them that they were hard to please.

'You asked me to identify the van and I gave you the numberplate, what more could I do?'

The Superintendent had bent over him.

'This may seem very funny to you, Nield, but that is not the view that we take. You probably don't know yet, because it hasn't reached the papers, but last night two of my men stopped that van that you saw on a road on the outskirts of the town, and when they looked in the back they found the body of a girl.'

This had certainly checked Conrad's humour.

'How terrible.'

'She was unconscious, she's in hospital, it's touch and go whether she recovers. She is there because you were such a bloody selfish, smug fool that you couldn't come forward to help us, and you couldn't even answer our questions honestly when we asked you. It is an offence to obstruct the police, Mr Nield, and it is an offence to waste police time, and I think we could very probably get you on both those charges. So just you think about that before you start getting smart-aleck with us.'

It had been very painful to be addressed like this, by a large red face stuck only six inches in front of your own. And it had been terribly unfair, as they were quite incapable of understanding.

'It is your own damn fault, Superintendent. You deliberately let me believe that you suspected me of committing this crime, taking my clothes away, searching my house and all that. I thought that the girl who had been murdered was the one I'd given a lift to, so in that case why should I attach any importance to seeing that van. I told you as soon as I knew how things stood.'

'Why didn't you tell me that you'd stopped in that lay-by on your way home on the twenty-ninth? You deliberately lied to me about that.'

'I forgot, it just went out of my mind. You asked me if I'd seen anything and I told you I hadn't, which was true.'

But they had been deaf to reason. What had happened was that they had made a mess of their investigation and saw a heaven-sent opportunity of pushing the blame on to somebody else.

'You had all the information which we needed, and you didn't give it to us.'

'Frankly, Superintendent, you don't encourage people to help you if you take this sort of tone with them. I object to your attitude, I object very strongly.'

And the Superintendent had turned gloomily on his heel and thrown over his shoulder an invitation to Conrad to take the matter up with the proper authorities. Like his Sergeant he was incensed by the idea that this fellow, who had fouled up their investigations and wasted their time, was going to get off scot-free. He did not believe in his own warning about possible charges, the police had better things to do, but he longed to be able to get at the man in some way.

'Of course,' he added, swinging round suddenly and confronting Conrad again, 'you can always say your piece at the trial.'

'You don't mean I'll have to appear in court, do you?'

The Superintendent smiled. That had made him think.

'Certainly you'll have to appear in court. You must expect to be examined very closely about all your movements that evening. It is your evidence that places that vehicle on that road at the relevant time. If the defence counsel can shake the jury's confidence in you as a witness then he'll do it.'

'All that about the girl will come out?'

The Superintendent enjoyed answering this. 'Everything will come out. Abandoning her there at that time of night, scattering her clothes all over the ground, even attempting, from what she told us, an assault on her. What the jury will be asked to decide is whether they can trust the evidence of a man capable of behaving like that.'

And Sergeant Rosen had joined in the game. 'I have a shrewd suspicion that you won't have to wait until the trial. That young lady has got her head screwed on. It's my belief that she went straight from here to the newspaper office yesterday. One of the reporters there has been very interested in your involvement in all this.'

No, it had not been a pleasant interview. As Conrad walked along the road he imagined that he heard the voice of the defence counsel: 'She has stated on oath before this court that you placed your hand upon her knee. Please tell the jury what was in your mind when you did this.'

'Address yourself to the jury and answer clearly, Nield, why did you tell this girl that you were a representative for an electronics firm?'

Conrad was pulled out of this unpleasant reverie by the sight of a poster advertising the *Bickleton Herald*, with the headline 'Police Vigilance Rewarded', and he went inside the shop and bought a copy. There it was, on the front page: 'Girl

249

witness tells of ordeal on moor.' He folded the paper up small and hid it under the parcel of his confiscated clothing.

By an odd coincidence the first person he saw when he went through the College gates to collect his car was Milne. He looked astonished to see Conrad.

'Hullo, Conrad, this is a surprise. I understood the police had taken you off. There was a story going round that you'd been arrested.'

'Sorry to disappoint you.'

'Oh, I say, I'm delighted, of course, but what on earth did they want you for?'

'To give me these –' Conrad indicated the parcel of clothes – 'and to take another statement. It seems they've got hold of the man who did it.'

'Jolly good.' Then, 'You mean it was just for that they pulled you away?'

'Just for that.'

'And made you miss the end of the interview?'

'That's right. Maddening, isn't it? Who got the job, by the way?'

Milne hesitated. 'It was a very near thing, Conrad. I heard about it afterwards from Ted Goodey. He said that initially it was between you and Cyril, but Cyril lost favour because of his failure with the submission. According to Ted they were on the point of asking you in when Miss Birdsall told them that the police had taken you off, so they had another confab and finally offered it to Porter. It seems that Tony and I were not really in with a chance.'

At the beginning of this speech Conrad had fixed a gentle smile on his face in anticipation of whatever news Milne was going to give him. He had made up his mind that the only dignified response was a world-weary affability, the resigned acquiescence to a capricious fate that experience teaches the wise man, but when he heard Porter's name he had difficulty in keeping the smile in place. Fate had surely no right to push caprice to such an extreme.

'Porter, eh? Well, one should not be surprised. It's a tradition in this place to give every post to the least suitable applicant. Even Aspinall would have been a better choice.'

'I suppose,' said Milne, 'the rest of us had better start looking for jobs somewhere else. It won't be easy at our age.'

The hard edge of the *Herald* dug into him, reminding Conrad that it would be even less easy for him than for the others. What sort of job would he get when that had been sniggered over for a day or two?

'Let's take our troubles one by one, shall we, Philip? I've had a hard day and I think I'll just go home, have a few drinks, and put my feet up. I suppose you'll be doing the same.'

He hitched the parcel under his arm and ambled towards the College car park. Mortifying to find that all his efforts against Cyril had merely tipped the prize into the hands of the man he least wanted to get it. Those bloody policemen had no idea how they had messed things up for him. They would be laughing, of course, enjoying their triumph. He pitched the parcel into the back of his car and started the engine. What he had to decide now was what tale to tell Stephanie. She'd better not be too reproachful. If she had told that policeman, as she ought to have done, that he had an important interview and was not to be disturbed he would have been Director of General Studies now. He would remind her of that once or twice.

He drove carefully home and parked his car in the garage. Then he retrieved the parcel from the back seat, and let himself in at his front door, waving cheerily to old Mrs Berriman from next door but one, who was peeping at him from behind her curtains.

'Hullo, Stephanie,' he called, keeping his voice as cheerful and matter-of-fact as possible, 'I – er – I didn't get the job. A pretty close-run thing, I was told, but I didn't get it.'

She must be upstairs, she had not come out to meet him. He raised his voice and projected it towards the landing. 'You could have helped me a bit more, Steph, by not sending that bobby round after me. It doesn't exactly help –' He had climbed halfway up the stairs, but she still had not appeared. Where the deuce was she? She could hardly have gone round to Margery's at this time, for God's sake. She might have taken the trouble to be in to greet him after an interview as important as the one he had had.

He looked in the kitchen. No sign of any preparation for dinner. This was very odd. She had not said anything about going out. He went into the living room and looked round. Her work-basket was gone.

Then he saw an envelope, with his name on it, propped against the clock on the mantelpiece. He took it down and slit it open. His hands were trembling.